Other Series by H.P. Mallory

Paranormal Women's Fiction Series:
Haven Hollow
Midlife Spirits
Midlife Mermaid

Paranormal Shifter Series:
Arctic Wolves

Paranormal Romance Series:
Underworld
Lily Harper
Dulcie O'Neil
Lucy Westenra

Paranormal Adventure Series:
Dungeon Raider
Chasing Demons

Detective SciFi Romance Series:
The Alaskan Detective

Academy Romance Series:
Ever Dark Academy

Reverse Harem Series:
Happily Never After
My Five Kings

GOLDY

Book 2 of the Happily Never
After Series

By

HP Mallory

10 Chosen Ones:
When a pall is cast upon the land,
Despair not, mortals,
For come forth heroes ten.
One in oceans deep,
One the flame shall keep,
One a fae,
One a cheat,
One shall poison grow,
One for death,
One for chaos,
One for control,
One shall pay a magic toll.

Goldilocks:
Born a thief and a cheat
She meets fate with a smile
And brings a giant his doom
On a distant isle.

ONE
Kassidy

The magnified roar of a bear shakes every leaf on the trees around me and turns my legs wobbly for a too-long second.

I force myself to keep moving, clinging to the burn in my muscles, the ache of my back as I struggle to carry my precious cargo, the scrape of air in my lungs. All these pains remind me I'm still alive. And they remind me I want to *stay* alive, no matter the cost, even as hopelessness threatens to overwhelm me.

I knew the risks going into this mission, knew this nightmare scenario might be waiting for me.

But, fuck, all the same.

Knowing and experiencing are two different things, and I can't help the shudder that rocks through me as the furious bear shifter behind me bellows its displeasure into the sky.

The path is so overgrown, I can scarcely follow the twisting brown ribbon of dirt winding in front of me. What's more — night is closing in, something which will prove to be more a hindrance to me than to my pursuers. Bears have amazing night vision, and it's doubly true for werebears.

Well, fuck me.

I shove my hand into the satchel bound to my waist, a satchel enchanted by Tenebris a long time ago

1

in order to hold massive quantities of… you name it. The number of items and the breadth of said items the satchel can hold is mind-blowing, but you wouldn't be able to know just by looking at it.

It takes me thirty precious seconds of searching to find the pair of enchanted goggles I managed to filch off a traveling merchant. When I slide them on, the night comes into clearer focus, everything highlighted in fluorescent green, and I leap just in time to avoid stumbling over a fallen log. Instead, I use the mossy oak as a springboard, launching myself toward the wall, just a few feet away.

The smack of body against the brick drives the air from my lungs, and I dig my fingers and the heels of my boots into the worn lines of mortar between the stones in order to hold on. I heave in one breath, then two, only giving myself a few seconds to recover before I'm climbing. A surge of hope rises in me as I scale the fifteen-foot wall. I'm so close to escape. If I can scale this wall and make it to the other side, I'm home free. I can make my way back to Bridgeport and liaise with Hook for safe passage to Delorood.

I've been a good climber my whole life, since very soon after walking. First, to escape the bastard who'd sired me, avoiding beatings by remaining out of reach, and then to keep up with my adopted brothers: Sabre, Titus, and Draven, who had the unfair advantage of flight. Even with my fingernails threatening to break and the flesh of my fingers already screaming, I know I can handle this wall.

The roar ceases, and the silence is so deafening, I whip my head down to see what's happened to my pursuers. What I find below draws a squeak from me.

The two bears, one black and the other slate gray, have disappeared, leaving men in their place — very tall and very... strong who also happen to be as naked as the day they were born. I can't see much beyond the tops of their heads, though, but what I can make out with the aid of my goggles frightens the shit out of me.

These fuckers are huge! Easily six-feet-six or more, with more muscle than your average carnival strongman. And they're scaling the wall after me, closing the distance quickly, the dark one in the lead.

My mind squeaks a panicked litany even as I force myself to climb higher, faster.

Oh shit, oh shit, oh shit...

The dragon shifters — Malvolo, Herrick and Reve — had tried to warn me against this mission, saying that next to dragons and hellhounds, bears are the toughest customers around. You'd have to be a moron or have a death wish to fuck with them. And yet, here I am — with no death wishes so I guess that leaves the other alternative. Am I moron? I guess the jury's out on that one.

I don't really have time to think about it though, because these enormous and enormously pissed off assholes are catching up. Only a foot or two beneath me now, even though I'm climbing as quickly as I can.

"Ah!" I yell when one of them makes a grab for me, wrapping long, sure fingers around my ankle. He tugs, and the force is almost enough to dislodge me from my perch. If he succeeds, he'll send me careening

3

back to the ground to break my back or split my head open like a ripe melon, depending on which way I land.

I cling tenaciously to a brick which pops out of the wall a bit more than the others, giving me something on which to wrap my upper body around. I squeeze until blood runs down my fingers and my knuckles are long past the point of turning white. And then I get an idea. Hopefully not another moronic one.

Clinging to the exposed brick, I take my free foot and smash it, as hard as I can, on the fuckers fingers which are still wrapped around my ankle. Yes, it feels like I'm about to snap my ankle but I do it anyway because I'm not going to last hanging like this. Now the second part of my hopefully not moronic plan: I free one hand from the stone and bring it down to where it's just above the enraged guy's face. He looks up just at the moment I shake my hand and all the blood from my palms and fingers floods his face.

The hot spray of scarlet hits him in the eyes, just as I intended.

"Fuck!" he yells in an accented voice as he draws his grasping hand back to clear his vision, growling all the while. I seize the opportunity and drag myself the last few feet up the wall, scrabbling to reach the top.

The ledge of the wall is about three feet wide, but sturdy enough to stand on, especially for me because I'm about the size of a large child. Yeah, I wasn't around when the gods were handing out height but you know what? Being so little (I'm maybe five feet tall on a good day) has it benefits—I'm small and I'm quick and both attributes make for a good thief.

And I also have great balance — I've been forced to balance on the point of a spire once — so this walk along the top of the wall is a jaunt through the park! When I reach the end, I evaluate the drop down. Even jumping feet first, I'm unlikely to survive the fifteen-foot fall, and if I did survive it, my legs would be broken and I'd have no chance of escaping those fucking bears.

And those bears will kill me if they have the option. I've no doubt about that. The fuckers are beyond enraged.

Climbing down isn't an option, either. My hands are shredded to shit and once on the ground, if my pursuers climb onto the ledge, they'll be in a prime position to rain things down on my head or unload a crossbow bolt or two right into my face.

And I like my face as it is, thank you very much.

Fuck, Goldy, you've really put yourself in a bad one, this time, I tell myself.

I'm aware! Think you can contribute something useful? If not, shut the hell up!

Yeah, I like to have conversations with myself. Hey, there's truth to that old saying about 'being your own best friend', right? Well, at this moment, I'm pretty ticked off with my best friend because she left me in a shitty situation, without many options.

What to do, what to do, what to do…

I stare out at the pitiless winter sky, wishing for the millionth time I'd been born a member of the Order of Corvid, like my adopted brothers. If that had been the case, I could just take the form of an overgrown jay, raven, or rook and fly away from this fucking place.

5

Instead, I'm earthbound. And that leaves me with only one real chance at escaping.

There are more big oak trees just below me. If I aim right, I could snatch a limb on the way down, swing off the limb like a trapeze artist and hit the ground hard, but not fatally so. I know how to land. And I know how to roll. I just wouldn't be very good at fending off two hungry man-bears who want to tear out my throat.

Well, fuckety-fuck, Goldy, what's it gonna be?

This is going to tear up my hands even more so than they already are, but that's a small price to pay for a clean getaway.

Yep, I've made up my mind and I'm going for it.

I'm preparing my leap when the first of the shifters clambers onto the top of the wall with me. Him! All six-foot-enormous of him! What the hell is the idiot thinking? He's a fucking bear, not a tightrope walker!

"I hope you fall off!" I yell at him, just… because.

He doesn't say anything but as I watch him, he seems somehow…balanced and graceful on his feet. With a nervous gulp, I adjust my measure of his height. Six-nine or six-ten, shorter by only a few inches from the tallest shifter I've met to date.

Oh, ye Gods! Look at that cock!

Yeah, he's completely nude, and I don't really do well around naked men. I just… I'm not used to them, that's all. And now I'm totally off-guard for a few stunned seconds. And this fucking naked man-ballerina is making his way towards me as if he's not afraid at all of falling off this fucking wall.

6

His tan, muscled torso gleams lightly with sweat and my blood has caked on his face, in an arc around each of his eyes so he looks like some kind of weird, naked mime or a weird, naked raccoon. I can't keep my eyes from tracking downward, tracing the contours of his abdomen down to his...

Dear God. That thing... there should be a warning sign tacked to it.

I have to yank my eyes away from the sight of the very full and very large cock that nestles against his thigh. I have to imagine the winter air is painfully cold on his bare skin, but it's not dissuading the monster between his legs. I've only ever seen one other cock in my life, and it was similarly large and belonged to a dragon shifter. Are all men built like this—with enormous man meat? If so, I think I'll be holding onto my virginity until the end of my days.

Which won't be too much longer if you don't hurry the fuck up, Goldilocks, I remind myself with a bewildered shake of my head which sets my golden curls bouncing all over the place.

"Can't you cover yourself with something?" I yell out at him as I start forward again.

"Yes, I'll soon be wearing your fucking skin!" he yells back in a Scandinavian accent, voice deep and angry. "I'm going to skin you from head to toe, thief!"

I don't look back, but I can hear the sound of his steps. He continues his advance, taking slow, measured strides toward me. I glance back to get a read on his proximity.

Black shiny hair atop his head, he's long of limb, bulging with ready muscle, scars and burns crisscrossing his biceps and forearms. He's got a

7

square, heavy jaw; a narrow, aquiline nose; and captivating brown eyes. They narrow on me, watching me dither on the edge of the wall like some frightened damsel.

"Hand over the Ambrosia and you don't have to die," Black Bear's companion says as he pulls himself onto the ledge, his voice a deep rumble like distant thunder. His slate-gray hair is an odd contrast to the rest of him, giving the impression of advanced age, while his body looks like it could belong to that of a young blacksmith.

His presence doesn't trouble me unduly. The ledge is narrow, and, if I'm lucky, at least one of them will fall off and die a slow and miserable death.

"Not a chance!" I've worked too hard and there's too much at stake to give up now.

Gray-Bear's mouth screws into a tight line. "I'm only going to give you one more chance to hand the Ambrosia over now and I'll extend my leniency." So he must be the one in charge?

"Fail to comply," Black Bear adds. "And there'll be lots of fucking pain and even more death."

I pause at that one and scrunch up my face as I glance back at him. "How can there be even more death?" I call, shaking my head. "You can only die once."

He frowns at me and I just offer him a shrug and a smile to say I know I've bested his argument. As to his threat… Pain, I can handle. And death is a risk I'm willing to take.

So I shove my hand once more into the satchel and grope around until I find the hilt of a broadsword. I draw the sword from its jeweled scabbard before bringing it forth from the bag.

"You want the Ambrosia, beary-bears, come and get it," I challenge, raising the sword to its ready position. It's not my preferred weapon, but it will do. I just have to fell these fuckers and then I'll be free. And maybe I'll wear *their* fur since Black-Bear made that overly rude comment about wearing my skin.

"Last chance, girl," Black-Bear says and he's now maybe six feet from me.

"Stop stallin', Nash," the second one growls, his hazel eyes glaring murder at me.

"When we reach you, we're going to split open your belly with our claws and watch your insides trail to the ground!" Black-Bear, otherwise known as Nash, yells at me.

"Is that part of the extra death I was promised?" I respond with a little giggle. I like it when my comments are wittier than those of my enemies.

Nash takes another step forward and I strike with my sword, carving a furrow into his bicep. The blade goes in deep, but he doesn't cry out. He's a tough motherfucker, more so than I expect. He continues forward, and lashes out at me. I duck his swing, dancing back a few steps to stay out of reach.

Yeah, that wasn't such a great idea because I find myself balancing precariously on the edge of the wall, one boot threatening to step out into open air. One shove is all it would take to end me right here and now.

I move forward, brandishing the big sword, but the truth is that the thing is made for someone way taller and stronger than I am (I got it from Malvolo, an enormous dragon shifter) so it throws off my balance and I have to drop it, so I don't go tumbling off the wall.

"Fuck!" I yell as I start to lose my balance. At the same time Nash's huge, calloused hand locks around my wrist and tugs me back onto the stone ledge, steadying me before I can fall.

Um, what? Black Bear just saved me after threatening to kill me more than once?

For a protracted moment, we just stare at each other. I can't seem to tear my gaze away from his beguiling eyes. What is he doing? I'm his enemy. Why did he save me?

Oh, maybe he's going to push me off the wall to kill me once and then maul me when I'm down, to kill me twice?

"Surrender," he orders in a soft but fervent whisper.

"I never surrender!" I say just as quietly.

Then I use all the strength I've borrowed from one of their guards and I take a step forward, driving my fist into his gut. The attempt shocks him and he lets out a startled "oomph" sound. But, most unfortunately, he doesn't double over, like I expected. And that doesn't make a whole lot of sense because the bear I leached energy from only ten or so minutes earlier was big and strong, with lots of power to spare.

But just making contact with this guy's abdomen does a number on my knuckles, and, as I glance down, I realize I've split them wide open.

Damn it—at this rate, my hands are going to be useless for weeks. Maybe I can track Tenebris and buy a healing potion from her. Yes, it's *that* important I heal myself and quickly—a thief's best tools are her hands, and I can't afford to lose the use of mine.

Well, unless my double death makes that a moot point.

So while the blow didn't do much but surprise this giant, it did loosen his grip on me, giving me enough time to twist out of his grasp and sight my target again. An oak, many feet below, with its bare arms stretched toward the sky. The branch is about eight or nine feet off the ground. Perfect. It's not going to be a pleasant impact, but I'll survive and, honestly, I'd rather take my chances with the tree than Black Bear.

I dive off the wall, praying the wind doesn't shift me off course. For a moment, that seems to last forever, I'm flying, arms outstretched to catch the branch. God, sometimes all I want in the world is a pair of wings.

Then I reach my target, hands clenching tight on the bark of the tree, using the last of my borrowed strength to make the move possible. I swing my weight around the branch, using my momentum to roll my body in a spin, digging furrows into the tree. It sheds bark like shingles, dropping them to the ground below with a sound like clattering stone. The effort it takes tears my palms to ribbons and tears spring to my eyes. I blink them back, stopping the sob building in my throat. Escape now, indulge the pain later.

I leap down, the eight-foot drop making my bones shiver in protest, but I grit my teeth and bear it.

Ha-ha... bear it.

And now I've got to get the sword before I make my getaway. It sticks blade first into the ground, quivering like a javelin as I snatch it up, and shove it back into my satchel. I start moving again, slower than before. It's hard to find a part of me that doesn't sting or throb in some fashion. But I'm free at last.

I race, as fast as my legs will carry me, for the break in the trees. The break will lead to a path that winds back to Bridgeport, the seaside town. I have a reservation at the inn there and a meeting with Hook arranged for the next day. And then I'll be sailing as far away from these angry fuckers as I can!

I've nearly reached the path when a figure steps in front of me, bringing me up short. I have to dig my heels into the packed earth to stop from smacking into his chest. He's monstrously tall and pale like the other two, but that's where the similarities end. He's got a squarer face, an angular cut to his jaw, and blue eyes instead of brown. Deep brown hair gathers around his face in waves and brushes his ears.

I don't see the fist that lashes out, but I feel the impact on the side of my face. It sends me flying backwards, literally picking me up off my feet. My head knocks into the trunk of another oak tree and stars explode in my vision. The last thing I see, before darkness sinks in, is his triumphant smirk.

TWO
Kassidy

Bile claws its way up my throat as I swim back to consciousness, and my body heaves, threatening to spill the leftover fish I had for breakfast all over my front. I swallow it back, but the sour taste just prompts another gag before I can cough down the worst of the nausea.

When I try to open my eyes, a silver spike of winter daylight drives into my vision. I gag again and screw my eyes shut tight. My ears are ringing, and my head feels like a struck bell. I can't lift my head more than an inch or two without feeling the return of the nausea. I settle back down against the ground—stone I think it is, owing to the feel and the coldness against my cheek—and try to gather what information I can about my surroundings with my eyes shut.

I've been out for at least ten to twelve hours, if the sun is shining. And that's bad. Really bad. It can only mean the man who punched me nearly put me into a goddamn coma. I don't think I've had anyone lay me out that hard, not even the dragon I was unfortunate enough to spar with.

Cold bites my body. And from the fact that I can feel the cold on my legs and arms, I realize I've been stripped down to just my undershirt and underthings. The thin cotton offers almost no protection from the

13

elements and I curl my legs unconsciously, trying to get them nearer to the heat of my core. My boots, belt, satchel, and weapons are all missing as well. My bare feet are numb and my toes won't curl when I try to move them. Shit. They've left me to die of frostbite out here. Maybe they think it's what I deserve.

Gods, what if they do try to kill me twice, just to prove a point?

Oh, shut up, Goldy.

I try to lift myself up as I force my eyes open and they rebel against the light so I close them once more. It's not as if I haven't been trapped in the cold before. I've survived worse, though I had my brothers to huddle against for warmth, at the time. Now, my progress is impeded by manacles on my wrist. The fuckers chained me up?!

The portion of skin beneath the heavy iron is so cold, it actually feels like a low-grade burn. The body is tricky like that sometimes. I've seen people freeze to death because their body tricked them into thinking they were burning up in the snow.

I open my eyes slowly, centimeter by centimeter, until they grow accustomed to the light. When only mild discomfort greets me this time, I'm grateful. I test the length of chain the manacles are attached to. There's no give. I'm tethered to a stone column, one of many in this courtyard, and the column is double the size of an oak trunk. Even if I've somehow retained the strength I stole from one of the werebears, there's no way I could snap this thing in two. It's probably designed for holding a bear in place, and my scrawny human self won't make a dent in it.

Swallowing back the desire to gag again, I sit up, and my head pounds with the effort. I'm definitely hurt, but I'm still not sure how badly. I was fairly sure I'd snapped my neck when I hit the ground but such clearly isn't the case because I'm not paralyzed.

As I become aware of voices nearby, I crawl to the backside of the pillar, trying to hide. I recognize both voices, though I've only heard them speak a handful of words. But, I'm good with faces, names, and voices. Another trick of the trade when you're a thief. It can be deadly to hit the same mark twice.

"It's cruel, Nash," Gray-Bear, the one known as Leith, mutters.

I dare a peek around the rounded edge of the pillar. They're standing about ten feet away, talking in low voices that nonetheless carry across the stone courtyard. There's not much between me and them, except for a burbling fountain and a few stone benches. They're thankfully clothed this time, and they pose a striking contrast to one another. The taller of the two, Leith, is dressed in a simple white linen tunic that ends at his knees, beneath which he wears woolen trousers and suede boots. His slate-gray hair is pulled back into a low tail behind his neck, but pieces have already come loose, as though the wind tossed it into motion.

His brother—Nash—is dressed in leather armor and chainmail, with only brief flashes of tan, rippling bicep or thigh muscle showing between the pieces. His midnight hair is cropped close to his head with a design of swirls shaved into the closely-cropped hair. Anyone trying to grab a fistful of it would have a hard time. The brown-haired bear is conspicuously missing.

15

My traitorous body clenches with want at the sight of the two of them, especially Nash. He oozes masculine confidence, something I've always liked in a man. That, and a good sense of humor. But Nash's finely-cut face doesn't look like it's seen a day of laughter in its life.

He follows Leith's pacing form with a glare.

"Cruel? It's the law, Leith. You don't get to bend it because the miscreant happens to have a mossy cleft between her thighs."

A mossy cleft? And just like that, whatever desire I might have felt for him is gone.

"Don't be crude, Nash. I merely mean to point out she's human. And she won't survive the usual punishment. Didn't you see how small she is? She won't live through even half of it. We'll flay her down to bone, not to mention she's already hurt."

"Then she should have thought of that before she stole from us." Nash insists stubbornly before turning on Leith and shaking his head, in obvious anger. "I don't see why we're arguing about it. If she were a man, you'd have ordered her punishment already."

"Yes, but she's not a man."

My sluggish brain catches up with the words as I slowly start to make sense of things. They mean to punish me for the theft of the Ambrosia. I don't know much about werebear society, other than the fact that all werebears are of Scandinavian, and more pointedly, Viking origin and they're a small and reclusive band of mariners who favor the coast and shun outsiders.

I also know they're the only ones in all of Fantasia who know how to create Ambrosia. And Ambrosia is valuable. It's a bread-like substance imbued with magic that can extend life and heal injuries. It's for that reason I've been sent. The Guild knows there's a war on the horizon, and we need every advantage we can get. And Ambrosia would be a good advantage to have—something we can use to heal our soldiers.

I'm not sure what the two of them mean by punishment, exactly. A lashing, maybe? If so, I could probably survive it, especially if I'm able to touch one of them at some point and leach his life force in order to heal myself. Still, it doesn't mean I relish the thought of being whipped.

I really don't like pain.

I lean further out from behind the pillar and my chain rattles, betraying me. Both their heads whip toward me in unison, eyes narrowing in an eerily similar fashion. I try to scrabble back into the shadow, but too late. I've been seen.

Fuck fuck and fuck!

Nash rounds the pillar first. I glare defiantly up at him, refusing to let him see how frightened I really am. The shivers that rack my body are as much from cold as from fear. Damn it all but where are the dragon shifters when you need them? They'd make quick, charcoal work of these fuckers in two seconds flat.

"The thief is awake," Nash sneers.

"You're a prick, you know that?" I shoot back at him, not wanting him to realize how nervous I am. It's better not to cower. "A big, dumb…"

A snarl cuts me off. It's like a ripping sound issuing from Nash's chest. He bares his teeth and his canines are already extended into fangs, like he's going

17

to tear me to shreds. I fall silent, mentally beating myself for baiting him. I'm chained and at every physical disadvantage. All I'm going to succeed in doing is getting myself killed.

Maybe even twice.

Leith rounds the pillar next and shoulders Nash out of the way; he's growling as well, but at Nash instead of me. The two lock eyes and I can practically feel their wills clashing like two boulders, stubbornly refusing to give. Nash eventually tears his gaze away from Leith, growl tapering off to a grumble.

When Leith shifts his eyes to me once more, I've regained my footing, though I have to use the pillar for support. The courtyard seems to be spinning and my head starts pounding again.

Shit, shit, shit. I'm definitely hurt and I need a healer.

"What's your name, thief?" he demands.

"Thief," I answer with a shrug that gives me an even worse headache.

He growls louder.

I consider for a minute. Do I give him my name? It's not like I'm an especially well-known thief. There's no bounty on my head, like there is for Tenebris, so it's not as though he'll be able to sell me to a neighboring kingdom for gold. Still, I'm leery.

"What's *your* name?" I ask instead, holding my chin high.

Leith's eyebrows raise slightly as if he's surprised I've turned the tables on him. "I am King and my name is Leith Nord. This is my cousin, Nash Ericson."

18

I blink. Royalty? Royalty were the ones who came after me? I'm surprised, to say the least. In fact, it's so strange, I can't even formulate a proper response. All the royals I've ever met have been naggy, doughy sorts, depending on more capable men and women to do their bidding.

"And the asshole who punched me?" I manage at last.

"He's the asshole?" Nash manages through his teeth.

"Sorren Nord," Leith answers.

"Your brother?" I ask.

Leith shakes his head. "Also my cousin. I have no siblings."

"Now who the fuck are you?" Nash demands.

I decide to give them my thief name rather than my birth name since it will be harder to link me to my Guild name, in case they try at some point. "Goldilocks."

A small smile tugs the corner of Leith's full, kissable mouth. He doesn't intimidate me as much as Nash does. Even though he appears just as strong and immense, there's kindness in the set of Leith's mouth and eyes. That doesn't mean he won't hurt me, of course, but it also doesn't look like he wants to. It's more than I was expecting. Far more than I deserve for breaking their laws.

"Goldilocks, hmm?" Leith says as he looks at me, or more pointedly, my hair. "Wonder where you got your name?" then he smiles in a way that says the inside joke is just ours. It's a bizarre response and then I suddenly wonder if he's trying to make nice because he figures it will get him further than if he's an asshole like Nash.

Well, he's right.

"So we're in quite the quandary, Goldilocks," Leith continues, his hazel eyes narrowed on me in a way that makes me feel like he can see right through me. I don't like the feeling.

"Why is that?" I ask, wondering what his game is.

He shrugs. "Because you broke a hefty law by stealing from us."

"Right," I answer. "About that, I have lots and lots of stuff in my satchel," I start. "Maybe we can trade for my… mistake?"

"We aren't interested in trades, thief," Nash spits back at me. "Besides, I already raided your satchel and took what little interested me."

"Great," I say with faux good humor. "Then when is my release date?"

"There will be no release," Nash snorts. Then he turns to face Leith. "You know the law, Leith. Follow it, or I will."

"Watch your tongue," Leith barks at him.

I clear my throat, nerves starting to eat at me because I can see by Leith's clouded expression that he's torn. And if he's torn, that means he can be convinced by Nash. But I'm still not really sure what it is Nash is trying to convince him of. "What does the law say?"

Leith's expression is tight. "Our law states that anyone guilty of stealing the Ambrosia must pay with blood and flesh in recompense."

Um. What?

20

"What does that mean, exactly?" I ask tentatively.

"It means you will receive ten slashes of bear claws from each member of the royal clan, and if you survive, you'll be put to work to pay back your debt," Nash says coldly.

"How many members of the royal family are there?" I ask, scared for the answer. And how long, exactly, are their claws?

"Three," Leith answers. "Nash, myself and Sorren makes the third."

Ice drops into my stomach and I have to hold my breath, lest I begin to hyperventilate as his meaning sinks in. Ten slashes from bear claws from the three members of the family? That's thirty swipes. Leith's earlier words float back to me and I now understand the truth of them. I won't survive even half of that punishment.

"I won't survive," I croak, shaking my head.

"Exactly," Nash responds.

"I understand you think I'm just some thief," I start, shaking my head as the urgency of my predicament weighs down on me. "But I'm much much more than that."

"Save your speeches, thief, we aren't interested," Nash says.

"You don't understand!" I rail back. "I can't abandon my brothers to the fight that's coming."

"Prepare to face your punishment, little Goldilocks," Nash continues and by the glint in his eyes, I can see he's going to enjoy this.

He seizes me by my undershirt and spins me around, shoving me roughly against the stone pillar.

GOLDY HP MALLORY

It's so cold against my skin, I almost scream. He holds my cheek against the ice-cold pillar while he tears my undershirt all the way down my back and the flimsy thing slides down my arms, fluttering to the ground. I cross my arms over my chest, trying to cover my nudity, even though I'm facing the stone. I then brace for the pain I know is coming.

How am I going to get myself out of this? My mind races.

Kassidy, think of something! Otherwise, Nash is going to kill you! You have to think of something!

I'm trying!

"Nash," Leith starts.

"It's the law of our clan," Nash interrupts him, anger tainting his voice. "I didn't make the laws! They've been in place for a reason so we aren't going to be the ones to break them!"

Don't let them hear you scream, I think desperately. *Bite your goddamn lip off if you have to, but don't give them the fucking satisfaction, Kassidy.*

The searing pain of claws I'm expecting doesn't come. There's the sound of a blunt, heavy impact, and then Nash is snarling again. When I dare to peek out from the corner of my eye, I see Nash with his hands in a defensive position as he fends off the sledgehammer blows Leith's raining down on him. At first, they seem pretty evenly matched, until Leith manages to get inside Nash's defenses, knocking him hard onto his ass.

"Enough!" Leith roars. "Have you forgotten *I* am king?"

"The law demands blood!"

"There's another option," a third voice drawls.

22

All assembled turn to face the new arrival. I don't recognize his voice, but I can guess who it might be. Sure enough, when I swing my gaze to the archway at the edge of the courtyard, *he's* standing there — tall and pale and just as impassive now as he was when he hit me. He's not looking at any of us, instead examining his nails as though they're of more note than anything we're doing.

Of course, I'm not doing much, chained as I am to this pillar.

Leith straightens from his defensive crouch and grimaces at the newcomer. "What the bloody fuck are you talking about, Sorren?"

"There's a precedent in the law for non-bear offenders," Sorren responds with a shrug, his Scandinavian accent just as pronounced as is his cousins'.

"What precedent?" Nash demands.

"Do you recall the tale of Queen Oliviette?" Sorren asks.

Leith appears completely nonplussed. "The barbarian queen?"

"The very same." Sorren elaborates for my benefit, reading the confusion on my face. "Queen Olivette was from a land of savages. She led her armies into battle against us, stealing from our royals. She was human, like you, and also like you, she was captured." I can't tell from Sorren's expression if he's having a go at me. "When it became quite apparent she wouldn't survive the punishment, the kings of yore employed a ritual called the Rite of Three."

A smirk alights on Nash's lips, and I really don't like that grin, no matter how attractive he may be. His eyes sweep over my body speculatively. I would give him a one-fingered salute if it wouldn't expose more of me to his gaze. Instead, I clutch my hands tighter around by breasts.

Leith makes a dubious sound. "Yes, could work. But we need her consent. I won't do it if she's unwilling."

"Unwilling to do what?" I ask, ashamed of the tremor in my voice. "What's the Rite of Three?"

Leith exchanges a glance with his cousins. Nash looks positively eager to tell me and Sorren remains ambivalent, as though the answer is inconsequential.

Leith faces me then and sighs. "Queen Olivette surrendered her body to three princes for three subsequent fortnights in exchange for mercy for her and her people. It would mean you would pay your debt with your body, instead of your blood."

"You would become a mistress to the three of us for six weeks straight, spending all your time in our beds," Nash adds as he looks me up and down, clearly appreciating what he sees.

My stomach pitches and my eyes prick. This is my only choice? Die or surrender to the deflowering from men I don't know? Give them something I've never shared with anyone? Not to mention the time away from the cause, from the Guild. Six weeks is a long time! With Morningstar threatening to break free from his prison any day now, I'm needed now more than ever before.

This isn't fair!

I search Leith's face. If it were just him, I could live with it. He's been kindish thus far and would likely be gentle with me if I asked. But the agreement isn't limited to just Leith. Nash and Sorren will each have a turn. I don't know Sorren well enough to decide if I dislike him but I most certainly dislike Nash. In fact, I can't stand him!

The look of anticipation on Nash's face clinches the decision for me.

I turn my back to all three of them, clutching the stone pillar for dear life. Tears squeeze from the corners of my eyes as the cold burns into me.

"I'll take my chances with your claws."

THREE
Leith

Foolish, foolish girl.

She can't know exactly the effect her words will have on Nash, but I can see the impact the moment they fly out of her mouth. The impertinence, the snub and implied insult of her refusal will send him into a fit. She doesn't know that Nash's beast is the worst of all of ours, forced to the surface by his father's punishment years ago. Nash stayed in his bear form so long, he almost couldn't come back. And now, the bear is more at the helm of Nash's body than the man.

Even though Nash and Sorren are my cousins, we are close enough to be brothers. And, yes, I share the same surname with Sorren. Our grandfather bore three children—a daughter and two sons. One of those sons was my father—Albrecht Nord and the other son was Sorren's father, Teague Nord. Sorren never had a claim to the throne because he was born a bastard, out of wedlock. As I have no children of my own, should something happen to me, Nash will be next in line through the bloodline of his mother, my father's sister.

The question of the throne is a sensitive one as Nash has always believed it should have been him seated on the throne, not me. He discounts the fact that I bear the same name as my grandfather, and he doesn't. He always believed his ability as a fighter and defender of our kingdom was enough to ensure his title, but the old ways are what they are and the kingdom is handed down through the father's line, not the mother's.

Rage spasms across Nash's face and he lets loose a growl that shakes the stones around us. He stalks forward, blunt human nails sharpening into dark, curved claws, and he strips the flimsy underdrawers from the little thief's body, leaving her completely bare, her pert little ass facing us.

It's distracting, to say the least. She's thin, but not in the way so many peasant girls are. She's never been starved, but there's no fat on her because she's spent her life doing hard labor. Her legs are sturdy, though not long. I linger on the muscled curve of her thigh. She looks like she could take the brunt of a man's passion between those thighs.

How long has it been since I've seen a human woman that could withstand a night in my bed? Too long.

Just above the curve of her hip is a gleaming tattoo. The gold ink stands out like a brand against her skin, depicting a shield pierced by both a broadsword and a wand, encircled by twinkling stars.

A Guild tattoo.

This woman is a Guild member. Fuck.

That fact stuns me for a half-second as the implications sink in. I haven't seen a Guild member in fifteen years, since the end of the last Great War, when the kingdoms of Fantasia—ours included—voted to contain Morningstar and his armies behind a seal, trapping them in the ether. Most kingdoms then summarily banned magic and sought to disband the Guild.

We all know they're still kicking around, of course. No royal decree will stop the fanatics of the Guild from insisting Morningstar will rise again. But I never thought to expect this. I thought the Guild was now just a band of fundamentalist fools, too tenacious for their own good, holding onto their need for vengeance with white-knuckled stubbornness. About as indoctrinated as the disciples of the new Wonderland religion, the worship of the Seven Joys.

But the arrival of this improbable girl throws the Guild into new light. It's not just the old guard anymore. They've inducted new blood. The girl can't be much over twenty, just barely old enough to remember the first war. She would have been recruited afterward. And that logically means there must be others. Yes, the Guild must hold onto more of its strength than we initially thought.

And if they're sending a thief to acquire the Ambrosia we refuse to trade, it means it's just as she said—she's no opportunistic pickpocket looking for money or immortality. We get those periodically, avaricious types who seek longevity for themselves. They're often other shifters and occasionally fae, which is why the girl slipped past our guards unnoticed. We've been certain for years that no human was foolish or suicidal enough to try it.

She's proved us wrong. Worse, she nearly got away with it. If not for Sorren's network of tunnels beneath our village, she would have made a clean escape with her bounty. She's tried to steal away with seventeen kilos of Ambrosia, enough to break down and spread among a small standing army. Which means only one thing.

The Guild intends to take the offensive, bringing war to Morningstar, should he and his brethren emerge. Fuck. What sort of retribution are we inviting from the Guild if we kill her?

Not that I'm planning on killing her because I'm not. And on that subject, I have a cousin to take control of…

Nash draws his arm back, ready to flay the skin between her shoulder blades before I catch his wrist.

"No, Nash!"

He whips his head toward me and he's already partially shifted, straight nose elongating into a more ursine shape. The ruddy brown of his eyes bleeds into the golden brown of the bear's.

"Unhand me, Leith. She asked for it, she'll damn well get it!"

"Look at her, Nash!"

"I'm fucking looking!" But he's looking at her ass. Not that I can blame him—it's quite high and round.

"No, *look*!"

Nash's fury doesn't abate, but he does what I ask, raking his gaze over her body. My own beast rises to the surface, some latent possessive instinct pushing to the fore as I see clear appreciation in his eyes. He sees what I do. The strong, toned physique, the small, pert breasts. I wish she'd move her hands so I could see the lovely pink of her nipples once more. I ache for a taste of her. Ache to taste the cleft between her thighs, to see if she's as sweet as she smells. Test my teeth against firm, quivering thighs as she reaches her peak, pussy clenching tightly around the two fingers I intend to push inside her.

I press my beast down with a soft snarl of frustration. I master my instincts, unlike Nash and Sorren. I control the bear; it does not control me. It's the reason why I'm the only one fit to rule our clan. Nash's impulses would lead our kingdom to ruin. And Sorren can't discern right from wrong, not since the incident. Besides, a bastard has no right to the throne — it's not a rule I came up with — it's one that's long existed.

So, it falls to me.

Nash finally spots the Guild marking, after lingering on her ass for a long stretch. And he reaches out to trace the tattoo with a claw. Goldilocks flinches like she's been struck, letting out a soft yelp. She's clearly terrified of him. Of all of us, no doubt.

Gods, when did we become such bastards? She's a tiny thing, for fuck's sake. Thirty or forty years younger than we are. Time should teach us the meaning of leniency. Instead, it's only hardened us into inflexible monsters.

Remorse flickers in Nash's dark eyes for a second before he spins her around. "When and how did you get this?" he demands as his eyes drop to her breasts and she colors instantly, reaching up to cover them, which leaves her bare down below. I spot the thatch of golden hair that covers her cleft and I feel my cock stir.

"The fucking Guild gave it to me!" she yells at him, face distorted in anger as she covers her breasts with one arm and her pussy with the other.

30

"Last I knew, the Guild didn't employ thieves!" Nash insists, his eyes narrowed on the space between her thighs. I'm more than sure he got a brief view of the golden hair between her legs and he wants another.

Goldilocks's eyes flash with fiery defiance, her jaw ticking in a way I can't help but find attractive. Gods, her eyes are the loveliest shade of green I've ever seen. Too light to be called true emerald, not pale enough to be called sage. Almost the color of verdant grass. The color is comforting, like returning home.

"Then you're behind the times, *Ericson*." She says his last name with the intent to remind him it's not my last name—the king's last name. At least, I'm guessing such is her reason. She lets derision seep into her tone, unwisely baiting Nash again. "The Guild started employing thieves when the rest of Fantasia forced us to play dirty! We have sellswords and pirates now as well, if you're interested."

She shakes her head, tossing her golden curls, trying to come off as flippant. I can still smell the acrid bite of her fear, so I'm not convinced. Neither is Nash.

"So, if you're done interrogating me, you can get back to the punishment," she hisses at him, straining as far as her chains will allow her to get into his face.

For a second, I'm sure he's going to kill her. Tension crackles hot and wild in the air between them. But then his gaze flicks down to her mouth, a soft growl building in his throat. And then I realize I mistook him. He's not going to kill her...

Unless something stops him, he's going to drive her to the stone and fuck her right here. There's too much of the bear in him to overlook her challenge. He'll fight her, win her, claim her.

I hook an arm around her narrow waist and draw her to my side, out of Nash's reach. The snarl escapes him, a sound of protest instead of desire. He'll thank me later, when he realizes how close he came to ravishing her. If any fucking is going to happen, it needs to be on her terms or not at all.

I dip my head so I can speak quietly into her ear. She shivers at my proximity and I sneak a guilty glance down at her chest. The rosy buds of her nipples are peaked, taut and yearning. Is it from the cold, or the pressure of my body?

"Surrender, girl," I coax. "Surrender to the Rite of Three. It's not such a high price, in the end. Six weeks in exchange for the rest of your life."

"And if I become with child?" she demands.

The thought suddenly thrills me to my marrow but of course I can't tell her as much—I'm not even sure why it does. Yet, the idea of her stomach swelling with my child… it's a visual that fills me with warmth. "I swear on my honor, as a werebear and a king, we won't finish inside you."

She cranes her neck to look me in the eye. "You promise?"

"Yes. We won't sire children with you. After your time is served, you bear no further obligation to any of us."

She releases a shuddering breath and then turns to face me, pushing close to me so most of her petite body is covered by my coat. The top of her head barely reaches my sternum. I tense, waiting for her to reach for my weapon or otherwise try to harm me. I know she's fast, and stronger than she appears. But she just continues to shiver.

She must be frozen. Nude in this weather? It's almost as cruel as the lashes she's being faced with. I shrug out of my jacket and drape it over her shoulders. Cold slices through the thin cotton of my shirt at once, but I bear it. I have the blood of my beast to warm me. Her human constitution won't last under the elements for long.

"All right," she says in a quiet, somber whisper, "I'll do it. Under one condition."

I'm relieved. I didn't want to see her come to harm. "Name it."

She raises her eyes to mine. A look of aching vulnerability crosses her face. Without thinking, I slide my hands up to cup her jaw. I want to erase that expression, to replace it with pleasure.

"I'd like…" she starts but closes her eyes as though she hates the words exiting her mouth.

"What do you ask?"

She opens her eyes and those green gems glitter in the sunlight. "I'd like to choose the order."

"The order?"

She nods. "If… if I agree to do this, I'd like to choose the order of the three of you."

"Very well. What do you prefer?"

She swallows hard. "You first. Then Sorren. Then Nash."

Out of the corner of my eye, I see Nash's face twist, clearly insulted at being placed last. Sorren's face betrays nothing, impassive as ever. What in the name of Avernus is going on in his twisted mind now?

I face the small girl again, imagining her splayed before me, imagine feeling the down of the hair that covers her cleft and the taste of her when I stick my tongue deep inside her hole. "Done."

She sways in place, clutching my coat as though it's a lifeline. Then, she drops her gaze to the stones at her feet. "So... am I supposed to do this chained? Is a bed too much to ask for?"

Right.

Rutting her here in the courtyard is rather barbarous, even for a bear. I reach into the pocket of my abandoned coat and produce the key. I slot it into the lock of the manacles and twist until they fall away with a clatter. I wait for her flight, but it doesn't come. She just steps closer, huddling into my side. She's shaking—either with cold or fear, perhaps both. I don't like it. She shouldn't fear me. Not because I'm not worthy of fear, but because no one in my bed should dread being there.

I decide here and now, I won't touch her until she asks. It'll be a long, frustrating night in my quarters, but at least it will keep her from antagonizing Nash.

"We should go," I say.

And so, we leave the frigid courtyard behind, stepping into the warm interior of the castle. I'm only half paying attention to the corridors as they fly by, trying to figure out what's going on behind those beautiful emerald eyes.

But she's as inscrutable as Sorren.

Scary thought, that.

FOUR
Kassidy

Stop being such a damn girl, Kassidy. You're going to get through this! And you're going to show these bastards you can't be backed into a corner!

As pep talks go, it's not my best. Still, there's a ring of truth to it. I *am* acting like a damn girl. If I were a man, this wouldn't make me squeamish in the slightest. If they were three werebear women, offering to fuck me in exchange for my freedom, it would be the sort of lascivious thing told in drinking establishments, instead of my worst nightmare.

It's not as though you plan to go through with it anyway! I rail at myself.

I don't?

No, you fucking don't!

No, I'm not going to have sex with any of them. And, good thing I was smart enough to ask for Leith first because he seems the nicest and, thus, the easiest to dupe.

I take a deep breath as the headache that's been pounding through my head since Sorren punches me continues. Not to mention my palms and fingers which are scraped up and a bleeding, disgusting mess. I'm not in any shape to be having sex or draining a powerful werebear. The truth is that I should be resting and allowing my body to heal.

But that's not an option so I stick with the plan.

35

I'll let Leith strip me, perhaps touch me a little, but when his clothes are off and his guard is down, I'll steal every scrap of strength I can from his body and then I'll bolt. But this time, I'll go a different direction in an effort to avoid Sorren. It's a solid plan.

So why am I still shaking? Leith's hand rests at the small of my back, giving me a gentle push forward. He's not groping me, though he only has to slide his hands down a few inches to palm my ass. And he's made no motion to do that or anything else.

Yet, my heart is pounding and my palms are clammy. It's not as though he's shouting at me or threatening me. And he's a hell of a lot nicer than Nash is.

I don't want to admit the truth, even to myself when the thought finally occurs to me. But it's there, nonetheless.

It's not fear making me quiver. It's anticipation.

The expectation of those big, calloused hands sliding over my body, erasing the chill that grips me. I want to know what it feels like to be the object of a man's desire because I've never played that role before.

And when I watched the way the three dragon shifters doted on my friend, Neva, I couldn't help but wish the same for myself. To have that sort of power over a man, to bring him to his knees. It's a power only select women have and Neva had it in spades... obviously.

I wish I had it in spades too but, I'm just... me. A girl with wild, corkscrew hair, small but pert breasts and a tiny, child's body.

But back to this whole fucking subject.

It isn't as if I've never been touched before. I mean, I might not be much compared to Neva but I'm also not ugly! Peter and some of his boys flirt with me incessantly. Peter has even stolen a kiss or two — sweet, brief things as light as butterfly wings. They'd made my stomach flip with girlish excitement.

But this… this is different. The feeling in my stomach is molten, hot and moving south, so I'm aching in places I've never ached before.

We reach a door at the end of another long corridor and Leith stops walking, withdrawing another key from inside his coat pocket — the coat I'm still wearing. Just the feeling of his hand through the fabric that rests against my thighs makes my breath catch. He's going to touch me there — between my thighs. In fact, he'll probably do so much more if I let him.

Well, I'm not going to let him! I remind myself.
Right.
Not even a little touch?
No!
I mean, it couldn't hurt just to feel him…
No!

The door is heavy oak, intricately carved with symbols from a language I don't know. Most people speak the shared tongue of Fantasia, but certain subsets are bilingual. I wish I knew what it says. Leith pulls the door open and gestures for me to step inside first.

My steps falter at the threshold. This is it. No going back now. Maybe it *would* have been better to do this in the courtyard. Being inside this room with only the corridor as my means of escape translates to the fact that I'm more likely to face a bottleneck situation, if I get cornered from either direction. I don't have any of my gear, so I couldn't possibly fight, especially if there ends up being more than one bear to fight, even with Leith's borrowed strength that I intend to steal from him as soon as I can. The courtyard would be humiliating, but it would at least give me more places to run.

The interior of the room is more spacious than I imagined. It's at least twelve feet by twelve feet, and modestly furnished. The walls are gray stone, the rugs mossy green. The bedcovers are a muted brown, stretching across a straw mattress that's big enough for at least three men of Leith's size. Bare wooden beams crisscross the ceiling, and wooden furniture litters the room. The fireplace provides a crackling ambience, as well as enough heat to warm me to my toes.

When the door closes with a click behind me, I jump. We're alone now, just the two of us. I can't seem to tear my eyes away from the bed for long. I'll be on it soon. And he'll be on it and then we'll be on it together...

Gods, but I feel like I'm going to throw up. And this fucking headache won't go away anytime soon. And I'm tired and hungry...

Leith circles me, sliding two fingers beneath my chin so he can get a good look at my face. His eyes are searching and not unkind.

"Sit," he says, pulling a wooden chair from its spot by the fireplace.

I sit. The heat of the fire washes over me, cradling me in comforting warmth. It would almost be worth fucking him just to stay in this room for a while. I'm so tired. My body aches. I just want to sleep. And eat something.

Leith crosses the room, rummages in one of the drawers in his desk, and emerges with a small box. As he walks back over to me, its contents rattle as I wonder what the bear is up to now.

He withdraws two vials from the interior. One, I recognize instantly — the shimmering tangerine hue is hard to mistake for anything else. It's poppy juice, the newest drug being bandied about the wealthier circles in Fantasia. Leith doesn't strike me as a pill-popper, though, and I can't imagine the quantity needed to dose a werebear.

Leith unstoppers the vial and dips a finger inside it, withdrawing it just as quickly. On his finger, a perfect dewdrop forms. The stuff smells like raspberries. He offers me his finger. "Take it."

"I don't want to get high," I say, shaking my head. I've never had any sort of drug or potion or whatever. No reason to start now. In my line of work, if you don't have your mental faculties about you, it could mean your death.

"One drop won't incapacitate you. It has pain-relieving properties. Trust me, you're going to want it," he continues as I wonder what he's going on about.

Gods, is his cock that big that I'll need a painkiller to take it? Is he going to rip me in half? Will losing my maidenhead hurt that much?

"It won't be pleasant to clean and seal your wounds," he finishes as I shake my head inwardly at myself.

Kassidy, you need to calm the fuck down if you're going to get yourself out of this situation alive!

I almost refuse, just to be contrary. But in the end, practicality wins out. It'll be easier to escape if I'm not in pain. I grip his finger, flicking my tongue over the tip before guiding the rest of it inside my mouth. Tangy sweetness coats the inside of my mouth at once and I groan a little in the back of my throat. The stuff absorbs almost instantly. Now I understand why it's so popular. Even a small amount feels incredible.

Leith shudders, hazel eyes bleeding to the gold-brown of his bear form as he watches me, no doubt wishing something else of his was in my mouth instead. I give his finger another lick, hoping to distract him. The more eager he is, the less likely he'll be to notice my ploy before it's too late.

He draws his finger from the heat of my mouth and clears his throat. "Give me your hands."

I present them dutifully, wincing as I finally get a good look at the damage done. The only reason the pain isn't overwhelming when I awoke was the cold. The numbness might have been uncomfortable, but it was better than this.

Leith plucks a pair of tweezers from the box and bends his head over my hands, removing bits of bark and dirt from all over my palms and fingers. Even with the poppy juice in my system, it still stings.

"Why are you doing this?" I ask, frowning down at the top of his head.

"You're injured."

"So what?"

40

"So I'm not a cad. Did you think I'd just flip you onto your knees and rut you while you were in pain and wounded?"

"Yes. That's exactly what I was expecting." It's all experience has taught me to expect. Aside from Sabre, Titus, and Draven, almost every man I've met has been a pig. Drunks, layabouts, letches, and whoremongers. Even Peter doesn't take women seriously.

The only three men I ever met who were worth a damn, aside from my brothers, are the dragon shifters. But they're already spoken for.

My silence is answer enough. Leith snorts, picking more debris from my wounds.

"You must have had bad luck with men?"

I almost tell him I've had no experience with men, or even *a* man, whatsoever. But I'm afraid that information might put him off, and then I'll have to rework the whole plan. So I stay silent.

When he's through, he unstoppers the second vial — this time a light topaz color — and dribbles the contents onto my hands. Where the liquid touches me, the flesh begins to mend immediately. The blood soaks back into my skin and the open wounds begin to seal. By the time the liquid has seeped through my fingers, my wounds are almost sealed. They look weeks instead of hours old.

"What is that stuff?" I ask, quiet wonderment thick in my tone.

"Liquid Ambrosia. It's the most concentrated form."

"Hmm, it seems to be helping my headache too," I say as I feel my health improving with each passing second.

He smiles at me and I feel my breath catch. Leith is a beautiful man. On the inside and the outside — well, as far as I can tell anyway. It's almost a shame that I'm about to betray him. Almost.

"That form of Ambrosia is very difficult to make," he continues. "Be grateful for it, Nash wouldn't have wanted me to give it to you."

"Yeah, well, Nash is a cock."

Leith drops his head back and opens his mouth as a deep chuckle shakes his whole body. It makes me smile and I find myself instantly growing warmer towards him. I imagine he makes a pretty good king.

Stop smiling at him, Kassidy! I reprimand myself. *And stop thinking he's nice! He's not! He's going to force himself into you in a minute with that gigantic appendage of his…*

No, he's not, I argue. *Because I'm going to zap him of his power well before then!*

Well, maybe wait to zap him until after you feel the tip of that behemoth cock inside you?

What? No! What's wrong with you?

It's just… you've never felt the tip of a cock inside you before.

And I'm not going to fucking well start now!

Just a little feel of it?

No, and you shut up!

"Goldilocks?" Leith asks and looks at me with a question in his eyes.

I shake my head. "Sorry… I, uh, was just having an argument with myself."

42

"You were what?"

I shake my head harder this time. "Nevermind." Then I stare down at my hands, clenching them experimentally. "Wow, the wounds are basically healed!" This is exactly why we need that Ambrosia! Does he know how many casualties the Guild could prevent if he'd just give us what we need?

"Yes."

But I am grateful to him. Grateful he's not a tyrant. Grateful he's trusting enough to let me get close so I can betray him. I don't relish the truth of what I'm going to do, but it's necessary, all the same.

I'm not ready to lose my virginity to a man I don't know and I don't want to have sex with Nash, or Sorren, for that matter. But, the biggest hurdle of all is that I don't want to lose valuable time here for weeks on end when I could be doing Guild business.

Time to stop stalling.

Right. I have to get that Ambrosia and escape.

I'll probably only have fifteen to twenty minutes to find my things and slip away. I stand, shedding Leith's coat in one fluid movement. It leaves me bare before his gaze.

His eyes sweep over me before he can stop them, lingering on my breasts and the vee between my legs with a frankly animalistic hunger. But he doesn't make a move toward me.

"This doesn't have to happen tonight, Goldilocks," he says, voice dipping into an even lower octave. The timbre of his voice thrums through me, making my legs weak. "You are still healing from your injuries. I don't relish causing you pain."

I tilt my face up, trying my best to imitate Neva, my former traveling companion. She was a dancer at a raunchy tavern and I watched the way she looked and acted around her dragon lovers. She radiated sensuality without even trying. I'm hoping I learned a few things from her. And now's the time to find out.

"Kiss me, Leith," I murmur. "Taste the… oasis of delight that is… my mouth."

A slight chuckle emanates from deep within him and I feel myself flush.

The oasis of delight that is my mouth? I groan. *You're lucky he's still standing here, willing to do this!*

Oh, shut up!

"Leith," I whisper, narrowing my eyes to make them appear more… sultry. "I want to… take… your disproportionally large… man snake into…"

"Stop," he interrupts with a shake of his head as he tries to hide his smile but loses and another chuckle escapes. "Perhaps it would be best if you… didn't continue to speak."

"Oh," I say as my eyes pop open and I find him staring down at me with the expression of amusement.

"You don't have to try to impress me," he says in a soft voice as he reaches forward and brushes his fingers down the line of my face. "I'm already impressed."

"You are?" I swallow hard, not really sure how it could be that I've impressed him. With what?

"Yes," he nods. "I'm impressed with your tenacity, your courage," he says as I hang on his every word. I'm not used to compliments so I'm eating this up. "I'm impressed with the way your eyes burned bloody fire at Nash," he says on a chuckle. "And I'm impressed with the way this eyebrow arches mighty high when you're affronted," he continues as he reaches up and runs the pad of his index finger over my left eyebrow. "And I'm impressed by the beauty of your eyes. I've truly never seen their equal," he breathes as he trails his finger down the tip of my nose. "And your little, pixie nose," he says, before he brings his finger to my lips. "And the rosebud that is your sweet mouth."

The sound that comes from him then is half growl, half moan. It weakens my knees and I feel like I might fall. He scoops me into his arms before my legs can buckle, crushing me to his broad chest. His mouth comes down on mine and I practically convulse in his arms. Everything in me clenches tight with need.

What is this man doing to me?

I don't know, but he really says the sweetest things…

His mouth is hot, desperate. And his kiss doesn't stay innocent long. His tongue flicks along the seam of my mouth and I gasp, giving him the opening he needs. He tastes every inch of me with tongue and teeth, almost like he's trying to eat me whole. Now is the perfect time to snatch his power, while he's so distracted.

But I can hardly think past a haze of lust.

I want him.

Oh my Gods, Kassidy, I want him!

Please just the tip of that enormous cock! Please please please!

Gods, why do I want him so much? We're strangers. Enemies even.

Without even realizing what I'm doing, I seize one of his big, calloused hands and guide it between my legs. He groans even louder when his fingers touch me. I'm beyond slick already, embarrassingly wet. I need him to touch me or I'm going to combust, leaving nothing but cinders on his mossy rugs.

He groans into my mouth, sliding my folds open with two fingers, exploring me. His thumb finds the bud at the apex of my sex and strokes it with incredible precision.

"Gods," I pant when he lets me breathe. "Oh, Gods, Leith. I... I'm going to..."

I never get a chance to finish the sentence.

Blinding white ecstasy ripples through me like a wave and my entire body goes as taut as a bowstring. My mouth opens, and I barely recognize my own voice screaming his name as the first orgasm rides me. I don't stop screaming either. I bury my nails into his back and scream my fucking head off as my body ripples with pleasure.

My knees finally give out and then it's only Leith holding me up, still crushing me against his chest. His teeth test the skin of my neck, and the sweet pain-pleasure of it threatens to bring me to orgasm again. He grinds his front against me, letting me feel all those inches of his cock.

And I want them. I want every single inch inside me. I know I shouldn't. Maybe it's some werebear magic he's using on me. The Huntsmen of the Order Aves are all supernaturally alluring—maybe it's the same with bears.

What if he's bewitching you? I think. *What if this burning need you're feeling is just artifice, just a response to his magic?*

That thought gives me the presence of mind to return to my original plan, instead of allowing him to hoist me onto the bed and fuck me into oblivion the way I want him to. I slide a hand up his bicep, trail my nails — what's left of them, anyway — up to his neck, twining my fingers into the hairs at the nape of his neck. I tug lightly and draw a half-growl from him.

"On the bed," I pant.

He grunts in agreement and lifts me off the floor, carrying me the last few feet to the bed, before depositing me on it roughly. I bounce a little and then settle. I expect him to reach for his trousers, to bare that huge cock and line himself up with my entrance. But again, he surprises me.

He sinks to his knees at the edge of the bed, nudging my legs apart, spreading me until my glistening sex is revealed to his ravenous gaze. And he stares at me. Stares at the flesh between my legs for a good few seconds.

"Wha… What are you doing?" This wasn't the plan! As far as I understand it, he's supposed to climb on top of me.

"No questions," he says as he spreads me open wider, running his nose along my inner thigh and inhaling like he's gauging the bouquet of a glass of wine. He slips the fingers that were inside me into his mouth and makes a hungry sound. Fuck, it's so wrong. But it's sexy as hell.

"But… I thought you wanted to fuck me?" I ask, clearly and completely confused.

"I do," he says as he looks up at me then back at my sex. "Fuck, I do."

"Then?"

"Tomorrow night. Tonight I want nothing more than to taste you. I want your flavor in my mouth, on my tongue."

Again, my resolve wavers. He's not going to fuck me tonight? He's going to give me the sensation I've been waiting a lifetime for, the thing I can never find with my own hand? Release. Powerful, incredible release, beneath his fingers and tongue.

Well, that's really not so bad, right?

I mean… I guess not.

Yeah, let him have my… flavor as much as he wants tonight and then tomorrow night when he tries to stick me with his timber, I'll suck the life out of him.

Er, maybe suck is the wrong word…

His tongue swipes between my folds and shatters all my careful contemplation. His tongue is somehow impossibly better than the press of his fingers. It traces the contours of my clit, bringing me tantalizingly close to the sweet ending I'm so eager to experience again. When he sinks two fingers into me a minute later, I'm almost sobbing with pleasure.

Yes, yes, yes, you perfect and enormous man-king!

Yes, you wonderful man-bear!

Oh, Gods, I want more.

I want his cock, Kassidy, please!

I tug his hair hard, sure I must be hurting him, but I can't bring myself to care. This feeling is so intoxicating, it's hard to think past it. When another orgasm tears through me a second later, tears leak from my eyes. The rush of emotion is completely foreign to me. It's frankly off-putting, and it gives me renewed focus.

If you're going to do it, do it now!
Before you start to care about the fucker!

I press my fingers to his scalp. The head isn't the best place to do this—I usually prefer the torso, where the energy is strongest. Failing that, a limb. I've taken energy from a dragon via his ankle; taking power from a werebear from his scalp is hardly the strangest thing I'm likely to do.

His power is ready and waiting just beneath his skin, pulsing with desire, ready strength, and the restrained rage of his beast. No worries about draining him to the point of death. Unlike fragile mortals, he'll survive what I'm about to do.

And that's a good thing, because I don't want to hurt him.

He has been very good to me, considering.

I roll my hips once more, groaning for his benefit. Then I reach deeper, snatching his power. It's a strange sensation, stealing from him like this. It doesn't precisely feel like theft, the way it does when I lift a coin purse or an artifact… or Ambrosia. It feels like… downing a glass of rum. It leaves me tingling, full, and elated.

Every person has their own flavor, so to speak. Ordinary humans taste bland, like water with a lemon twist. Barely any substance to them. I don't like draining humans. We have so few years as it is and most have no power to make up the difference, like I do.

Witches vary, but they always crackle on the tongue. Wickedness tastes bitter or sour. Good witches

49

taste like liqueur: sweet and thick, but with a stinging aftertaste.

The only dragon I've stolen from tasted like ozone and char, with the ominous energy that comes just before a firestorm and the devastation afterward.

Leith tastes like resin, pine, and bitter greens. It's a sharp flavor, but I like it. I take it in until I'm metaphorically full, the energy stretching the wall of my internal reservoir.

The werebear startles when I begin, but it's too late. He's paralyzed for the thirty seconds it takes for me to drain his power. There's no way to take it all at once, I simply don't have the capacity for something like that. But I take as much as I can, until I feel like I might burst, until a faint sense of psychic nausea settles over me.

If I do this to humans, it kills them. Period.

But not Leith. He still has enough energy to lift his head, a look of accusation on that handsome face before his eyes roll back into his head and he slumps, unconscious, to the floor. Guilt claws at my insides. He doesn't deserve this, but I have no choice. I have to get out of here with that Ambrosia.

I have to do it for the Guild.

Look, his cock is still hard.

So what?

So, maybe you could just climb on top of it and test it out for a bit?

You're sick, you know that?

Just the tip?

No!

I slide off the bed and push a pillow beneath his head. Then I take his coat, swipe the bottle of liquid

Ambrosia and slip it inside one of the pockets. Tying the garment tightly around myself, I creep to the door and open it a crack. There's no one waiting in the hall for me, not even a sentry.

Leith has tried to protect my modesty.

I'm such a fucking asshole.

I pad to the end of the corridor, checking around the corner again. No one.

Taking a deep breath, I lope forward.

My mission is clear. Find my satchel and bag, sneak past the guards, Sorren, and Nash, and make good my escape—all in fifteen minutes.

FIVE
Nash

I'm about thirty seconds away from exploding into fur, fangs, and teeth.

My bear pushes hard against my tenuous control, urging me down the long corridors toward Leith's rooms. As the Chieftain of our clan, he has numerous rooms on the uppermost level of the castle, but he makes the largest his bedroom.

I'm just going to talk to him, I try to reason. Even I know it's a fat lot of pig toss. I'm really going so I can catch a glimpse of *her.* The golden-haired renegade that almost got away. Grudgingly, I have to admit she's impressive. Too impressive.

The Rite of Three is a bad idea. It allows her too much freedom to escape to try to accomplish her bold scheme all over again.

At the very least, Leith should manacle her to the headboard before fucking her.

He won't though, and that's at least part of the reason I'm going to stand like a deviant by his door. Leith has always been too lenient with women.

If she tries to sneak away after the deed is done, I'll be waiting. Maybe it will quell the seething jealousy if I can hear her sounds of pleasure reverberating off the stones of the castle walls. Then at least I can imagine it's my cock inside that tight fud, coaxing moans from her throat as she cums over and over.

I press back hard against my bear half. All it wants to do is storm inside and claim her. That's all that part of me has wanted to do since the foolish thief pushed her face into mine, defiance shining in those exotic green eyes. She doesn't know the show of dominance was the surest way to rile my beast. If we'd been alone, I'd have pressed her back into the stone column and hoisted her up, thrusting into her as hard as I fucking could.

For the love of all the Gods, I might have done so if Leith hadn't stopped me. Sorren sure as hell wouldn't have. He's never been the same since the incident, and his morals are a long-distant memory. But he'd have watched, the dirty bastard.

I should thank Leith for stopping me. The thief clearly loathes me and won't welcome me inside her. I'm a monster, yes, but that doesn't mean I must *act* like one.

When I reach the end of the corridor, I find Leith's door slightly ajar. I pause a yard away, straining my ears for the sound of their mating. The slap of his hips into hers, the ragged breaths, the moans. But I don't hear anything. Leaning slightly forward, I sniff the air. My bear growls its approval. I smell release. Sex of some sort *has* happened. But the scent is mostly unfamiliar.

I've been alive long enough and through enough mating cycles that I unfortunately know what my cousin's release smells like. And the smell of his seed is conspicuously absent. The thief's is the only aroma that lays thick and intoxicating in the air. She's achieved release once, possibly twice, but Leith has not.

I find that questionable and. more so, troubling.

I wait several more seconds for one or both of their voices to sound in the room beyond. When only silence greets me, I creep forward, daring to push the door open a little more so I can peer inside. If they're rutting, I'll go. Or at the very least, I'll do my best not to watch. Or at the very very least, I'll do my best to hide so no one will find me doing my best not to watch.

I'm expecting to find her beneath him, writhing as he drives his cock into her repeatedly, mercilessly plundering her lithe body. Failing that, to find her atop him, riding his cock, small but firm tits bouncing as she rocks against him. My cock hardens painfully at the mere thought.

I find neither in the room beyond.

The bedsheets are rumpled, but there's no golden-haired thief tangled in them. Instead, I see Leith lying prone on the stone floor, a pillow shoved beneath his head. His eyes are closed, face slack. Is he dead? If she's killed him, I'll rip her from sternum to pelvic bone and leave her outside the gates so the crows can pick her clean.

Crossing quickly to his side, I kneel, groping to find a pulse in his neck or along his wrist. I soon find one, weak but still there. The relief that realization brings still isn't enough to quell my fury. The thief is going to pay for this. Leith extended a hand of mercy and she's bitten him for it, betraying his trust the second she had the opportunity.

I'll find her and deliver her just punishment. Thirty swipes from my claws. I don't care how long it takes or how far I have to track her. She *will* pay for this.

I find a group of servant girls to tend to Leith before stalking off to the armory. The thief's things were taken there, and she's not likely to leave without the spoils she came for.

It's a five-minute journey from Leith's quarters to the armory, if one is moving at a dead sprint. I go double that, skidding to a stop outside the armory door in two minutes. I shoulder open the door, tensed and ready to do battle. She's already proven herself formidable, and I refuse to die because a tiny thief ran me through with a polearm.

The morning sun glints off rows of metal weaponry, shields, and armor. There's no sign of her here. Perhaps I've beaten her to her quarry. But when I round the corner to the section set aside for leather armor, games bags, staves, and other assorted supplies, I find the knave's pack and satchel conspicuously absent. Hurling a swear word at no one in particular, I turn on my heel, loping toward the courtyard.

Where the bloody fuck are our guards?

They're meant to protect against something like this. How could she bypass them so easily? They're all trained shifters, the strongest we could find from our far-flung tribes, brought here to be honored with service. And yet she bowls through them or slips past as if they're not even there! Leith will hear of this and the useless lot of them will be flogged!

It's disquieting, to say the least.

Before I flay the skin from her bones, I ought to pry from her the answer as to how she managed her escape.

Beyond the courtyard are the gardens, a maze of overgrown shrubberies, rambling rose bushes, and veritable forests of stone and ivy that Leith is too busy to keep. Before rule fell to him, gardening had been a mild obsession of his. Now the place is derelict, all but abandoned—a shadow of its former self. Much like Leith, himself.

The chase with the little larcenist brought out the most life I've seen in him for years. Her apparent acquiescence made him happier than I could have imagined.

Maybe, if things had turned out differently, he might not grasp at opportunities for escape quite so fervently. Sorren is the eldest of us, but due to his bastard heritage, he'll never take the throne. And owing to the incident, he's not in the right frame of mind, were he given the opportunity to take the throne.

I'm older than Leith, but owing to the fact that my relation to my grandfather, the original king, is through my mother—his daughter—the clan decided Leith had a stronger claim, since he's descended from our grandfather directly through his father's blood. Sometimes I wish neither Leith's father, nor my own, had died and then this tenuous question of rulership would be a moot one.

I traverse the gardens easily. After so many years of navigating the property in search of my absent cousin, I know it by memory alone. It gives me an advantage the thief lacks.

The sky retreats to a dim gray haze overhead as I enter the maze, boughs of leafy green blotting out most of the winter sun. A thousand overgrown branches reach for me, and I slide a blade from its sheath, cutting away the obstacles in my way. A tightly-knit golden curl hangs from one of the thorny plants up ahead and I know I'm on the right track. She's been this way — and if the scent just barely discernible over the earthy smells of the garden is correct, she's been here recently. I'm not far behind her now.

I bare my teeth in anticipation, though it's more snarl than smile. I want answers and I'm damn well going to get them.

And then I'm going to kill her.

The scent of blood hits me next, overpowering even the reeking colony of fungi that has taken root in the pits of the Poseidon statue near the exits. We've put the statue up to appease Triton, who's gone and lost his damn mind, exiling his youngest and bringing storms to ports who don't pay him fealty.

Delorood is getting hit the worst, and though we don't live incredibly near, Leith thought it prudent to give the fish-fucking bastard a gesture.

I slow, taking the next corner at a walk just in case there's something nasty waiting for me around the bend.

Prudent, I realize, when I turn the corner and find Sorren leaning casually against one of the hedges, staring down at his feet in... well, it isn't quite glee. Sorren hasn't been able to muster an emotion positive enough to be called happiness or joy in twelve years. But he's definitely amused, in so far as he can be. His amusement is always cruel and at someone else's expense. I've seen him in such a mood before, when he tests his traps on prisoners.

My cousin was once a highly sought-after engineer, a master of architecture, an innovator who pioneered advances that improved life all over Fantasia. He'd taken his lot in life — the disgraceful stain on a proud werebear royal bloodline — and made it something worthwhile. Of the three of us, Sorren was the only one who went to war with the Guild.

And then, the incident happened. Now, he's little more than a shell. A hollowed-out vase collecting filth and brackish water. He still constructs his traps and works on his experiments. It's really the only thing that brings animation to his face any longer.

I flick my gaze to the left and see the mirror that cuts out the hedge path to the left. The magic on the glass is so transparent, even I wouldn't have noticed it, except for the fact that the mirror's been broken. A shape roughly the size of a human head has cracked a hole in it. The blood runs from the broken shards down the glass to pool scarlet on the stones below. More blood lines a gap in the stones, bloody handprints made by dainty human hands.

The thief has fallen inside Sorren's mirror and from the looks of it, she tried to lift herself back out again. Sorren will have put a stop to that.

"Did you cut off her hands as she tried to get back out again?" I ask dully. It should horrify me that such is even a possibility, I suppose. But if I continued to be appalled at Sorren's soulless antics, I'd never stop feeling nauseous.

"No," he says, a chilly smile curling his thin lips. "I thought Leith might be cross with me if I did."

Restraint from Sorren? Will wonders never cease? I'm beginning to wonder what magic this thief wields over my brethren. Leith, the responsible justice-dealer, wanting to show leniency. Remorseless, sadistic Sorren, sparing her pain? It shouldn't be possible.

I approach the hole cautiously to peer inside. It's one of Sorren's mirror traps. He's created at least a dozen in the last ten years alone, obsessed with the need to trap Vita should she ever return to the mortal plane. There's a small labyrinth playing out beneath our feet all the time. I'm always leery of falling into one of Sorren's traps. He can open the entrances to them damn near anywhere.

Sorren leans over to peer into the hole with me. "Why? Do you think I should've taken a pinky for posterity's sake?"

I shake my head once in disgust. "You should have just killed her, Sorren. This is cruel."

"Killing her would be a waste," he insists.

"A waste?" I ask, looking up at him.

He nods. "I still want my turn with her. All that pale, flawless skin is like a canvas. I could scar it so prettily."

I can't let that happen to her. And that means I have to go in after her. It's what Leith would do, if he were conscious. And once he regains consciousness, he'll be pissed off if he knows I didn't go in after her.

Fucking fuck.

I let the bear push to the fore—I let its fury dominate my mind, a cushion against the madness that's coming. But I don't let it take over me completely. I don't want to shift.

Then, I leap into the hole after her. There's a ten-foot drop to the bottom, and glass shards stab into my boots and up at my ankles when I land. I smell still more blood; the scent is incredibly potent in the enclosed space. She's hurt and she's hurt badly.

The tunnels are well-lit, the phosphorus lamps that line the ceiling cast an eerie green glow over the tunnels and the shifting monsters in its walls. Streaks of red line the mirrored glass that surrounds me in every direction. All I have to do is follow the trail. Or follow the screams bouncing through the tunnels from a ways off.

With another snarled curse, I'm off, crunching through glass and blood to save the stupid thief from herself.

SIX
Kassidy

The monster looms out at me from the eerie green void and takes a swipe at my head, its bone claws flying toward my already battered face with improbable speed. Hateful, beady eyes are set in a face too ugly to be real. It's part bat, part snake, and part ape. This abomination shouldn't exist in nature and yet here it is, bearing down on me, all the same.

Its roar shakes the tunnel, rattles my bones, and sends terror clawing down my spine. Another involuntary scream rips from my throat. Every instinct in my body tells me to run.

But run where? Every new corner I turn prompts another monster, each more horrifying than the last. That is, if I don't run headlong into mirror first. Ground particles of the broken glass line my neck and face like stinging glitter, cutting tiny furrows into my skin with every movement I make. But even breaking the glass doesn't stop the monsters from coming.

I lash out blindly, my knife connecting with the wall in a screech of protesting metal and glass. My knuckles drag across the hard, broken surface, splitting again. Blood oozes, hot and wet, between my fingers and my grip on the knife falters. It drops to the floor, only to be consumed by the inky spill of black matter below. I try not to look at the blackness below my feet. It's too much. A monster—it's all eyes and huge, fanged jaws. I keep expecting it to gnaw one of my feet off, boot and all.

But it won't bite me because it's not real.

None of this is real. If these were flesh-and-blood monsters, I'd have snatched their powers by now, turned them into nothing. But my mind doesn't care about pesky things like logic or sanity.

My lungs burn, my throat stinging as I breathe in still more of the glass particles. I can't stop my traitorous heart from bruising my ribs. There should be nothing to be afraid of here! But knowing and accepting are two different things and I shriek, barreling forward in a vain effort to find an exit.

Thirty meters down the corridor, I encounter another hidden mirrored wall, impacting it so hard, I see stars. The surface breaks, raining glass and a thousand refracted images of a serpentine beast striking down at me from all angles.

All I can do is throw my hands over my head in an effort to protect my face from the onslaught of jagged mirror pieces. Blood flows in rivulets down my arms. I've lost so much already. The only reason I'm not already dead is the massive power-up I took from Leith. What will happen to me when that power fades? There's no life here to drain, no power to steal. How far does this blasted thing stretch?

I have the notion that I could wander this place for days and never find my way out.

Will they truly allow me to die like this — gibbering and insane, afraid of my own shadow? Maybe they intend to let me waste away in here, starving to death with nothing to keep me going but my own fear? Is my crime truly worth that? I've only tried to save the lives of thousands. So what if I've stolen and lied to do it? The ends justify the means and all that… right?

Something moves in the green murk behind me and I whirl around, ready to face the next monster, pulling another of my daggers from the interior of my coat. I was surprised to find most of my things still intact in the armory and now I'm grateful for that fact.

I bring the knife to bear with a defiant snarl and lunge, aiming for the location where the eyes should be on an average sized human.

My blow glances off leather armor and in the next second a real, substantial hand twists the blade from my grasp. I let out a surprised scream, my irrational hindbrain convinced that one of the monsters has somehow crawled from the walls to attack me. I bring up a knee and flail wildly, all my training going out the window in my panic. I score my nails down leather but they barely leave marks.

A hard, armored forearm crosses my chest, holding me in place like a steel bar. My back slams into an equally armored front, my head coming to rest below a strong chin. The head of my attacker dips and a familiar voice growls into my ear.

"Stop fucking kicking me, thief! I can just as easily choke you and carry you out unconscious."

Nash. It's Nash.

Relief washes over me at once. I can't deny I'm happy to see him, happy to know the monsters in the mirror haven't become real. Yet, Nash is his own type of monster. But, he's one I can handle.

My chest still heaves, budging his arm a few inches every time. Every lurch of my heart is painful, and hits like a drum whenever I spy a monster in my periphery. I'm starting to think unconsciousness would be a mercy at this point. I bite my tongue before I can say so. It feels like admitting surrender, something I never want to do in front of a predator. Sabre and Titus taught me proper shifter etiquette — well, they taught me what not to do around huntsman, who are pretty much the only shifters I've ever feared. My brothers taught me that shifters often react like their beast half. Showing weakness to Nash is probably the worst thing I can do, under the circumstances.

And then there's just pride. Let the ferocious bear shifter carry me over his shoulder through the courtyard like a war prize, *again?* I don't think so. I'll never live this down as it is—I'm more than sure Nash will mock me over the fact that he had to come in here to save my ass.

Nash's sigh stirs the hair at the nape of my neck. Warm breath dews on my skin and the proximity of him makes my heart lurch once more. It's just now begun to strike me that there's a very muscled, very attractive man holding me close to his body. His mouth hovers just above the shell of my ear. I'm struck with an image of him teasing the shell of it with his tongue, rolling the lobe between deliciously sharp teeth.

My hips squirm involuntarily, pressing my ass against his front. I'm lucky he's wearing armor, or I might have given him the wrong impression. Thankfully, he misinterprets my action as fear. He slides one rough hand over my eyes, blotting out the verdant shadows, the mirrors, and the monsters within. When he speaks, his voice is gentler than before, but still edged with impatience.

"Take a deep breath and hold it until you feel your lungs are about to burst, then release it."

I do as he says, drawing in a shaky lungful of air. It's easier to breathe when I can't see the monsters. I hold the breath until it burns my lungs and then I expel it, repeating the action without having to be told.

He's right. I know this trick already, but in my blind panic, sense flew right out of my head. Titus, Sabre, and Draven drilled this into me from the moment I started training. Slow your breathing, and your heart has to follow.

Nash grunts his approval when my heartbeat slows to a gentle trot and my breathing becomes less wheezy. "Good. Now, let's get the fuck out of here, Goldilocks."

"Don't call me that," I mumble, as idiotic as it sounds since I already told them my name. But, hearing it now on his tongue is too personal, too much for me to handle. "Call me thief like you've been calling me."

"You're lucky I'm speaking to you at all, *Goldilocks*," Nash retorts, scorn edging his tone. "I'm within my rights to kill you for attempting to kill our king. Weren't content with stealing away our wares, were you? You had to attempt regicide, as well."

Regicide?

No, he's got it all wrong!

"I didn't try to kill Leith," I say hotly. "He should be fine after a few meals and a good night's sleep."

"What did you do to him? Poison? Witchery?"

"Neither," I manage to say.

"Who and what in the name of Avernus are you?"

That is an excellent question—one I've been searching for the answer to for a lifetime. I've traded a dozen different appellations over the years and none of them seems to fit. Sister. Warrior. Criminal. Thief.

Friend. In the end, every descriptor peels away like skin after a bad burn.

Underneath it all, I still feel like a helpless little girl, hiding in the lone, stunted sycamore tree in the backyard, trying to escape the notice of my father's drunken rages. I nearly killed him at age eight, sucked the life right out of his body after he attempted to gut me like a trout. In the end, though, I didn't wield the blade that ended him. That was Sabre, after the Guild convicted him of attempted child murder.

I say nothing in response. Nash's growl comes out on an exhale, but it lacks volume. It sounds more like a frustrated sigh than anything. He starts moving forward, shuffling us slowly through the maze. Even at the reduced speed, it hurts every time we hit a dead end. Thankfully, Nash seems to know his way around, so it happens seldom.

I don't understand how he's doing this. The monsters are sanity-rending. Even when I tried to close my eyes and navigate through the hall, I only ended up with more bruises and cuts to show for it.

"Don't they bother you?" I ask at last, curiosity momentarily overcoming my dislike for him. "The monsters, I mean?"

Nash laughs, and it catches me off-guard. It's the first time I've ever heard him sound pleased about anything. The sound is downright touchable, a warm, rolling thing that sounds simultaneously boyish and filthy. It's a laugh I could imagine him giving after a particularly good tussle between the sheets.

I'm ashamed when my clit throbs hard in response. I want to roll my eyes at my own body for being such a greedy creature. Haven't I already had enough pleasure from Leith? I don't need Nash's attentions, too, especially when I hate him as much as I do.

"There's no bigger monster in this maze than me, thief. Don't forget that."

It's hard to judge distance without my sight, but I do my best. Counting the shuffle-steps we take, I determine we've walked about a mile and a half before Nash speaks again.

"When we get out of here, you're going to explain how you escaped and what you did to Leith, and then you're going to face punishment."

"Punishment?" I repeat. "Then the Rite of Three is no longer on the table?" At this point, I'm pretty sure that option is out the window. Once Leith gets his energy and vitality back, I doubt he'll ever want anything to do with me sexually ever again.

But, what if he does?

Hmm.

It seems incredibly demeaning somehow, to trade sexual favors for my freedom. I know other Guild members have done worse. Hell, Jezebel is practically known for it. Still, the prospect makes me uncomfortable.

Nash chuckles. "Were it up to me, I'd fuck you and then slit your fucking throat."

I turn around to glare at him. "Well, luckily for me, it's not up to you because you're not the fucking king."

He glares right back at me. "I don't care if you choose the lashes of our claws or if Leith offers it still, his bed, but if you try something like this again, I will kill you."

Maybe I should count my blessings and just keep my mouth shut. Unfortunately, that's never been a strong suit of mine. No matter how fraught the peril, my tongue wags in defiance of danger.

"Well, my mind hasn't changed: I still don't want to fuck any of you."

Nash shrugs, his hand inching up my torso a fraction as he does so. He brushes the underside of my breast with one calloused hand. Given I'm wearing nothing beneath Leith's coat, it's incredibly distracting.

"Then don't fuck us and, instead, take your lashes and see if you survive."

Nash's head dips and he presses a searing kiss to the hollow beneath my ear. My entire body jerks to attention, nerves crackling like I've been struck by lightning. He lets his mouth linger on my skin, a sensual promise. As he slides his fingers along the underside of my breast, a moan gets caught in my throat. My head lolls back and I dare a peek at his face.

And he stares right back at me, heat in his eyes. I immediately look away.

The green cast of the mirrored halls is mostly gone, weak wintery sunlight washing away the unnatural glow as we step out of the maze. We're in a patch of forest I don't recognize. Nearby, a stream burbles, and something small scampers through the underbrush.

Nash's face is incredibly handsome when it's not twisted with rage, and he looks older than Leith without the juvenile, stubborn twist to his lips. His dark hair beckons to be touched, his lips to be kissed.

"Would it be so bad, thief?"

I jerk myself from his grasp, and he lets me go. Or maybe I'm bleeding too badly for him to keep a good grip on me. Either way, he allows me a foot of space so I can think. I'm not stupid enough to go loping into the forest. I'm injured again, bleeding from more places than I can count. He wouldn't even have to run after me; he'd just have to trail behind until I succumb to the dizziness that's sucking at the edges of my equilibrium.

"I'm not sacrificing my maidenhead to any of you," I mutter.

I don't turn to see how he takes that revelation. I just start trudging up the hill toward the gates of the compound, hoping that when I eventually fall, it'll be somewhere other than in Nash's arms.

SEVEN
Kassidy

At some point, I must have passed out, because when I come to, I'm in a warm, familiar room.

A cursory glance around the place confirms what I already suspect. I've been returned to Leith's bedroom. And there's a large wooden tub in the center of the room—large enough to fit three of me.

Leith is nowhere to be seen.

The place seems so empty without the massive werebear inside it. I spend the first ten minutes unwilling to climb out from beneath the covers. It's very warm and comfortable here, and the novelty of it almost makes me want to smile. Never have I been able to afford such luxury.

Almost all of what I steal goes to the Guild's coffers, and what little is left is just enough to get me a night or two at a local inn along the way and maybe a hot meal.

Even when I live with Titus and Sabre at the House of Corvid, it's not bursting with amenities. Huntsmen learn to live on little and shed creature comforts as a way of life. Draven only enjoys so much wealth because he's assigned to guard Princess Carmine, on King Leon's orders.

I consider rolling back over and sleeping the rest of the day away. After what I've been through recently, I deserve a full night's rest. When I turn my head, however, my cheek lands on something smooth and cool that crinkles beneath my touch. I jerk upright at the unfamiliar sound, then feel silly when I see it's only a bit of parchment. Neat, looping scrawl reads:

If you are well enough to attend, your presence is requested by your king. Attire will be provided for you.

The handwriting is clearly masculine so I assume it's in Leith's own hand. But, why all the pomp and circumstance?

Maybe because he's a king? I answer myself.

Frowning, I search the room for a timepiece and find none. With no windows to speak of, I can't tell day from night. It was afternoon when Nash and I emerged from that evil maze. Is it evening now? Or have I slept through the night and ignored Leith's invitation, snubbing him once more? I can't imagine I'll get away with doing so much longer.

And what am I doing in here anyway? Didn't I make it clear to Nash that I wasn't choosing The Rite of Three? I thought I'd been clear about that when I trudged away from him?

And, yet, here I am again.

I sit up and stretch my aching muscles, noting as I do that someone has tended to me while I slept. I'm naked beneath the covers. Almost every part of me is bandaged, so I appear more shrouded corpse than girl at the moment. I imagine it was Leith who cared for me. Or maybe it was the maids. Somehow, I can't picture Nash crouched over me like an attentive nursemaid, picking glass from my wounds and swaddling me.

Swinging my legs over the side of the bed, I take stock of myself. My face has been healed magically by Ambrosia, no doubt, though the rest of me seems to be in various states of recovery. Not going to waste more of the precious healing foodstuffs on me again, I see. Probably wise. I'm good at getting myself cut up, and they seem less than eager to part with their precious Ambrosia.

As to what Ambrosia is? I have no idea. All I do know is that it's magical and the Guild wants it to heal our fallen soldiers.

My toes curl into the soft surface of one of Leith's rugs. It would be heaven to stay here for a time, if it didn't mean a bear would charge in at some point and mount me.

The door swings open and I snatch the bedcovers with a shriek, jerking them over my nude body as quickly as I can. The woman standing in the doorway blinks at me, nonplussed. She's taller than me, but that's not a difficult feat to achieve. All supernaturals are, and most humans as well.

This woman does seem a little short for a bear, though, standing at only about five-foot-four or so. She's petite, with small but defined curves and an athletic build. Her maid's uniform only reaches mid-thigh. She's all lustrous earth tones and looks like she could blend perfectly in a forest. An oval face, with skin the color of teak. Her hair is mahogany, falling down her back in perfect ringlets, unlike my mass of unmanageable curlicues. Her eyes are chestnut, with a ring of ebony around the iris.

"I'm sorry for frightening you, mistress," she says meekly. "Shall I go?"

My heart settles back into a somewhat normal rhythm. Gods above, I'm getting jumpy. I blame Sorren's death trap for it. I'm seeing monsters around every corner. But, this girl is no monster. A werebear girl, probably, but a girl nonetheless. I hug the duvet closer to my body and try to grasp at the last shattered remnants of my pride.

"No, it's fine. Come in."

The girl steps into the room, her eyes immediately dropping to the floor as though she's not worthy to even look at the place. She doesn't raise them again until she reaches my side, and when she does, I can see the questions in her gaze. Why am I allowed here? What makes me worthy to spend a night in Leith's bed when he's not even fucking me?

I wish I had an answer to give her.

In each hand, she clutches a large bucket filled almost to the brim with water, a sponge floating on the top of one and a bar of soap in the other. Around her elbow is a folded dress, almost identical in color to the one she's wearing.

"I am Celesse, and the king wanted me to check to see if you're awake."

"Why?"

She nods. "I've been assigned to act as your lady's maid this eve. King Nord requests I bathe you and help dress you for supper," she murmurs. "If her ladyship isn't too fatigued."

With that, she walks over to the large basin in the room and fills it with both buckets. Then she looks up at me.

Ladyship? Ha. I'm pretty much the furthest thing from a lady this woman is ever likely to see. And that begs another question: why is Leith still trying to be kind to me? I've done nothing to warrant it, in fact I've done exactly the opposite. I should be chained to the pillar in the courtyard again, if nothing else.

"I'm fine, and I can bathe myself. Thanks, though."

I will probably need help into the dress, admittedly. It looks more elaborate than my traveling gear, and I am still aching after my time in the maze.

"And your dress?" she asks.

"Yes, I could use help with that," I answer and drop the covers at last, figuring she'll see my nudity since she's going to have to help me into the dress. I hobble over to the bath and carefully unwind the bandages covering most all of me. When I take them off, I'm surprised to see that I'm fairly healed all over. So maybe Leith did feed me more of the Ambrosia than I'd thought?

I seat myself in the hot water which feels like heaven as I settle into it and pick up the sponge. I scrub at the blood that's leaked through my bandages and the stuff that no one bothered to clean off.

"There's soap for your hair on the other side of your bath, mistress," Celesse says.

I glance over the lip of the tub and spot it immediately. I lather up my hands and after dunking my head back into the tub, I lather up my hair and give it a good washing. Once I rinse the suds away, I feel like a new person.

"Better, mistress?" Celesse asks.

"So much better," I answer as I offer her a smile and stand up, allowing myself to drip dry while Celesse dutifully retrieves a towel from the far side of the room and places it in my outstretched palm and watches as I pat myself dry.

When I step out of the bath, she moves to help me into the dress. I want to protest, but it's pretty obvious I'm going to need help. Even in perfect health, I'm not sure if I'd be able to get myself into the complicated looking thing. So, I hold still as she first helps me into a weird looking contraption she calls a corset. She wraps it around my middle and tells me to lean forward to pull my tits up, not that there's much to pull up. But the swells of flesh the thing creates are quite… nice. Celesse then pulls on the ties until I feel like I can't catch a breath and I'm going to pass the fuck out.

Next is the gray dress. She drapes it over my head and it settles over the corset nicely. Instead of hitting me mid-thigh, the way hers does, it hangs below my knees. Sometimes, I hate being so short. She looks at it and frowns before pulling a pair of scissors from her apron pocket and cutting the hemline so it hits me on my lower thighs. Reaching under the bed, Celesse pulls out a pair of equally simple gray slippers and I slide my feet into them. They're warm and comfortable and exactly the right size.

"Who did these belong to?" I ask, irritated by the fact that Leith has women's slippers beneath his bed.

"You, miss," Celesse answers. "I brought them up earlier when you were asleep. Along with the towel and the tub.

"Oh," I say, feeling stupid for asking and even more stupid for my jealousy, which was probably fairly obvious. "Thank you."

Celesse swings open the door to Leith's closet and I catch the glint of a mirror before she guides me in front of it. Her beaming face is reflected back at me from the glass. Then she grabs a wooden chair and sets it up in front of the mirror.

"Sit, if you please," she says.

I do as I'm told and Celesse begins fussing with my hair, pulling at it with a comb, which she also produces from her apron pocket. When she's finished, my ringlets are still wet but at least they're tamed and she has them pulled behind my ears, courtesy of a wide blue ribbon. It's the first time I can really see my face.

As I stare at myself, I'm completely gobsmacked at my reflection. I almost look... like a woman. For the first time in my life, I have the semblance of curves. The cinched bodice and low cut of the dress give the illusion I have modestly-sized breasts instead of the mosquito bites that can be generously called tits. The dress bares half my shoulders, emphasizing my clavicles. If I can ignore the swaths of bandages that still cover me, I almost look pretty. Not stunning, like Neva, but attractive enough to warrant a second glance.

"You're lovely, miss," Celesse pronounces. Then she spins me around and marches me right out the door, into the corridor beyond where a new batch of guards stand waiting for us. It seems Leith has learned his lesson where I'm concerned.

The guards appear to be wearing the same sort of armor Nash has, though it doesn't appear new, like his. Each of the men is easily two to three hundred pounds of muscle. Their bear forms must be massive. I'm not eager to be chased or injured again today, so I stay within the column of them as we're marched up the stairs and escorted through the courtyard.

I feel less like an honored dinner guest and more like a condemned prisoner being led to the gallows. Leith is sure to be furious with me. Maybe *I'm* the main course tonight. Filleted thief, with a side of bitter greens.

Ha, funny, Kassidy.

Well, I'm trying to break the mood! I rail back at myself.

It's not easy to be funny when you're terrified.

True. Stick to being terrified.

When the doors swing open, I'm expecting to find all three of the cousins assembled and ready to take off my head. Instead, it's only Leith, dressed in a sharply cut cobalt blue coat, matching slacks, and a pair of shiny black boots. It's a compelling combination, paired with his hazel eyes, lightly tanned skin and gray hair. He sits at the head of the table, but he stands as I enter the room.

I boggle. How the fuck is he still capable of being a gentleman? I can tell my thieving is still having an effect on him. He's paler than normal, and he looks a little drawn. Still, he pulls back a seat to the left of his as we approach. Before I can sit, Leith raises a finger.

"First things first," he murmurs.

He pulls a large square box from his coat pocket and opens it. Inside is an ornate necklace made of braided gold and silver, with a ruby the size of a grape at its center. I'm practically salivating at the sight of it. For an instant, I forget how hungry and uncomfortable I am. This thing's market value is off the charts! If I could sell it, the money could fund our endeavors for a few months, at least.

"Spin around," Leith says. "I want to see how it looks on you."

Me? He's giving the necklace to me? After I drained him of his life? Why? There has to be some sort of catch. Is he taunting me with valuables, knowing how much I want to steal them?

"I don't think it goes with the dress," I hedge.

A wicked smirk tugs at his mouth. "Fine. Strip down and I'll have Celesse bring you something more appropriate."

My face heats as his eyes dip appreciatively to my breasts. He licks one corner of his lips, and I know exactly where that filthy mind has settled. He's thinking about how hard my nipples are beneath this bodice, how I'll sound when he latches onto one. How I sound when I come, the way my body trembles beneath his touch.

Heat also gathers between my thighs, and I know he'll be able to smell it if he wants to. Damn it. Why does this man make me so wet?

Saying nothing, I turn so my back is to him, hiding my embarrassment. He steps closer, and the heat of him presses into my back. I obligingly sweep my hair aside so he can drape the chain around my neck, letting the ruby settle between my newly enhanced breasts.

The moment the necklace latches, something is wrong. The remainder of my ill-gotten strength seeps out of my limbs and fatigue washes over me so hard and fast, I almost collapse. I'm saved from impacting the stone floor by Leith, who hoists me into his arms for a few moments before settling me in the chair.

"What… the fuck did you… do to me?" I demand. Or, rather, I try to demand—the words come out slurred, barely intelligible. What's the bastard done to me? Drugged me?

When it wears off, I'll kill his ass.

"Relax," he says, resuming his seat and his smile. "It's just a sealing charm."

"What the fuck's that?"

"It will hold your powers at bay, in case you're of the mind to use them on me again."

Okay, so he is pissed. This whole bullshit dinner setup was merely to throw me off so he could get the fucking necklace on me and ensure my powers were taken away. The fucking bastard!

I scrabble at the chain at my throat, desperately fumbling for the latch. I can't be without my powers. How in the name of Avernus am I supposed to escape without them? My powers are the only thing keeping me safe. I feel naked without them, and intensely vulnerable.

The latch won't budge, no matter how hard I try to undo it. It's as though it's rusted shut, which is impossible because Leith had no problem fastening it around my throat.

And then I understand—I'm going nowhere.

"It won't… come off!" I damn near shriek, if I possessed the energy to do so.

Leith looks unperturbed. "It wouldn't be an effective tool if it could be undone at will. It's coded to respond to touch. Mine, specifically, or Nash's."

"Sorren?"

He shakes his head. "I don't trust Sorren with this sort of… responsibility."

I shiver. I don't want to admit it to him or to myself, but Sorren scares the piss out of me. At first I thought Nash was the scariest of the three, but how wrong I was! Sorren is in another league of scary.

It's yet another reason why I don't want to go through with this Rite of Three bullshit. I get the feeling that Sorren would rather carve out my liver and eat it than have sex with me.

Leith chuckles darkly. "Yes, Sorren is a bit… disturbed."

"Yeah, understatement."

Leith nods. "He's been that way since the incident. He used to be a good man. A brilliant one, in fact. But now, all that intellect is corrupted, turned toward the pursuit of pain and peculiar appetites."

"Why do you let… him live, then?" The question bursts from me before I can hold it back.

"Let him live?" Leith repeats, frowning.

I realize he wants me to explain. "If he's so… dangerous, why let him… wander around here like…

he's … harmless?" Then it occurs to me. "Does Sorren wear one… of these horrible… contraptions as well?"

Leith's face darkens. "No. Sorren can't shift any longer and that particular necklace is meant to help young shifters who are just learning how to wrestle their powers."

"Why… can't he shift any longer?"

Leith nods as if he expects the question. "That ability requires…" He pauses. "Well, it isn't my story to tell. If you want the full story, you'll have to get it from him."

When Avernus glazes over with ice!

I'm not going near Sorren again, if I can help it. "I'll pass."

Leith pointedly ignores my disquiet and continues. "You don't have to sit there looking petrified, Goldilocks. I'm not going to hurt you."

I try to read a lie in his face but find none. His handsome, chiseled features are set in lines of utter sincerity. He means it. "Have you put… this thing on me… so you can force… me into my punishment and… make sure I take it?" I ask, wanting to get down to bare bones and find out what the fuck is going on.

"To which punishment are you referring? The Rite of Three or the lashes?"

"Either," I answer with a shrug.

"Well, the answer to both questions is no. I would never force myself on a woman who didn't want me and I'm not eager to kill you."

"Why not?"

He chuckles. "You aren't very good at trying to convince me to keep you alive, are you?"

"I just… don't understand why you're… being nice to me. If that's what… this is."

Well, the necklace isn't exactly 'nice' but he hasn't killed me yet so there's that.

"I shouldn't be nice to you?" he asks as he leans back in his chair and regards me with interest. He reaches forward and picks up a chalice filled with wine. It's the first time I've noticed it and when I look at the table before us, I realize it's covered in food I hadn't noticed before.

That's how riveting Leith is. He pulls all my attention when usually, I'm much better at paying attention to my surroundings.

I frown. "Um… yeah?" I start. "I tricked you an' took your life force."

A faint smile curls Leith's full mouth. "Ah, yes, that's quite what you did, isn't it? Just as I was giving you the orgasm of your life, too, as I remember." He chuckles again. "I've been fucked to the point of exhaustion before, but never quite like that."

Stupid heat creeps into my cheeks again. Damn him for making me blush. I've never felt like such a fucking girl in my life. I'm Kassidy Aurelian, expert Guild thief, calm under pressure, someone who takes shit from absolutely no one.

I've also never known a man's body so intimately. Maybe that makes all the difference? It's hard to stay unflappable in the presence of a man who has worshipped your pussy, and treated you like a damn goddess though you'd done nothing to earn it. Actually, I've done everything opposite of earning it.

Yet, somehow, I get the impression Leith would do it again, right here and now, if I asked him to.

I have an enticing vision of Leith sweeping the plates and food off the table and hoisting me onto it, hiking the silly dress up to my hips before he ducks between my thighs.

His nostrils flare subtly and his eyes grow darker, his voice taking on an even huskier bass when he speaks.

"You smell like you still want me."

I swallow hard. "I don't."

He chuckles and leans in closer, inhaling even deeper. "Your body reveals your lie."

"Well, ignore it… because it doesn't know… what the fuck is going… on since you put… this fucking… necklace on me."

"It's not just your body."

"What else?"

He shrugs. "It's in your eyes, Goldilocks. Stop looking at me like that, or I'm going to drag you to my chambers again to finish what we started."

Why does that sound like an excellent idea? It must be the exhaustion. And the influence of the damn necklace.

Keep telling yourself that, Kassidy.

Oh, you shut up! I don't have the patience to deal with you right now!

I tug my plate forward and seize my fork, stabbing it viciously into my pork chop. I saw off a piece with the serrated edge of my knife and pop it into my mouth. The raspberry sauce adds a twist of tart flavor to the meat and I practically moan. I still don't understand why Leith's being so kind (well, aside from stealing my powers with the necklace), but I'm not going to let that mystery get in the way of appeasing my hunger.

Leith watches me, picking apart a fluffy roll with his long fingers. I can't help but think how good they felt inside me, even as I gorge myself on pork and sautéed onions and mushrooms. I can't remember the last time I ate this well.

"Why are you... being so... nice to me?" I ask finally as I face him, needing to take a break from the food because the corset is so tight, I can barely breathe. "And no bullshit... I want the truth."

He shrugs. "I don't blame you for trying to steal the Ambrosia."

"Why not?" I ask, shocked.

"I understand what a difference our Ambrosia would make to your mission and your people. It's admirable the Guild is still fighting, even after all this time."

"If you know it... could help the Guild... and you seem... to like that... fact, why won't you just... give it to us in an... effort to help us?" I demand. "We're trying..." I suddenly lose the ability to speak because I'm so exhausted.

"Take your time, Goldilocks," Leith says. "The necklace has incapacitated you and you need not rush."

I nod and breathe in deeply before I continue. "We're trying... to save the lives... of every human and non-human in Fantasia. And yet... here you are, sitting out of not one, but... two wars, selfishly...

hoarding one thing that… could tip the scales in… our favor."

For the first time since we've met, Leith's face hardens with real anger. "You wouldn't be so quick to judge if you knew what was at stake here."

"Tell me… then, because… I'm sure whatever is at… stake here isn't… worth not helping us."

"Ye know nothing of which you speak."

"Then enlighten… me, Leith."

His hazel eyes grow more haunted, the set of his jaw even angrier than before. "We stayed out of the war once before and we were left alone. That's all we want. We are a solitary people, and we are few in number now. We live simple, peaceful lives and we rarely fight wars. Your Guild fought Morningstar for almost a decade and you only achieved a stalemate. Your generals are scattered to the wind — you're fractured, and no one is willing to aid you this time."

"That's not true!" I try to argue but he continues.

"Besides, none of the champions have risen yet. They've been prophesied all along but where the bloody hell are they?"

I try to speak up, to tell him Neva is one of the Chosen Ten, that word has been spreading such is the case, but he doesn't let me speak.

"Let's say for sake of argument that I gave you what you seek, then I'd be definitively throwing our lot in with yours. I'm not willing to sacrifice my people on the altar of your ideas, I don't care how damn beautiful you are."

The compliment barely registers and I quickly shrug it off, like water off a duck's back. I'm too angry with him to be flattered. Doesn't he see we'll have a fighting chance if he just hands over the Ambrosia? I can understand the vicious pragmatism, I really can. I've had to make difficult choices during my time as a Guild thief—I've done horrible, immoral things in the name of duty. But this is different—this is callous to the point of being inhuman.

"There is… a Champion who has arisen…"

He laughs. "Who? And why have I not heard of this news?"

"Her name is… Neva… and she's my…friend."

"And how do you know she's one of the Ten?"

"Rumors are… spreading. The only… reason you haven't… heard them is because… you're isolated here."

"Then you don't even know this to be true? You're basing it all on rumors?" he demands.

"You're a fool," I whisper. "Morningstar *will* set… sights on you next. If you… don't give the Ambrosia to us, he'll… take it for himself. We—the Guild—are the… only reason he didn't pursue… you more ardently… during the last war—because he… was too busy trying… to decimate our armies."

"Perhaps," Leith says, a bitter smile twisting that handsome face into something just a little less pretty. Suddenly, I can see the weight of years on his frame, years of bitter hardship and disappointment. "Perhaps I'll get lucky and your so-called champions will put in an appearance before it becomes an issue, eh? But without the prophecy of the Champions proving true, you are little more than a band of believers." He pauses and takes a drink of his wine. "And that's not enough for me."

We fall silent, and he starts eating his now thoroughly shredded roll, dunking the salvageable chunks in the raspberry glaze. I slump in my chair, stewing as he finishes his dinner. The walls of my full stomach are stretched uncomfortably against the bodice of this fucking corset, and nausea threatens to bring the whole meal back up again.

I stand, when it appears the conversation isn't going to resume. "I've had enough," I say.

"You've barely eaten."

"I can barely… breathe in this… fucking outfit!"

He looks at me and chuckles. "I must admit, I do prefer you in your trousers. It's easier to see the swells of your ass."

I ignore the comment and the way it makes me want him even more than I currently do. Instead, I cast him one final look. "You should… have more faith. The… Champions are coming… I know it."

"I don't put stock in miracles, Goldilocks. Diminishing returns and all that."

"Maybe that's… exactly what… you should do," I insist. "Expect… miracles because… without them, what's… the point of living?"

His face is as blank as a winter sky. I can't explain why, but I don't want to leave him with things the way they are between us. He's a good man and he's a good king. He just is stubborn. But, he's also been kind to me and I don't want to overlook his kindness. Were it up to Nash, I'd be dead by now… probably.

I approach Leith and he looks up at me in question. When I reach him, I lean in and give him a chaste kiss on his cheek. His hands seize my biceps and he pulls me to him. Without my powers, I'm only as strong as the average woman my age. I can't resist him. And the truth is, I don't *want* to resist him. I savor the warm slide of his mouth over mine. A sort of feminine pride swells in my chest when I feel his hardness pressed against my thigh. I've never had a man want me. It's strangely gratifying.

I break the kiss after several seconds, and he allows me.

"I'm tired... and I can... barely breathe in... this fucking thing," I say as I glance down at the dress.

He chuckles.

"Will... you think about... what I've said?" I ask.

"Yes, Goldilocks, I will."

I nod and then start for the door. I'm not sure where I'm going to sleep — if I'll have my own room? Hopefully one of the maids will be able to tell me.

Regardless, I have to get the Ambrosia, even if I selfishly condemn the bears to take part in a war they want to avoid. Too much is at stake. Leith will see reason, eventually. And if he doesn't, that's on him.

I stride out the wide set of doors, feeling his heated stare on my back.

EIGHT
Sorren

The little bird preoccupies my thoughts more often than not these days.

I frown down balefully at the jumble of gears and wires in my hand. What a great pile of troll toss this project is shaping up to be. I'm never going to finish the device at this rate, not while she dominates my thoughts so thoroughly. Such a tiny thing to cause such a stir. Even in my human form, I can crush her easily.

I smile a little to myself at the thought. She has a body meant to take pain. I'm eager to see how much of it she can take.

Leith and Nash will never allow me to hurt her though. Not until she does something unforgivable. They're both too attached to the little dove. Even Nash, who won't admit as much, even to himself. But when I get my turn in the Rite of Three, I will see to it that she learns the line between pain and pleasure.

She'll jump, gasp, possibly scream when I drip molten candle wax down the contour of her back. Her pale, creamy skin could pinken so nicely beneath a cane. She'll get the lashing Nash promised beneath a crop. Perhaps, if I can manage it, she'll feel the sting of ginger root in that pert little ass of hers. All while my cock pumps in and out of her tight wetness.

89

I set the mass of gears and wires onto the long, unvarnished workbench that dominates one wall of my little lair. Leith has gifted me many trinkets, hoping to keep me locked away with my books and experiments, instead of mingling with people. He's ashamed of me. Ashamed of what I've become. And, because of what transpired with Vita, I can't even bring myself to feel anger at his scorn.

I know what I am, what I've become. And Leith isn't wrong for hating me.

There's nothing inside this hollow chest except cold. Nothing can change that now.

The lair truly is enormous, as large as any cathedral built for that newfangled religion coming out of Wonderland these days. The Church of the Seven Joys. It's hogwash, plain and simple. Everything that comes from Wonderland is poppycock or madness. Still, I have to admire the craftsmanship of their buildings. High, vaulted ceilings, not unlike this place, but built with steel and glass instead of craggy stone.

Many would consider me mad, I suppose. I no longer operate strictly along the strange mores and etiquette by which humans and shifters live their drab, little lives. I see no need for it any longer. But it's not insanity that plagues me. Not like the March Hare, Hattie, or even that damnable cat who pops in every now and then to pester me. He seems to enjoy the experiments I've done on mice. At least, that's what he says.

No, my disease is too clear-cut and dispassionate to be true madness.

When I step out of the lair, it's evening. The sky burns with a million spheres of white light. It's theorized by some astronomers that the heavens are bitterly cold; I would very much like to find out if such is true.

Winter winds whip my hair into my face and the cold worms its way past my coat, easily cutting through the shirt and jerkin. I shrug both off and stride into the wind. Cold doesn't bother me much anymore. It simply brings my outside level with the temperature of my inside.

I'm going to find her and, somehow, I will convince her to agree to the Rite of Three. I need to have time alone with that comely body. It's strange, really, that she should compel me so. I haven't felt the stirrings of sexual desire in a long while.

No, it's not sexual desire I feel. It's fascination— desire is too warm an emotion. Still, no female has held my attention for long since the incident. I fuck, on occasion, if I find my mind too full. Release has a clarifying effect on my overburdened head.

Will this obsession clear when I've fucked the little dove? I can only hope so. I have designs I must tend to, and she's impeding them. And that angers me.

It's a mile walk to the castle, and another mile to wind my way to Leith's room—the one he sleeps in. The chieftain of our clan has more rooms than he knows what to do with. Silly really.

As regards Leith, he's had her, with his fingers and tongue at the very least. I've caught wind of the gossip on my brief forays to the castle for supplies.

91

I'm pleased to hear it. She seems to like him, for some reason I can't fathom. Still, it opens the door to the possibility she'll agree to fuck Nash and me.

But when I arrive at Leith's room, I don't find either of them inside. I do find that the clever dove has fashioned a rope from the bedsheets and anchored it to the hooks that hold the drapes back.

A chilly smile tugs at the corners of my mouth. Clever female. Her persistence is quite amusing. Totally futile, but amusing, all the same.

I balance on Leith's window ledge. He prefers quarters near the ground floor, so it's only a piddling four-story drop. It barely rattles my bones when I hit the ground. Raising my head, I sniff the air and find the warm waft of her scent lingering like perfume. Her fear is a sweet aroma.

I follow the trail around the side of the fortress, expecting it to veer toward the wall. Instead, it loops around twice, wandering toward the edge of the garden, around our factories, the small school building on the periphery of the compound and then back again. My face breaks into a genuine smile. Oh, she's clever, using our noses to keep us spinning in circles while she conducts whatever business she's up to now.

She can't fool me, though. I find her new trail eventually. It's muted, yes, but still detectable. She's scrubbed herself thoroughly in one of our fountains, erasing the sweat from her skin, the musk of fear and arousal she's feeling even now. I doubt Nash or Leith will pick up on it. The scent of their own anger or anxiety will cloud her subtle aroma. Not an issue I have to deal with, thank the Gods.

If they, in fact, exist.

I locate her in the small rectangular building that hides in the shadow of the castle's west side. She's found the aviary. The calls of the doves therein sound weary, even to my ears. She murmurs gently to one as I approach.

"Come on… stick out… your leg for me," she says and I can tell by her speech that something's off about her. It's then that I spot the necklace. Leith has disarmed her of her powers, how interesting. I actually prefer her when she could put up more of a fight.

"I know… you're tired," she continues, addressing the bird who blinks up at her in confusion. "But it's important."

The sooty gray dove obligingly extends its leg and allows her to attach a message to it with a piece of twine. I lean against the doorway, my bulk barely squeezing through. I make an effective door, caging her in with the birds. It's fitting. A little goldfinch among doves, so much smaller and fragile than she believes herself to be.

"They can't talk back, you know," I say dryly. "This isn't Wonderland."

The little dove lets out a breathless squeak and rounds on me, hand slipping into the folds of her gray dress. It's the uniform of a servant, but I quite like it on her. The bodice lifts her modest breasts and the neckline highlights them to their best advantage. I want to bite the swell of flesh, mark her with my blunt human teeth as a signal to other males that she's mine.

But Leith shall be quite angry if I do that, so I stay my desire.

Her eyes go round in her face and she backs away from me. Her fear doubles, the scent of it filling the interior of the aviary. My cock twitches. Pretty, pretty goldfinch doesn't want to play. I'll have to convince her otherwise.

I rip the message from the dove's leg, without injuring the beautiful creature. I'm the only one who comes here, to feed the birds and talk with them. They know I won't hurt them—it's the reason why they all fly towards me as soon as I walk in.

I unroll the small piece of parchment and read: *"Dear Neva, I'm trapped in the werebear fortress near Delorood. Please send help if you can. I'm not sure how much longer I'll last. K."*

When I look back at her, she's pulled a cleaver from the inner folds of her dress. I smirk. Oh yes, I like this feisty little bird. Not a shy squeaking mouse, this one.

"Who is Neva?" I ask as she watches the birds circle me and come to land on my shoulders as they're wont to do when I feed them. Unfortunately, I haven't any of their birdseed with me at the moment. "And why have you signed your name with a K?"

"None of your... fucking business, asshole," she growls, eyes glaring at me, even as she struggles to catch her breath.

I smile. "It *is* my business. You are our prisoner, little dove. We can't have you pleading for rescue, now can we?"

I rip the parchment in two. She makes a small sound of protest in the back of her throat but says nothing as I let the scraps fall to the floor.

"Why do... you keep... dragging this out?" she whispers. "I'm not... going to give... myself to... any of you." She takes a breath. "I'd rather... fucking die."

I take a lazy step forward and she stiffens, backing as far as she can go, startling violently when her back hits the wall.

"Seems a silly choice?" I ask with a shrug. "Leith will treat you gently. Nash is more spirited, true, but he's not cruel."

"But you... are cruel," she counters. "They've... told me... as much."

I smile wanly. "Yes, they would be correct." My eyes travel down her pert and luscious little body. "Your body is a canvas, little bird. Beautiful and unblemished. I want to mark it, want to teach you that pleasure and pain balance on a knife's edge."

"You get... the fuck away... from me," she says, eyes blazing with emerald fire. There's an underlying tremor in her voice. "I will... gut you like... a fucking trout, do... you understand?"

"You wouldn't be the first," I say.

She looks at me in confusion and I shrug off my coat, all the birds on my shoulders returning to their roost. I allow the heavy woolen garment to drop to the floor. Some poor maid will have to clean the hay and birdshit from it, but it's not my concern at the moment. I strip off the shirt and jerkin next so she can get a good look at the ruin of my chest.

My front is crisscrossed with whip scars and brands from Vita's torture. A horizontal line stretches across my navel, where they spilled my guts onto the floor. The wound was sealed since then, of course, but the scar is a livid pink to this day.

But the worst wound is on the left side of my chest, directly over my heart. It looks as though someone took a spoon and dug until they reached my ribs. The skin has barely closed over the bone, and it leaves my left side misshapen, damaged forever.

"Oh, Gods," she breathes, taking an unconscious step forward. Her unoccupied hand flutters anxiously, as though she wants to touch me. I pull back. "What happened?"

"The war happened."

Her brow furrows. "But... Leith said..."

"That we didn't join the war? No. The werebear clan didn't participate. *I* did."

"You did?" she asks, eyeing me narrowly, as if searching for a lie. She won't find one.

"Yes."

"Why... would *you* join... our cause?"

"I wasn't always... like this," I answer with a shrug.

"That doesn't... answer my question."

I breathe in deeply. Even disarmed of her powers, she's still so incredibly ornery. I like it. I like her. "It seemed the right thing to do."

"Why?"

I shrug. "I was a mere bastard, never to claim the leadership of the clan. My father warned me that if I ever left the clan, I'd be exiled. Stripped of any rank I'd achieved and left penniless. I left anyway."

Pity washes over her face. It's the first time I've ever seen the expression from her. "I... I'm sorry."

96

I shrug. "I'm not sorry. I can't be, actually. Not after what Vita did."

She shoves the knife back into the folds of her dress, keeping hold of the handle but apparently feeling confident enough to sheathe it for now. Those emerald green eyes rove over my chest, pity softening her entire face. If I were still the man I'd been then, her pity might anger me. But anger, like passion, is too warm an emotion for me to feel it now.

"The incident… that Leith… mentioned," she murmurs. "He said… it wasn't his… story to tell."

"Ever honorable, Leith is," I drawl. "Do you want to hear the tale?"

She nods mutely, eyes fixed on the divot gouged into my chest. I trace the puckered edges of it absently.

"On one condition," I start.

"What?" she demands.

"I want to touch you," I answer and I glance down to her thighs.

"No."

"I won't hurt you," I say. "But if you want something… personal from me, I want something personal from you."

She's quiet for a few seconds. I motion to the blade in her apron. "You can hold that to my throat, if you wish."

"You won't… try to fuck me?"

I shake my head but I can smell the proof of her arousal in the air. She wants me to touch her, much though she might say otherwise. "I want to feel you… the inside of you."

"With what?"

"This finger," I say and hold up the index finger of my left hand.

She reaches for the blade and pulls it out of her apron. I smile as I approach her. "I was captured in the war," I begin as I reach forward and pull her dress up to her thighs. She holds the tip of the blade to my neck but I'm not worried. If I wanted to, I could rip the blade right out of her hands and break her in half. But, I don't want to. "After my capture, I was taken to Morningstar's camp," I continue as I trace the line of her inner thigh until I reach the searing heat of her pussy. I brush my fingers across her undergarments and find them soaking wet.

"You're wet," I breathe onto her face.

She closes her eyes as I rub my fingers across that sensitive little nub.

"The story," she moans.

"Ah, right." I take a deep breath. "The bitch goddess, Vita, requested me to be her newest experiment," I continue as I push her panties to the side and run my finger up and down her soaking wet cleft. She immediately throws her head back and moans. My cock is swollen and demanding but I won't give it what it desires most. I promised her I would not.

"She tortured me for a fortnight and then," I continue as I circle her opening with my finger and she rocks against me. "Look at me," I demand when she closes her eyes.

They immediately pop open and grow wide as I push my finger into her ever so slowly. She's so incredibly tight. "Mmm such a tight and wet little dove," I breathe the words. She moans.

"When Vita's trinket was ready," I lean down and whisper against her. I push my finger into her further until I feel something odd. A piece of flesh that disallows me from pushing into her further. "Ah, the little dove has never had a cock before," I say.

She swallows hard. "No."

"And, tell me, do you want one?" I run my thumb over her clitoris and she immediately throws her head back in a moan. "Tell me, little dove, do you want a cock in you…"

"I…" she starts and loses her nerve.

I lean further over her and bring my lips to hers, so close she tries to kiss me but I pull back. Instead, my eyes burn into hers as I fuck her with my finger, only going in as far as her body will allow me. "Do you want a big cock thrusting into that tight little pussy?" I whisper.

"Yes," she moans back at me.

"Do you want *my* cock, little dove?"

"Yes," she sings as she rocks against my hand, her juices running down my fingers.

"Do you want my cock ripping through that little sheet of flesh inside you? Forcing its way into your depths?" I whisper against her lips as my thumb works feverishly at her clit.

"Yes," she screams as she gushes all over my hand. "Please fuck me, Sorren!"

I pull my finger out of her spasming channel and suck her juices off as she watches me. I grin. "I'm sorry but I made you a promise."

"A... promise?" she breathes as she sits up and realizes she's still holding the blade. She places it down, beside her.

I nod. "I told you I wouldn't fuck you. Therefore, I won't."

She swallows and appears confused. "But... I asked you to."

"I know."

"Then?"

"I will fuck you on my own terms," I answer as she looks at me as though I've lost my mind. She glances down and sees my cock is raring against my pants.

"I... don't understand."

"It's not for you to understand," I respond. "All you are meant to do now is listen to the rest of my story." She gives me a strange expression but nods as she pulls her dress back down, hiding that naughty little pussy of hers that will figure in my imagination as I stroke my cock to completion as soon as I leave her.

"Please... tell me the rest," she says, a blush stealing over her cheeks.

"Very well," I say and clear my throat. But not before I suck the last of her from off my finger. "Vita carved open my chest and tore out my heart," I finish as the little dove's eyes go wide. "She placed a clock in its place."

She's frozen stiff, staring horrified at my chest. I grip her hand and she allows me as I pull her hand and place it against my bare chest.

Tick, tock. Tick, tock. Tick, tock. Spin, whir. Tick, tock...

The metronomic ticking only ceases its steady rhythm when blood rushes through one of the valves on the side.

"Oh, Gods," she breathes, looking up at me in shock. There is a gentleness to her that thrills me, that pulls me to her even more. "It really is a clock."

"Yes."

"How did Vita even...?"

"How else? Magic. The clock's been charmed for nigh on twenty years. Less than five years and I'll be dead."

"Dead?"

"Yes, all things come to an end, eventually."

"That's why you can't feel emotion," she murmurs as understanding settles over her expression and she studies me with new eyes. "It's why you're a monster. Your heart and soul are out of sync."

Clever girl. Not everyone would make that leap so soon. "Yes, that's why."

I trace her cheek with my thumb and she allows me; her skin is lovely, smooth, and flushed with heat. I'd like to kiss it.

"There's no hope for you?" she asks.

"None," I answer without emotion. "Not unless my heart can be recovered. And that's quite impossible, I'm afraid. Only a Chosen one could hope to go against its guardian, Discordia."

"Discordia?"

I nod. "She's one of the few enemy generals who's managed to linger, though I hear she's a former shade of herself without the others to back her. That only makes her *nearly* impossible to defeat."

"I've heard whispers," little bird says, words pouring out of her in a rush. Interesting but it seems she trusts me now — whether that's owing to the fact that she just orgasmed in my palm or she pities me because I have no heart, it's hard to say. All I do know is that one day, my cock will be inside her… deep inside her.

"Whispers?"

She nods. "That my friend, Neva, has shown her true power. She's one of the Chosen Ten." She nods as her eyes go wider. "If I could get a stone with some of Neva's power in it, I could transfer her power into myself and were I able to do that, I bet we could get your heart back from Discordia. Could that pay my debt for stealing the Ambrosia?"

I pause, considering the offer. I've made peace with the fact my time is measured by every tick of my heart. But if there's a chance, it's only logical I should take it.

"You would have trouble even breaching the gates of Discordia's palace," I say.

An impish smile rolls across her lips in the most intriguing manner. I can see why Nash and Leith want to fuck her. She's compelling, intensely so. If I leaned in to claim that mouth, how would she react?

"Just get me to the gates and into Discordia's stronghold and leave the rest to me." She tilts her head arrogantly. "There's nothing I can't steal. Even your heart, Sorren."

NINE
Kassidy

"Impossible." Leith folds his arms stubbornly across his chest, leaning against the gilt back of the throne. Guards and servants line the walls of the room but my attention is on their chief. "It's out of the question."

"Tough, but not impossible," Nash argues, facing off against his cousin.

I'm astonished that Nash and Sorren are taking my side against Leith. Until now, it's been my assumption that Nash would rather cut me to ribbons than aid me. Even his rescue in the maze was motivated by his desire to have me, not because he truly cares. But now, both stand their ground, facing the throne where Leith sits, straight-backed and glowering at the three of us.

Sorren's mouth stretches into that eerie little smile once more. Even knowing he can't help his soullessness, it still raises every hair on my body to see just how far from human he is.

And, yet, when I think of him in the aviary — the way he manipulated my body, the way I orgasmed and burst out a stream of liquid all over his hand — I didn't understand what had happened. But there was a gentleness to him then. It was in the way he refused to fuck me, even when I asked him to. And the way the birds trusted him — the way they landed on his shoulders.

Is it possible Sorren isn't the man I originally thought he was? The man his cousins think he is? As the thoughts plague my mind, he glances over at me and gives me a small smile, a secretive one and I feel myself suddenly yearning for him again.

As completely insane as it sounds, of the three of them, I want him the most at the moment.

"Don't you want to see me back, cousin?" Sorren asks, giving his full attention to Lieth, a hint of a sneer in his tone. The antagonism only makes Leith's face stonier. If Sorren's trying to appeal to his chief's empathy, he's badly missing the mark.

"Of course I do. You know I've been searching for cures. But there's nothing for it except to get your heart back. But, Sorren, if there was a way to beat Discordia, we would have found it. Only a champion can retrieve your heart. You know that. We all know it. And since there are no champions alive at present…"

"There is," I interject, cutting into the argument I can feel brewing. "At the… very least, I know there's… one champion."

"And how do you know this?" Nash demands.

Well, I don't know for sure. "Rumors," I answer honestly.

Nash shakes his head.

"Rumors are… usually true!" I insist.

If the rumors about Neva are true and she really is one of the Ten Champions, then maybe there's a chance. And if not… well, at least I die trying, right? It's all I can do for the people of Fantasia. If I fail in my mission, I intend to take this Discordia bitch down with me. If she's as dangerous as Nash and Sorren say, then I don't want to give Morningstar a single foothold he can use to claw his way back into the world, not one loyal follower who will rally support to him.

Leith's skeptical brow thrusts higher, until it's touching the slate hair that threatens to flop into his eyes. He looks particularly discomposed, having been dragged from bed by Sorren an hour ago. He'd been more than a little peeved ever since I'd refused to sleep in his bedroom, choosing one of the maid's rooms instead.

"And how do you propose to get this *chosen one* to cooperate? If, in fact, she even is a chosen one?" Leith asks. "I assume your Guild must have plans for her already?"

"I'm not… sure if the… Guild does."

Nash looks at me. "Do you even know where to find this person?"

In truth? No. I have no fucking clue where the Guild has stashed Neva. I was hoping the dove would be able to deliver my note to Peter or Cap'n Hook so they'd know I was looking for Neva.

Even if I were able to find her, she shouldn't be traveling out in the open. If the rumors are true, Neva's wanted for the murder of Queen Salome.

"I can send… word that I'm… looking for her," I turn to face Sorren with a frown. "Which was what… I was doing… with the dove, before… I was so rudely interrupted."

Sorren just smiles at me… lasciviously. "Rudely?" he repeats, eyes eating me up. "That's one way to put it."

Nash and Leith look at one another in confusion and I'm quick to change the subject. I turn back to face Leith. "Once Neva receives… word that I need her, all… she has to do… is use a siphon stone… and fill it with… a fraction of… her power," I start and then have to take a breather because the fucking necklace is stealing all my energy. Leith looks at me with guilt in his eyes. I take a deep breath and continue. "Then she just… has to give… the stone to Peter or to… Captain Hook and… they'll be sure… to hold it for me. Once… I get my hands on the stone, I… could absorb Neva's power… to get us past the gates of… Discordia's fortress. From there, I… trust you can… do the rest?"

Leith's face doesn't soften. "And just how am I supposed to trust you? You've deceived me *twice.*"

"Right," I say, expecting this line of argument.

But, Leith isn't done talking yet. "Every time I place my trust in you, I'm forced to regret it. If I extend my hand a third time, I'm fairly sure you'll just use the opportunity to escape."

"I'll do it," I say as I glance at Sorren and find him already staring at me. The heat in his gaze frightens me and I drop my eyes to the ground.

"You'll do what?" Leith demands.

I swallow hard. "As a show of… trust… I'll agree to The Rite of Three." I take a deep breath and nod. "If that's… what it will take… to repay my debt… to you for trying… to steal the Ambrosia… twice," I say, bolstering my faltering nerves. If I have to sacrifice my maidenhead to save hundreds of thousands, that's the price I'll pay.

"Hmm," Leith says and I'm surprised he doesn't agree right away. From the looks of it, Nash is surprised too.

I quickly change the subject. "Sorren says… Discordia has made… her home in… the bowels of Grimm. That… means it will be… at least a month and a… half by the time we… reach our destination. Long enough for… me to be with… each of you in turn."

"And we should believe you won't try to flee?" Leith asks.

I point to the necklace. "Not with… this thing on."

I can feel three pairs of eyes on me after I'm through talking. Leith tries to school his expression into indifference; Nash's undisguised lust heats my blood and I shiver as I remember just how good those searing lips felt against my throat. And then, there's Sorren. His attention still scares me, but if I'm honest with myself, I want more. I can't remember ever being as turned on as I was in the aviary. The things he was saying and the things he was doing…

Leith's eyes slide down my body, and his eyes darken further with desire. The promise is swaying him, but I don't see any acquiescence. I suppose I need to sweeten the pot—I need to make him understand I'm serious this time.

I reach back and unlace the bodice of the dress as well as I can—which isn't much. "To prove to… you I'm serious, I'll strip… down right… here and now, if… you like," I promise with a coy smile. I turn to face

Nash. "But I... need help... with the pulls of... my dress."

Nash, surprise registering on his face, nearly jumps in his excitement to help me, but Leith's growl interrupts him.

"Step back, Nash," Leith says, the weight of his authority bearing down on us.

But Nash doesn't drop the laces of my dress.

"Have you lost your damn mind?" Nash says, voice as rough as the scrape of gravel. His hands clench and unclench at his sides and he can't seem to tear his eyes away from me.

"You heard what I said," Leith responds.

Nash glares at him. "Yes, and you don't speak for me or Sorren. If the thief is willing..."

"Need I remind all of you, I'm Chieftain?" Leith points out. He turns a burning glare to me. "You will remain in your fucking clothing."

I frown. "But... I thought..."

"No, I'm not fucking you." He looks at Nash, then Sorren. "Neither are they."

"Oh?" I counter, seeing my chances slipping through my fingers. So I take a step closer to Nash. "I think... Nash disagrees."

Summoning the courage I have left to spare, I stand on tiptoe. I curl my fingers around the sharp line of Nash's jaw and angle my lips just so, stopping inches from his, giving him the option to kiss me.

Nash lets out a growl of pure animalistic want and his hands wind around my waist, drawing me roughly to his body before his lips are on mine. He holds me so tightly, I can hardly breathe. Without my powers, I feel

108

like a brittle twig, liable to snap in half any second. But I only try to press myself closer to his body. He's inhumanly warm, enough that even his leather armor feels pleasant against my skin. His hands are rougher even than Leith's.

Nash is a brute, no doubt about that. But compared to Sorren, he's a gentleman. And I can't deny he knows what he's doing as he presses every advantage he has, sliding his fingers beneath the untied portion of the dress. He traces a ticklish pattern across the sensitive skin along the small of my back and the curve of my ass. The sensation makes me squirm in his arms, gasping in surprise.

His tongue delves into my mouth, exploring every contour. He tastes incredible. Spicy, like the dance of cayenne across my tongue, spreading sparks in his wake. One hand palms my breast and, small as my breast is, he can fit all of it in his grasp. Rough fingers pluck at my nipple, kneading it to attention so forcefully, I cry out. My knees wobble, threatening to give out from under me.

"Nash," I pant, drawing back just enough to speak.

"Stop," Leith growls. A glance up at him reveals he's slid to the edge of his seat and is clutching the arms of it in white-knuckled fury. I can't tell if he's angry with me or Nash. But, he's definitely angry.

"I don't… understand," I start as Nash moves his mouth to my neck, and I gasp again as rough teeth scrape my skin with the promise of pleasure edged with pain. Sorren is right — pain and pleasure do balance on a knife's edge. Nash toys with the top of my

109

dress, pushing it down past my shoulder and baring my corset. "Isn't this… what you… wanted?" I ask Leith.

"No," he answers, his eyes furious. "I said, stop!" The bass of his growl is nearer now, and he yanks me out of Nash's grip so hard, it nearly wrenches my shoulder. I'm hauled back, cradled to the front of Leith's body.

Nash's protest rumbles like thunder in his chest and I see bear eyes staring out of that handsome face. He's close to shifting; I'm absolutely certain things are about to come to blows. Just like that first day, tension crackles between Leith and Nash, threatening to explode into violence.

Leith's hand comes up and he cuffs me on the ear. It's more the shock of the action than the sting of the blow that draws my breath. It's nothing I haven't felt a hundred times while training with my brothers. Sabre will actually box my ears if I fuck up too badly, and that hurts a damn sight more than what Leith's done. I just never expected Leith, of all people, to hit me.

"What the fuck are you thinking?" he hisses. "Don't bait him if you don't intend to follow through, stupid girl! Do you see those eyes?" I look at Nash's eyes and just nod. "They should tell you how little control he has. Push him and he *will* fuck you — right here!"

"I'm not… baiting him," I say on a breath as I face Leith. "I was serious; I agree… to the Rite of Three. All of you… together or apart, I… don't care."

Leith studies me with suspicious eyes. "Why the sudden change of heart?"

"I have to get out of here and rejoin the fight. If I can restore Sorren's heart, he can join me and the Guild." At least, that's my hope.

Leith blinks in surprise at this. "Sorren would join you?" Leith asks, shaking his head.

"Yes, I would," Sorren says without pause.

Leith looks at us both as if we've lost our minds. I realize I need to explain. "As fucking... terrifying as Sorren's... maze was," I continue. "It's a... brilliant trap. The... Guild could use someone... like Sorren... on our side."

"That's not your decision to make!" Leith rails at me.

But I shake my head and stand my ground. "He's already... told me he has... no obligations to your... people. He'll... never take the title... of chief. Even if Sorren fights... with us, your people wouldn't... be in danger, Leith. So, please, let me... do my part because... I now see doing so will... help my cause."

Leith's face softens, and Nash's eyes have returned to their normal, russet shade. Even Sorren watches me with interest. I note he's hard, just from watching me with Nash. Sorren is as huge as the others, and he strokes himself absently through the fabric of his pants, as though he isn't aware he's being watched or, maybe, he just doesn't care. I shiver. If I'm going to do this, I still want to save Sorren for last. Someone physically incapable of care or compassion should not be the one to take my maidenhead. I need someone gentle the first time—I need Leith.

"I understand your plight, I truly do. But this quest is madness. It will only get you killed."

111

"That's not… your concern," I interject.

He shakes his head. "If you truly want to return to your people, just complete the Rite and go home."

Anger courses through me. My pride smarts as much as my ears. I don't know how many indignities I can take, but I'm not letting this one stand. I've proved not once, not twice, but *three times* that I'm capable. It's only Sorren's intervention that's kept me within these walls. Nash and Leith can't contain me if I have my powers.

"Take this damn… necklace off me… and I'll prove to you… I can handle… myself in a fight… since you obviously… don't believe me," I challenge, jerking my chin up defiantly. "I'll… fight Nash."

Titus would tell me not to look a predator in the eye — doing so only provokes the predator in question. But, at the moment, that's what I want. I want Leith to come after me without reason or restraint. I want to prove him wrong. I almost beat him once before, and I was injured and exhausted. I can do it now at full health.

"How do I know you won't just drain us and flee if I free you from the necklace? You've done so before," Leith responds.

"My word as a Guild member, I won't. I'll win this fight using minimal magic and I won't drain a single one of you."

"Werebears rarely fight alone," Leith says.

I nod. "If anyone else comes at me, I'll defend myself against them, as well."

Leith is quiet as he considers it. If I know anything about shifters, especially machismo ones, it's that they can't turn down a challenge. "What is it that would be on the table when I win?" Leith asks as Nash scoffs at his wording.

I smile at him and he smiles back. Yes, I have Nash right where I want him. I face Leith again who frowns at me. "If *I* win, then you agree to come with me to Discordia's palace on the quest I mentioned earlier."

"And when you lose?" Leith demands.

"*If* I lose, the first one to reach me can do what he chooses with me."

Nash draws a blade from the sheath at his waist. "Sounds fair and reasonable to me."

"I agree," Sorren concurs.

"No," Leith answers as I face him with a frown. "If our kind wins, you remain here with us," he finishes.

"What do... you mean?" I demand.

"I mean, you make this your home," he answers as I wonder what his aim is. Why would he want me to stay? I've caused him nothing but headache.

"Deal," I say, figuring I have nothing to lose.

Leith expels a breath and comes to stand behind me again. The heat of his body against mine is intoxicating. The castle is drafty and I'm standing barefoot on the flagstone. When his breath tickles the hairs on the back of my neck, I have to restrain a sound. My nipples harden painfully, and I realize, with a rush of mortification, that my dress is still very much untied which means everyone can tell how much I like having him there.

Leith's fingers deftly twist the clasp open and he slides the chain from around my neck. The second it parts with my skin, I feel alive again. Strength seeps

into my limbs like the rush one gets from a good ale—
warm and pleasant, dissolving all worry. A strangled
sound of relief catches in my throat. I never, ever want
to go without my powers again. I hate feeling like a
fragile doll, just begging to have my face smashed.

I expect Leith to take a step back and let Nash rush
me. Instead, he shoves a hand into the thicket of my
hair and seizes it at the roots. The sting in my scalp
nearly brings tears to my eyes. Bastard. He's trying to
end this early, just to make his point. Well, fuck that.
And fuck him! I'm not going down that easily. If I end
up with a bald spot, so be it.

Leith tries wrenching my head to the side, to get at
my neck and shoulder. If he can get to the flesh there
with his bear teeth, it's all over. He doesn't even have
to tear my throat out to ensure victory—he just has to
snap my collarbone. An injury like that will lay me low
for a while without healing Ambrosia or the stolen
health of another.

Hooking my calf around his, I throw my whole
weight backward into him, using a portion of that
stolen strength that still remains in me. It's hard to do,
because he's so much taller and more muscled than I
am, but the move surprises him. He's knocked off-
balance and I exploit the momentary confusion,
bringing us both to the ground with a hard smack of
flesh.

And the ground is exactly where I want him
because it evens out my odds a little better. When your
opponent is three times your size, you want him on the
ground.

Leith's back takes the brunt of the injury and the breath explodes from his lungs on impact. It's enough to loosen his hold on my hair. I squirm off him in mere moments, taking a half-second to recover from the jarring fall. A quick scan of the hall shows Nash is in motion, watching me and coming closer. Sorren, meanwhile, lounges against one wall, watching the proceedings with a caustic little smile. One way or the other, Sorren will be pleased by the outcome of the fight.

"Guards," Leith calls as I face him with surprise. The door opens and two armed guards enter. He smiles at me and then motions them forward. "Attack her," he says. "But don't kill her."

One of the guards reaches me before Nash can, and I flatten myself to the floor, ducking beneath his swing, rolling and coming up to lodge my fist into his gut. He doubles over, and I take the opportunity to splay my fingers on his torso, soaking in some of the massive reserve of strength he possesses. As promised, I only take what I need, like skimming the cream off a pail of milk. He'll barely miss it.

I ram a shoulder into him as well and spin him just in time to shield myself from the other guard who joins the fray. I shove him lightly at the second guard and they both go toppling into the table. A chair dissolves into a pile of kindling beneath their combined weight.

It's finally Nash's turn. With speed that seems impossible, he's in front of me, striking before I can react. He hits me with an open palm instead of a fist. It's probably the only reason I remain conscious. When

Sorren had done the same, I'd gone down like a sack of apples. It helps that I'm not exhausted and injured this time. And I had the advantage of knowing the blow was coming. Still, pain ripples through the left side of my face and I stagger back a few steps.

Nash has his knife at the ready, a short thing only a few inches long. Unlikely to kill me, unless he severs an artery. It will still hurt like a son of a bitch if he manages to stick me. He doesn't have to kill me, just incapacitate me with pain. If I yield, I can be healed. And once I'm healed...

Tears leak from the corners of my eyes, but I lock down every other part of me. I've been through worse. Draven hits a lot harder, and Nash has a vested interest in not battering my body too badly. He wants me and everyone knows it. Can I count on that to win this match? I'm not sure. As much as Nash wants to fuck me, he also believes in truth in battle. So, no, I don't think he'll throw the tournament.

I turn, as if to run. Leith is regaining his feet as I sprint past him, and I barely escape his grasping arms. I vault the table, landing with a clatter among the dishes. The centerpiece is dashed to pieces, drawing a gash into the bottom of my foot. I kick the shards off the table and then leap upward, employing a favorite huntsman maneuver. The Guild is very given to acrobatics and feats of strength. It really is a shame I can't turn into a jay at the zenith of the jump and fly straight out the window.

Instead, I latch onto the chandelier that's suspended above the table and grin as the chain holding it tugs free under my weight. I bring the whole thing crashing down on Leith's head, knocking him flat to the floor once again. His arm folds beneath his body this time, and I'm afraid it may have broken. No time to be too concerned, though. I rise to my knees, seize the lax stretch of chain in one hand, and then whip it upward.

Chains are Titus' favorite long-range weapon. He has a whip fastened out of small links, and I've been on the receiving end more than once. This thing is huge and unwieldy, but it'll do the job.

I whip it once around my head and then let it fly, rattling through the air toward a startled Nash, who realizes his mistake too late. He starts a retreat, but not fast enough to avoid the blow. The tip of my improvised whip strikes him right between the eyes and he goes down hard. He lands on his ass then tips backward, his eyes going out of focus.

I wait for someone else to attack me, but no one does. They're all watching me warily.

Sorren brings his hands together in a slow, mocking clap. "Well done, little dove." Then he faces his chieftain. "Is it enough, Leith?"

Leith stirs beneath the knees dug into his back, and I obligingly stand. He shrugs off the chandelier and idly brushes at the hot splashes of candle wax on his skin. With a sort of grudging admiration, he peers up at me.

"Yes, I think that'll do, she's proven herself."

"So, we leave tomorrow then?" I ask, quirking a brow at him.

"End of the week," he corrects. "We'll need to prepare. There are disguises to be made and a regent to be selected in my absence. But yes, we will attend you." He looks over at Nash who is completely unconscious. Leith sighs. "A bloody band of fools, all of us."

"But you're my band of fools, aren't you, Chief?" I ask with a coy smile.

"Yes, that we are, thief. That we are."

TEN
Nash

She's bested me in battle. Knocked me out cold. That sealed things for me.

No woman has ever been able to defeat me.

And, now I want her. More than I've ever wanted anything in recent memory.

I'm not the only one who wants her either. Her bravado in the fight has made the three of us desire her even more than we already did. To be so teased with the Rite of Three—to come so close to being able to claim her, to mark her with our seed, and yet have it stripped away in the next second?

It makes me want to stake my claim and it makes me want to do so now.

But, alas, I can't. I'm not the only one of us with a claim to her, after all.

Leith wants her. I was shocked when he made the agreement that should she lose, she would have to make her home with us. But, as soon as he made the stipulation known, I agreed with it wholeheartedly. I don't want her to leave. None of us do.

Yes, Leith wants her, probably more than he should. But any dullard with eyes can see that she wants him, too.

She gravitates toward him without thought, staying near enough to be comforted by his presence, but not so much that she shrinks in his shadow. Not a hothouse flower, this little thief. She's a hardy thistle — stubborn, deeply rooted, prickly, and here to stay. If she does manage the impossible and restore Sorren to us, Leith will never let her go.

A soft growl builds in the back of my throat as he lifts her onto the back of his horse. Of the three of us, it makes most sense for me to act as her protector. I train with the men at arms every day, while Leith has grown indolent in his role as king. I don't trust her with Sorren, even if this mission does serve his ends. His interest in her disturbs me as much as it disturbs Leith.

But Leith *is* the Chief, the King, and we're traveling under the guise of an ambassadorial party. Fewer people will fuck with us that way, and disguised as his consort, the little thief won't raise many eyebrows. No one except her dearest friends will recognize her now.

She's fucking radiant, mounted on horseback, looking like the Barbarian Queen Oliviette herself. Her wild golden curls have been pulled into a tail at the base of her neck, with the more unmanageable bits braided tight to the side of her head to keep them out of her eyes as she rides. The muted browns and reds of her outfit suit her, and I'm more than a little intrigued by the way the light leather armor she wears clings to that compact little body of hers. The cloak hides the belt of knives she's tucked into her waist, so that the only weapon an unwary highwayman will spot is the jeweled scabbard of her sword.

"This thing is fucking ridiculous," she complains, kicking at the hem of her dress. "If we get caught in a fight, I'll have to tear it."

"Or take it off. That's always an option," Sorren adds unhelpfully, chuckling at the stern look she levels at him in response.

"If all goes well, we should be safe on the road until we reach your friends. Where are we meant to meet them?" Leith asks, diverting her attention from the smirking Sorren before a fight can break out.

"Denfur," she answers. "It's a town that borders Grimm to the east. Once we have the siphoning stone, we should be set to take a detour through the edge of Sweetland and make it into Grimm in less than a week."

After sending all of Sorren's doves with messages pinned to their legs, we finally received a response from the theif's friend, named Peter, that he had the stone she was asking after. It was at that point that we decided to make this trek.

It's going to be a month or more in travel, and I can tell the idea bothers Leith more than he's willing to admit. He says nothing, just swings his leg over Stellan's back and comes to sit astride, pushing our little thief to the back of the saddle. She looks comically small juxtaposed against his bulk.

"Are we ready?" he checks, as Sorren settles onto his own mount.

I'm already astride Zahn, who's pawing bad-temperedly at the ground as we wait. The mounts are only a necessity for the thief and Sorren, who can't resume his bear form with his false heart still in place.

But we'll be traveling in a pack to avoid any opportunistic thieving — except for the larcenist already in our midst.

"Not just yet," I say.

I bring Zahn to a stop and lean across the gap to reach for the thief. She stares at me and jerks backward a little when I offer her the small golden circlet I fish from my bag. She peers at it cautiously.

"What's this?"

"A coronet. It was our great-grandmother's. She had three consorts, as well. Take it."

The ripe, little thief takes it from my hand and regards it with a collector's eye. She traces a finger over the fine latticework of ivy that climbs along its base, brushing the facets of the red gemstones reverentially. They're set in the midst of the golden foliage like brilliantly colored fruit waiting to be plucked.

"Garnet, ruby, and red diamond," she murmurs, almost to herself. "Why three different gems?"

"For the three different men she loved." It seems blatantly obvious to me, but perhaps I'm too steeped in our ways. Many of them seem to horrify the little sneaky thief.

She settles the small coronet on her head where it blends seamlessly among the burnished shade of her hair, the scarlet stones standing out like drops of blood against the gold.

Leith shoots me a look over his shoulder as he urges Stellan forward. Goldilocks may not understand the significance of that crown, but Leith does. Three for one. A mistress for three of the Nord Clan. The message can't be clearer.

I want a fighting chance, and I am willing to share her affections if I have to. But I'm not letting her go. Not without tasting the forbidden fruit at least once. The memory of her kiss still scalds my lips, leaves me hungry for more. Leith may be her king on this journey, but I'll be her knight. Sorren will be her monster.

I can only hope it'll be enough to keep this infuriatingly stubborn woman alive.

***

"You don't have to sleep alone."

Goldilocks jerks in surprise as I approach, tucking herself more deeply into the shadow of a beech tree. Faint patches of moonlight pattern her face in shimmering silver to contrast with the gold of her hair. The slow pace of our travel worries her. She's looked pinched for a week now and I've noticed she isn't eating. She shivers most of the evening on her bedroll, rather than doing the sensible thing like scooting closer to the fire or — Gods forbid — asking one of us to share our beds.

Her reluctance to bunk with Sorren, I understand. But as for Leith or me...

She leans her chin pensively on her knee, staring into the gathering gloom. The trees form a shady bower over the neighboring portion of wood. She tells us she was raised by huntsmen. Not knowing what's out there in the dark must be killing her.

"You'd do everyone a favor if you decided to sleep with one of us, thief. Your rattling teeth are going to scare off any prey in the area."

Her bleak expression barely flickers. "If you don't like it, you all can move further away from me, then."

"Bloody fucking hell! It's a joke! I recall you had a sense of humor once. What's gotten into you?"

She curls her other knee beneath her chin as well and examines her toes with the solemn interest of a prospector.

"They're all going to think we're... having sex — the three of us."

The statement catches me off-guard. It's not what I'm expecting to fly out of those pretty pink lips.

"Who is?"

She gestures vaguely at the bower and beyond. "Them. The people in Denfur. The people at the inns, the taverns, the towns we pass through. Hell, even Peter and his friends. They're all going to think I'm... having sex with all three of you."

I sigh and try not to laugh. "That's what this is about then? You don't strike me as the sort who cares much for people's good opinions."

"I mean," she starts and then inhales deeply. "I don't, but..."

"Who cares what they believe? If they don't like it, fuck them!"

Her lips quirk into a coy little smile. "Fuck them, too? My, that's quite a few people I'm fucking now, isn't it?"

A bark of surprised laughter escapes me and I creep closer to settle myself in the tangle of roots at the base of the tree, keeping a foot of distance between us. She's frightened of us, still, and I'm not sure why. None of us have made a move on her. Even Sorren keeps his unnerving notions to himself and only stares at her after she's gone to sleep, something that deeply bothers Leith and me because we both assume it's just a matter of time before he… does something.

"I think you should worry less about what other people will think. All of us know better, so who does it hurt? You could do worse than being the perceived consort of three royals."

The puckered lines between her brows only grow deeper, and I have the uncharacteristic urge to smooth them away with a thumb before trailing it down her soft, ivory cheek. She's too young, too vital for all of this. Faces tend to stick in the expressions we wear most, and I don't want hers to be a roadmap of pain, stress, and misery.

"That's not the problem," she mumbles.

"Then what is it?"

She hesitates for another long moment and then gives her head a rueful shake. "It's nothing, Nash. Go back to the campsite. I think I'm going to sleep here tonight."

As if I'm going to let her freeze out here alone. I expel a sigh and begin unlacing my armor, dropping it to the ground in a neat pile off to the side of one root. I tug my undershirt off next, and she inches away from me, climbing to her feet. She backs away a few steps, as if she's afraid I'll fall on her right that instant.

"What are you doing?"

"Shifting. I can't do it with my clothes on if I want to keep them the shape they are. So either avert your precious eyes, thief, or don't squawk."

She continues to stare, which is a little gratifying. I'd been starting to believe she truly didn't appreciate my physical qualities — something I'm unused to from a woman. It's no secret I'm a handsome man.

But those emerald eyes trace the lines of my body with a feminine appreciation that pleases my beast. I'm so fucking tired of being outdone by Leith. If not for the bad luck of being born to the only female of the Nord clan, I'd be the king. And if that were so, Goldy, as she prefers to be called, would be in my arms, my bed, riding at my back.

The change hunches my shoulders forward. Snaps and pops echo through the clearing as my bones twist in a way that should be painful. The warm, addictive joy of ceding my human mind to the beast keeps the worst of it at bay. Muscle piles onto my arms, my legs, my flanks, and fur thrusts through my skin and rolls down my back. In thirty seconds, I've become the beast.

She's somehow, impossibly, more beautiful seen through a bear's eyes. These eyes can see colors the human mind ignores. And now she's painted in a spectrum of new, deeper hues.

I plant my bulk in the space she vacated, grimacing as the cramped confines squeeze my backside. Flopping onto my side, I hope she'll take the hint. At least this way I can provide her with warmth, and maybe she'll sleep properly if she's not afraid I'll try to fuck her.

A tiny smile tugs at her lips. "If I say no, are you going to sit on me?"

I incline my head and grunt. That's about as complex as communication gets with outsiders when in beast form. With another werebear, the body language would have given them a clear answer. But she's a human. An admittedly tough human, but still one who remains largely ignorant of the ways of beasts.

She considers me for a few extra seconds before shrugging. Then she drops back to the ground and tucks herself into my side. I sweep her as close as I can get her, so that my fur covers her on all sides like a heavy, warm blanket. Only her face remains free — and even then, she turns that toward my chest as well, nuzzling a cheek into my chest.

She releases a shaky exhale. "I like you better as a bear."

I grunt and emit a low growl which makes her giggle.

"Thank you, Nash," she says as her eyelashes meet the tops of her cheeks and she breathes in deeply. The smile still remains on her face as she falls into slumber's embrace.

Relax and sleep, little thief, I think back. *I've got you.*

ELEVEN
Kassidy

Denfur is a squalid little hole at the best of times, and doubly so when winter drives all the shady characters into its many inns and taverns, seeking warmth from the mess of caverns and tunnels within the mountain of Grimm.

It's perpetually dark in Grimm, seeing as how it's located in the depths of the mountain. The only lights provided are by overhead street lamps and the various lamps burning within the buildings. And it smells like shit as the air has nowhere to go and nothing to do but grow stagnant. The buildings are shabby, the rock roads unpaved, the muck scored by the wheels of a thousand carts. Grubby faces peer from dingy windows, dozens of beady eyes trailing our party as we make our way down its main street.

It's almost amusing to watch my companions' faces as the smell really hits them. The pungent aroma slams like a fist to the face every time I come here, and I don't even have decent scenting capability unless I've stolen it from someone else. Even then, there's only so much the human nose can discern. Titus, Sabre, and Draven truly hate this place.

Leith actually wheels his horse halfway around before he catches himself, grimaces, and forces himself and the horse to remain stationary as we pass a particularly thick patch of rot or feces or both. I try not to think too much about what's in the puddle Stellan is delicately skirting. Nash's face is a rictus of disgust, and even Sorren's blank façade has given way to mild distaste.

"You're sure this is the place?" Leith asks in an undertone, keeping his voice so low, not even the nearby bawd can hear.

She's leaning forward eagerly, big blue eyes drinking Leith in with very evident avaricious hunger. I've worn that look myself a few times, though never towards a man. It's the same expression I give something of value — something that will bring me lots of coin.

This woman clearly is more interested in men. She cases Leith, taking in the fine clothes, the trappings of wealth he displays openly, arrogantly, as if he's daring someone to steal from him. I know Leith well enough by now to know that's not his intent, even if it is what he projects.

The bawd doesn't know that though. All she knows is that he's one in a party of wealthy men — a man who's beyond handsome and will have ample coin to pay her. I know the way she thinks — perhaps she can swipe extra coin, if she can drive him to exhaustion in her bed.

For some ludicrous reason, I'm furious with her. I tighten my grip on Leith's waist and lean around him so I can pin her with a glare. It's incredibly stupid really. The King of the werebears isn't mine — obviously. It's not as though he's claimed me with his gargantuan cock, and there's been no talk of changing

129

that any time soon. So, I have no claim I can lay on him. There's no reason he shouldn't fuck this woman of ill repute.

She's a pretty thing, too. Blonde hair mussed, tall and slender, but with an ample chest spilling out of her dress. The coy smile she gives Leith shows she has all her teeth. I bet she's a local favorite. Undeterred by my irrationally possessive ire, she ignores me.

"Hello, beautiful," I hear Nash say from behind us.

"Don't get any ideas," I grumble. "She's probably got more diseases than you have coins in your pocket." Leith chuckles at that. "And that goes for you too, mister," I whisper to him and he stops laughing immediately.

"Spoiling all the fun," he whispers back.

"And saving you from crotch rot."

"I suppose I should thank you, but first I'll ask you where the bloody hell are we going?"

"The tavern we're looking for is further in. The Tiddly Tigress."

"The what?"

"Tiddly Tigress," I repeat with a sigh because it's one of my least favorite places. "It's Peter's favorite watering hole. We'll find him in his cups or neck-deep in trouble, I guarantee it."

Leith nods and spurs his horse forward, ignoring the bawd completely. She just stares after us, completely nonplussed. I'm sure she's never faced rejection once in her storied life. A grin curls my lips, a spiteful spark of glee kindling in my chest. I'm not usually prone to envy, but there's something gratifying in the gesture. I've been outdone by women like her all my life, men's eyes skimming easily over my boyish figure. Handy for my profession, but a bit of a sting to my heart as well as my female pride. I've tried to move past that fatuous, girly instinct but hey, I'm only human. I get lonely from time to time.

Yeah, so take that you stupid bitch! I think to myself.

Okay, Kassidy, calm down.

That's right! Go back into your crappy little house and stop looking at my men!

Only, they're not your men, I correct myself.

Well, they're more my men than hers.

I guess you have a point.

Nash and Sorren follow close behind, and neither of them pay her much mind, either, which just makes me grin harder. I bury my face into the hollow between Leith's shoulder blades to hide it.

I don't have to point out the Tiddly Tigress to Leith. We turn a corner a few minutes later, and there it is, in all its shabby glory. It's easily the tallest building on the street—three stories high, casement windows bolted shut against the foul smells, though I doubt it smells much better within the tavern. The wood paneling of the walls is blackened to pitch darkness in places, singed points dotting its face like seared-on freckles. The place has been set on fire a few times by drunken magical types with more power than sense.

Leith leads our little procession toward the stables set off to the side of the tavern. The footman is a short, chubby man with greasy dark hair and a hawkish nose. He gives Leith and the rest of us the same speculative look as the bawd, clearly planning to rifle

131

through our saddle bags for valuables the second we've disappeared inside.

"I know what you're thinking, Maslin, but I wouldn't do it," I start. "Not unless you want to lose a hand."

I lean away from Leith and I almost tip sideways off Stellan's back so I can make myself seen.

Maslin's broad, round face splits into a grin when he spies me. "Morningstar's sagging taint! Kassidy, is that you?"

"Kassidy?" Leith repeats, frowning at me.

Fuck. The cat's out of the proverbial bag. Oh well, I'll discuss that with him later. For now, I ignore the king.

"It's me." I raise a hand to my done-up hair and the circlet of gold Nash gave me. Not to mention my fine dress and the fact that I'm traveling with the best dressed, best looking men this place has probably ever seen.

I rummage in the folds of my dress and produce a coin purse filled to the cinched top with gold pieces. I flick it at Maslin. He doesn't look it, but he has wicked fast hands. He's nearly as good a pickpocket as me, so he snatches the sack deftly out of the air and grins.

"There's enough there to keep you honest, I trust?"

Maslin crosses his heart with a finger and gives me a sly wink. "Course, me girl, o' course! Wouldn't dream of stealin' from you."

I snort. Maslin is about as honest as a snake oil salesman, but I'm trusting fear to stay his hand if the money won't. Even in this elaborately sewn death trap,

I'm still dangerous and he knows it. Maslin is pure human. He knows if I get my hands on him, I can kill him. I won't like doing it, but if it comes down to it, I'll take his life to further the cause.

Actually, I'll take most lives to further the cause.

"You've got some explaining to do," Leith whispers to me.

"We'll see," I answer with a quick smile.

We leave Maslin in the stables, securing the horses in their stalls and rounding the side of the building, we pass a few more of the promiscuous women the town has to offer. One actually reaches out and playfully slaps Nash's ass as he passes. His eyes twinkle with good humor and he actually flashes her a sharp-toothed grin. Jealousy twists like a blade just beneath my navel and I curse my stupid fucking feelings. It's bad enough to be clinging like a vine to Leith, but at least we've been lovers, in a sense. I mean, I've done nothing but kiss Nash, but that's still something in my books.

Sort of crazy to think I've done more with Sorren than I have Nash. And, initially, Nash was the one who attracted me the most.

I lift the skirts of my ridiculous dress and stalk past Leith to take up the lead of our group, reaching the tavern doors thirty seconds before any of my companions. I shoulder them open with an unladylike grunt and slip inside, not bothering to hold the doors open for the others. They'll catch up or they won't and, besides, I'm not their fucking doorman, or woman. It's not my fucking business what they decide to do with prostitutes.

Stepping into the interior of the Tiddly Tigress feels like having a veil tugged over my eyes. The place is so dark, it's like swimming through ink. Only seasoned patrons of the bar know how to weave through the tables and chairs without toppling at least one. The only lights in the place come from little oil lamps scattered on various tables, but even those are almost rendered moot by the fug of pipe smoke that hangs heavy in the air. The lights are tiny pinpricks, bobbing in the gloom like drunken fireflies.

I draw on the last of my reserves, leaning into the power I stole from Leith's guard. It's enough to sharpen my night vision to a point where I can navigate through the bar without busting my shins.

The place is mostly empty at this time of day. It'll be doing a brisk trade come nightfall, but until then, there are only a few people in residence. There's a gaggle of genuine night hags hunched over a deck of cards in the corner, arguing with one another about who has the winning hand.

The smoke that hazes the air comes from a man in the middle of the bar. The pipe he's clutching is big enough to double as a club, in the event he needs to use it in a fight. The bowl alone is large enough to be a stewpot, and it's stuffed to the brim with snuff. The man himself is big enough to be a half-giant. Or maybe it's half-orc. He's got leathery brown skin and narrow yellowed eyes that trail me with interest as I pass.

My focus is on the men gathered at the bar. They all appear to be relatively young, but I know better. Every single one of them is old enough to be my grandfather, but because of a series of misadventures and a witch's curse, they're all frozen in the bloom of their youth. Useful for mercenary work, but a pain in the ass for almost every other occasion. Hard to have a wife and a family knowing you'll remain forever young while they wither and die in time. Quinn was the oldest of them when the curse hit, and even he's only twenty physically. Poor little Nibble is stuck at twelve. Peter's forever eighteen.

He's in the thick of them, leaning over the bar to flirt shamelessly with the beautiful, dark-skinned bartender, Layla. She's trying to do her work, scrubbing out the glasses, but I see the smile tugging at the corners of her mouth. I know she's got a soft spot for Peter. Always has, and probably always will. She grew up with him, after all. Even now that she's almost twice his age, she still looks at him with that same girlish wonderment she had when he saved her from pirates all those years ago.

He tucks a strand of her long, dark hair behind one ear and whispers something to her that makes her blush before she lets out a trilling laugh. I hate to interrupt. It looks like Peter might have a bedmate tonight, if he plays his cards right. But I have to say something to him before he drags her upstairs for a night of passion.

The door to the tavern opens again, letting a slice of lamplight cut briefly through the darkness before it clangs closed again. A brief glance over my shoulder shows that all three of my men have piled into the tavern.

My men? Ugh, I need to get a hold of myself.

"Pan, you great lout!" I call over the Lost Boys' raucous laughter at some joke he's told. "We've got business!"

Peter whirls, hand flying instinctively to his sword. His pretty face creases down into a scowl, mirth draining away to leave a peeved expression in its place. His fingers flex on the hilt. It never takes much to provoke Peter into a fight. Not only is he physically eighteen, he's stuck there mentally, as well. It means that he, along with the rest, tend to be quite reactionary. It's good they're all so skilled, or they'd have gotten themselves killed a long time ago.

He scans the dim interior of the tavern before his eyes land on me. The guarded expression falls away at once and his face splits into a huge grin that shows all his white, perfectly straight teeth. His big green eyes start at the crown of my head and scan me appreciatively down to the boots on my feet. He blows a whistle through his teeth.

"Damn, Aurelian. You clean up real nice. Knew there had to be a lady somewhere beneath all that armor and the layer of dirt."

"Oh, fuck off, Pan. And stop leering at my chest, you pervert."

Peter remains brazenly amused and bends at the waist, or as much as the forest green armor he wears will allow, giving me a flourishing bow. "If m'lady commands."

"Bastard," I mutter, sinking gratefully into the chair he pulls out for me.

"Born an' bred," he says with a smirk. "But you knew that already."

The rest of the Lost Boys crowd around the table as well, coming to stand behind Peter while Leith, Nash, and Sorren take the remaining seats. There's a tension that stretches taut between the two groups of men. Neither looks terribly happy with the other, sitting stiffly and eyeing one another with wariness. I can't understand it. I've never seen either group of men act this way before, and I've witnessed first-hand how they all typically act around other men.

It's Nibbles who breaks the silence. His round, boyish face lights up with a shy smile when he spies me.

"You look real nice, Miss Aurelian."

"Miss what?" Nash repeats.

Nibbles looks up at the enormous man and looks suddenly concerned. I wave my hand in the air to grab both their attention. "Sorren, Leith and Nash, we will discuss *that* matter later. In the meantime, meet the Lost Boys and Peter Pan."

I reach out and ruffle Nibbles' chestnut curls fondly, which only makes him grin wider. The rest of the Lost Boys mutter their greetings to the bears, none of them taking their eyes off me for long. It makes me feel a little self-conscious. I don't look *that* different in a dress, do I?

Leith grumbles something that sounds like a greeting or maybe it's a burp.

Embarrassed by the bears lack of friendliness, I fill the silence. "We're heading to Discordia's within the fortnight."

I turn and notice Sorren, who examines Peter's face with the expression a butcher wears before deciding just where to cut a hunk of meat. I rush to make further conversation before he can start getting any ideas.

"The Lost Boys are a group of sellswords who work closely with the Guild these days," I say to Leith and Nash because Sorren isn't paying any attention. "Their leader is Peter. This is Nibbles, there's Mayhaps, Riddle, and Quinn."

Only Nibbles smiles when I mention his name. Otherwise, the Lost Boys remain stone-faced. It's so unlike them. Usually I can't get them to be serious, even when it's required for a job. What in the name of Avernus am I missing here?

I rap the table with my knuckles, bringing the silent stare-off to a standstill. All eyes swivel toward me and I raise a brow expectantly at Peter.

"I've got the gold we agreed on. Do you have the siphoning stone?"

He drags unhappy eyes from Leith's face to mine. The tension in his expression eases when he looks at me. He shoves a hand into a pouch at his belt and withdraws a single smooth river stone. It's a moss green that blends almost seamlessly with his fae-made armor. It's about the size of a gold piece, and it looks utterly innocuous. Still, my heart quickens at the sight of it. It's possibly the most valuable thing in this bar. It's full to capacity with the power of an omnifarious, Neva, one of the ten chosen heroes that would fell Morningstar and his rabble once and for all.

Peter's grin creeps back onto his thin lips again, and I'm happy to see it. Somber Peter is a dangerous Peter. Between the startlingly red hair, the eyes, and the sharp cut of his cheekbones, he looks absolutely puckish and very much like himself.

"We're always happy to help you out, love. Just the usual price, and we'll be off."

I roll my eyes so hard, I think I may strain something. "Seriously? This again?"

Peter's white teeth reflect the bobbing flame at our table. "C'mon. You never used to mind. What's the harm?"

None at all, really. Three gold pieces for the group and a kiss on each of their cheeks. A kiss on the cheek which Peter will turn into a kiss on the lips and sometimes a grope of my tits. Well, he's only tried that the one time and since then, I caught onto him.

I reach into my pouch, drawing out the three coins. Peter sweeps them off the table and tucks them into his own pouch. "And the other half?"

Sighing good-naturedly, I lean across the table to kiss his cheek. He turns at the very last instant, as per usual, turning the chaste kiss meant for his cheek into a lip lock. There's certainly more... vigor in his kiss this time, as compared with the last time he did this little ploy. If there weren't a table between us, there'd be some body language in the kiss, too. My eyes fly open wide as his tongue skims my bottom lip.

A growl splits the air and then I'm reeling back, a hand fisted in the back of my dress like someone dragging a kitten by its scruff. I crane my neck to see Nash's face contorted in rage, the russet shade of his bear's eyes staring out from his human face. His teeth are sharper than usual, and he bares them at Peter in a snarl.

139

Then he lets go of me, and I go tumbling to the floor. I glance up just in time to see Nash's fist collide with Peter's face.

TWELVE
Kassidy

The punch almost knocks Peter off his feet. Almost. Peter's been at this game for over sixty years now and he's fought opponents that give me nightmares, just from the tales he's told. He may be impulsive and silly, but he's the best for a reason. If Nash weren't inhumanly strong and fast, the blow would never have even landed. As it is, Peter staggers back, nearly upending the next table over before he can steady himself.

His hand goes to his belt and, quicker than my eyes can follow, he's drawn his leaf-blade knife from its sheath at his waist. It's a favorite of his for close-quarters combat, when the sword would be too cumbersome or unwieldy. To hear him tell it, he stole the hand of Captain Hook with that very blade when he was a younger man. I never learned what the Captain's offense was on that occasion, or if it was just one of Peter's cruel whims.

The grin slashes across his face like a wound, the baring of teeth a fierce challenge to Nash's rumbling growl.

"You keep your fucking hands off her!" Nash's roar shakes the tavern walls and brings the other guest's activities to a standstill. The orc and the night hags eye us warily, clearly sensing the fight that's brewing.

"Testy, testy," Peter taunts. "Didn't do nothing she didn't want, little cub," Peter croons, a cruel edge of mocking to his tone.

Oh, fuck. He's in one of *those* moods. I hate it when he's like this. His teenage machismo doesn't rear its ugly head often, but when it does, he's a right bastard, just looking to spark trouble. Nash is a powder keg looking to blow.

Sure enough, the words land like a struck match and Nash is in motion again, charging Peter like a bull, another furious bellow shaking the tavern walls. I look to Leith but he just shrugs as though this isn't his problem. Bastard. And Sorren is… well, Sorren's no help. Guess I'm going to have to deal with this myself.

Peter dodges Nash's fist and then takes a glancing blow on his shoulder when the second comes down. He grimaces, but doesn't otherwise react. The knife flicks out and he readies it for a thrust.

Oh, fuck no. I'm not letting this happen. Not over something as silly as a stolen kiss.

I put on a burst of speed and knock clumsily into Nash, pushing him sideways into a table. Peter's blade comes down on empty air and Nash's howl of fury raises every hair on the back of my neck.

By this point, the rest of the Lost Boys have drawn their weapons as well and are squaring off against the remaining bears. Leith looks just as bemused as I feel; Sorren's smile is sharp-edged and curved like a scimitar, promising deadly things to follow. He can't shift, but the sword he carries will do the job nicely.

142

I grab a knife of my own from the table and hack at the layered skirt that binds my legs. I'm going to be useless in this fight if I trip all over it. I'm butchering the poor thing, but it does finally come off, leaving the remaining tatters tickling my thighs. It's so short now, it can barely be termed a dress at all. Maybe a long shirt?

With one hand, I clutch the knife, and the other lashes out to the nearest Lost Boy — I think it's Mayhaps, but I can't be sure, everyone's moving too fast — and I curl my fingers around his bicep, leaching his strength almost instantaneously. His knees buckle and I let go when his eyes threaten to roll back into his head. I want him down, not dead.

Riddle brings his slingshot up, loading it with what appears to be another riverstone. I know better. The violet stone is enchanted to burrow in on impact, making it just as dangerous as any arrow.

Why the fuck are they doing this? Nothing done so far warrants this kind of backlash. They're acting as if they want to kill each other. Over what? A stupid kiss? Yes, Peter overstepped his bounds, but it's not anything to go to war over.

I round on Riddle next, using the newfound strength and agility I've drained from Mayhaps to sink into a crouch and sweep his legs out from under him. He goes down in a flailing tangle of limbs and I slap a hand to his chest, siphoning enough strength to be sure he stays down. The shot he meant for Leith shoots up instead, blowing a hole in the tavern roof.

I wince. Someone's going to have to pay Layla for the damage.

Sorren is wading into the fray now, the naked blade of his sword glinting in the low light. I straighten from the crouch and take three running steps before bounding onto a table, using it as a springboard to come down like a proverbial bag of rocks onto Sorren's back, then riding him to the ground. I sink my hand into the tangle of brown hair on his head and mash his face into the ground.

I knock his face hard against the wooden floor and snarl, "Drop it!"

Sorren barely reacts to the pain; he gives me a grin that's more feral anticipation than smile. I knock his head into the floor again, harder this time.

"I said, drop it!"

"Or what?"

I grit my teeth and then reach deeper, toward the power within him. I'm expecting there to be less of it, since he has no access to his bear form. But it's all beneath the surface, at least as much as his cousins possess—if not more. The energy feels... cold. Like I've just dunked my hand into ice water. Drawing on it feels like breathing in winter air, the kind that slices into your lungs and makes you gasp at the pain.

Taking enough to make Sorren's grip relax leaves me buzzing with arctic power. I kick the sword away from his grasp, just in case he gets any funny ideas.

Most of the remaining Lost Boys have taken the hint and stepped away from the brawl, lest they face my wrath. Not Peter, though. He and Nash are still embroiled in a fight, each looking like he wants to take the other's head off. I don't know what the fuck has gotten into these two, but it ends now.

I seize the edge of one of the round tables, hoisting it easily off the ground with Sorren's stolen strength. Gathering as much power as I can muster, I sling it like a disc toward the warring pair. They both look up in time to see it coming and spring feet apart to avoid being hit. The table hits the far wall, shattering into dozens of broken pieces.

Looks like I'm the one paying for damages, then. Damn it. I'm going to wring both their necks for this, I swear.

I stalk forward, planting myself stubbornly between them. I'm not physically imposing. Both Peter and Nash are more than a head taller than me and probably weigh two to three times what I do. Neither advances, nor tries to shove past me.

"Enough!" I shout, voice echoing back to me in the stillness. "Nobody move, or so help me, I'm going to kick every single one of your asses!"

Every eye in the room is on me, and I feel the weighty stares on my back. This story will be all over the town by tonight. So much for keeping a low profile. What the fuck was Nash thinking?

I round on him and he at least has the good grace to look somewhat abashed. His eyes have returned to normal and he won't hold my gaze for long.

"You," I hiss. "You're coming with me."

Peter snickers. "Someone's in trouble."

I spin on one heel and slap Peter so hard, he staggers. My handprint glows a vivid pink against the pale cream color of his skin. He blinks huge green eyes at me in shock. 'Kassidy…"

"Don't you fucking start," I warn. "Keep your mouth shut, Peter, or I'll sew it closed."

I march away, catching Nash's arm as I make my way toward the front door of the tavern. He doesn't struggle, thankfully, though he could. With Sorren's strength, I think I could be a match for him, now, and beat him bloody for the stunt he just pulled. I don't, and he doesn't make me.

I finally pull him to a stop near the side of an inn, jerking him into the shadow of the building to get away from prying eyes.

"What in the name of the Gods was that?" I hiss. "Are you trying to get yourself killed?"

"As if that little, fucking rat could kill me," he snorts. "I'd have snapped him in two."

I give Nash a light slap, nothing like the one I gave Peter. It does make him blink at me, though.

"That isn't the point, Nash! You started it! And Peter's our contact, in case you've forgotten. He's delivering the best chance we have to steal back your brother's heart. Had you forgotten that?"

"He touched you," Nash argues stubbornly. "He tried to stick his tongue down your…"

I slap Nash's cheek lightly once more, and it succeeds in shutting him up. He glowers defiantly at a point just to the side of my face.

"It's nothing. Peter does this every time we see each other. He's a hopeless flirt and he's not discriminatory. Any woman will do. He's done this since I turned fourteen, and I had even less of a figure then. It's the way we agreed to pay each other. Three gold coins and a kiss on the cheek... though recently,

146

it's been on the mouth, as you've noticed. A kiss for each of the crew and then I'm off. It's just sport to him. He wouldn't have taken it so far if he didn't guess it would bother you."

Some of the tension curled in his muscles eases at my assurance. He's still not looking at me, though.

"You didn't warn us."

"Because it isn't your business what I do with Peter—or anyone else, for that matter."

Nash drops his hand to my waist, and I can feel the burning temperature even through the stiff material of the dress. My insides quiver oddly, like winged creatures have been let loose to riot. An unexpected surge of warmth pools between my legs as he leans forward, pressing our bodies tighter together.

"I want it to be," he murmurs, dropping his head so the side of his face brushes mine. His hair tickles my cheek and my sex tightens, anticipating the kiss he presses to my throat seconds later. "I want you."

"Nash..."

"Tell me you don't want the same," he says, reaching to undo the loose laces that keep the bodice of my dress up. He pulls at them slowly, deliberately, giving me time to protest. I can't. I don't want to. "Tell me you want me to stop, and I'll walk away."

My mouth is as dry as the Anoka desert, but that place between my legs is mortifyingly slick. It's hard to swallow, hard to form the words I know I *should* say. That this is a distraction we don't need, a pleasure I can't indulge. The words don't come—instead, a whimper escapes my throat.

"Tell me," Nash says. "Say you don't want it...
Kassidy Aurelian."

"Fuck," I grumble as I swallow hard.

"That's your real name?"

I nod. "That's my real name."

Nash smiles. "Then tell me you don't want to feel
my cock slipping inside you, Kassidy."

"I do want it," I confess.

My bodice slips, and my breasts spring free of the
constraints. Nash stares down at them with such
scorching desire that heat flashes through my body.

"I don't have the control Leith does," Nash says as
he looks down at me, his eyes serious.

"What do you mean?" I breathe against him.

"If we start this, I won't be able to stop. So if you
aren't sure, just walk away now."

I breathe in deeply and make a decision here and
now. "I'm not walking away."

THIRTEEN
Nash

Every part of my body yearns toward her, my skin hot and tight with the anticipation that comes with the change.

I've never hated my father more than I do in this instant. The bear is too close to the surface; it always is when my need runs high. She's not a werebear. She's not a delicate fucking flower, either, but she deserves gentleness her first time. Consideration, respect. Things my beast doesn't understand.

She pants, gasping enticingly when I skim my nose along her throat, press my mouth to that throbbing pulse point, and test my teeth against it. Her back bows, the curve of her spine flawless. It makes my mind flit to just what it would look like curved over a bed, my hand in her hair as I bury myself into her heat from behind.

Not this time. It can't be this time. But later...

"Nash... not here," she finally manages.

Her words don't register for a few seconds, because I'm too busy exploring the toned, elegant planes of her body. Only a few scraps of remaining fabric obscure her thighs. My cock strains the front of my pants, so hard it actually hurts. I want to be between those thighs, tasting her until she comes.

149

But she's right. I can't do this here in the back alley of the fucking tavern. She deserves more than this. Granted, I can't take her in my own bed, but she deserves a bed all the same. I manage to let my hands fall to my sides, releasing her.

The bear's furious roar resonates through my head. We don't want to let her go. We can rut her right here and right now.

Fuck off, I snarl at it. *Mine. Not yours. I will treat her with some damn respect.*

"Where can we go?" I demand.

She swallows audibly. "There's an inn right behind you."

I nod. "Lead the way."

She pauses for a moment. "What will Leith," she starts.

"Lead the way," I growl and she does as I order.

She shuffles toward the entrance to the inn. We catch some startled looks as we enter, Kassidy clutching her bodice to her chest for dear life. Still, the stupefied innkeeper's wife shows us to a room on the first floor.

The second the door closes, I can't keep my hands to myself. I have to touch her. Have to have her. Before I can seize her waist, however, she turns, lifting her chin and letting the dress drop with an almost defiant look on her face. It slithers to the floor and puddles at her feet before she kicks it aside.

Fuuuck.

She's wearing almost nothing beneath. Her nipples are a dusky pink and point toward the sky. The small breasts are incredibly pert, with just enough

150

soft roundness to cup in a palm but not enough to overflow it.

A growl builds in my throat. I can't remember wanting anything so much in my life. But... I don't want to hurt her.

"Kassidy," I begin, voice still more growl than anything else. "I can't be... my beast is... I don't want to hurt you."

A coy little smile plays at the corner of her full, kissable lips. "I'm a big girl, Nash. I'll handle it. It won't be something I can't recover from."

She's not lying. I can hear the honesty behind her words, she believes I won't hurt her. It's a confidence I wish I shared. But it does spark something inside me, something my father beat out of me over the course of years.

The desire to change. The desire to be better. To be the sort of man—the sort of warrior—Kassidy deserves to protect her.

I reach for her, pulling her into my arms. She's so small and dainty, still, even with all that ready muscle. If it weren't for her powers, I'd be confident I could snap her in two. She lets out a startled gasp when I shove a hand into her thick blonde mane and angle her head for another hot, possessive kiss. I almost smile. Her enticing scent swirls around me, carrying the musk of her arousal. She smells so fucking good.

Her hands come to rest timidly on my waist, gasping again when I pull her lower lip between my teeth. She moans when I palm one breast and then the other, kneading her nipples to painful attention. Her hips buck into mine, one of her calves hooking around the back of my leg, as she grinds herself into my front. I can feel how wet she is already.

I pull myself free of the kiss, give her earlobe a hard nip, and then growl the command into her ear: "I want you on the bed."

She hesitates, but I sense her hesitation is more nerves than anything else. But she does what I ask, backing to the edge of the thin mattress before draping herself onto it.

She watches me as I strip off my shirt, and then the trousers. Her swallow is audible when my cock springs free; she's obviously wondering if she can take my length or maybe my girth. I approach cautiously, trying not to scare her further. She doesn't back away or tell me to stop, which I take as a good sign. I stop just short of her and then climb over her, slipping a hand between us.

Her lithe body is warm and welcome against mine. She bites her lip enticingly when I press two fingers into her entrance. For my part, it's all I can do not to groan. She feels so damn tight. Just the *daydream* of feeling that pussy clenching around me is enough to bring me almost to the brink.

And then I feel the shield of her skin that points to the fact that she's never had a man before. "This is going to sting a bit," I whisper down at her.

She looks up at me and nods and I suddenly feel a swell of pride that I will be the first of us. It's my responsibility to ensure that she enjoys this, that it won't be something she'll hate. It's unfortunate I'm as large as I am but I'll do my best to ensure she enjoys it.

Her hips buck up toward my hand and a moan flies from her mouth. Leisurely, I pump my fingers into her. The wetter she gets, the less likely I am to hurt her. My thumb finds the bud at the apex of her sex and I lavish it with attention in short, shivering strokes.

"Oh, fuck..." Kassidy's words are almost lost in a gasp.

A slow moan rolls from her a few seconds later. Her hips won't stop undulating, meeting the thrusts of my fingers stroke for stroke as she chases an elusive climax. She buries her hands in my hair, short nails still pleasant as she rakes them over my scalp. A flash of pure, molten want shoots right to my cock. The pleasure dances on the edge of pain. I need to be inside her.

Her back bows, her lovely tits bouncing as she comes. The pleasure on her face transforms her from lovely to transcendent.

"Kassidy," I breathe.

She reaches for me when the shivers subside, dainty hand closing around my cock. The sound of relief her touch brings me makes her smile.

"Make love to me, Nash," she murmurs.

Hard to argue with that.

I brace my hand beside her head as she guides me toward her entrance, the head of my cock sliding inside. It's a struggle to push in gently, taking her inch by inch while giving her time to adjust.

"Are you ready?" I ask, when I feel the wall of flesh blocking me.

She nods and I push forward as she winces slightly. I start rubbing her clit as I push in and out of

153

her and the whimper turns into a moan. She opens her eyes and looks at me in wonder.

"That was the pain?"

I nod. "That was the pain."

I lavish kisses on her throat, waiting for her to signal me. I haven't been with a maid in years. Not since doing so earned me my father's wrath.

I was sixteen, led around by my cock as if the damn thing had a mind of its own. I hadn't known the girl was being groomed to be my father's second wife, to be married to him as soon as she turned eighteen. I hadn't known, and neither had she. Her parents hadn't told her. All I knew was that I wanted her, and she wanted me.

After that, Father kept me in bear form for so long, my human mind took months to return, even when I could finally shift back. I haven't fucked many women since then—certainly no virgins.

Kassidy rolls her hips experimentally, moaning when the motion drags the underside of my cock along a particularly sensitive spot. She snakes her arms around my neck, pulling herself flush against me with the peaks of her breasts rubbing my chest in a thoroughly pleasant way. I thrust into her, setting a slow pace. She deserves more than a fuck. I've never made love before. Not really, even my first time. But I'll damn well try, for her sake.

I'm expecting her to lie there and sort of take it, the way my first virgin did. She doesn't. She moves her hips in that rolling motion, meeting me stroke for stroke. And all the while she moans loudly, nails digging into my back when I push too deep.

154

She stares at me, those gem eyes boring into me with... wonder on her face. It's almost too intimate, more so even than the way our bodies are linked. She's looking at me like... a woman in love. And that just can't be right. Not yet, at least. She doesn't keep her eyes open too long. They close on the next thrust, her head rolling back as she moans my name, nails tearing furrows into my back.

The only warning I get is the soft flutter of her walls and then she's coming hard, back arching from the force of her climax. Her hair is messier than ever before, her eyes glazed over with pleasure, her mouth open in a perfectly lush 'O' — and then I'm there, as well. My hips buck, thrusting one last time before my vision flashes white and pleasure riots through my body.

It's an effort not to sag, boneless, on top of her. I'm abruptly exhausted after the fight and the fuck, and I'd happily sleep the rest of the day with her in my arms. I roll, collapsing at her side instead, sure she won't appreciate two hundred pounds and change of sweaty shifter on top of her after the coital bliss wears off. She's still shivering as the aftershocks roll through her.

It's not until I've settled myself that I realize the door is open and we have an audience. Sorren leans indolently against the doorframe, staring at the pair of us.

"Quite a show," he says with an unrepentant smirk. "Can't wait until it's my turn."

I yank a pillow from the pile at the head of the bed and lob it at him. He deflects it with a light laugh and it lands harmlessly at his feet.

"Fuck off, Sorren," I say.

"Leith told me to inform you he has the stone and we'll be ready to leave by sundown. Think you can recover by then, little dove?"

He leers at Kassidy and aims a very rude gesture in my direction.

"Get lost," I say. "Tell Leith we'll be down after I've had a bath and some rest. Tell him to get each of you a room and let's all get some sleep."

Sorren shrugs and pushes off from the door, sauntering back the way he came without even closing the door. With a growl, I untuck the covers and curl them around her, covering her nudity. It takes me a minute to get dressed. Enough to give Sorren a decent head start. It's not enough to let him outrun me, and I'm going to kick his ass for watching without her approval. The fucking barbarian.

"Nash?" Kassidy's voice is soft, but it nevertheless makes me turn.

"Yes?"

She smiles wearily at me, eyes already sliding to half-mast. She's going to pass out in seconds.

"I knew you wouldn't hurt me. Thank you."

"For the sex or the fact that it didn't hurt?"

"Yes," she says with a light chuckle.

I don't have time to ask her more, because her breathing abruptly evens out and she lets out that light whistling exhale she does when she's asleep.

FOURTEEN
Sorren

I trace the bags beneath my eyelids with a curious smile. The sensation is an odd one, almost forgotten. It's been years since weariness has plagued me in any way, shape, or form. Nothing but my traps have occupied my thoughts for any significant length of time. I eat, sleep, breathe, and generally operate like, well... clockwork. Nothing has scuppered my routine quite so thoroughly as this little dove.

I've spent the last two nights thinking about what it must be like to be inside her. She's impressive. Strong enough that I could spend the fullness of my depravity on her. She shouldn't have been able to find pleasure in the rutting Nash gave her. He thinks he's gentle with her, but his bear knows no such thing. Any other human would have screamed not from pleasure, but from the agony of his force. He took her hard and she loved every second of it, the tenacious little dove.

My cock swells just thinking about watching them, imagining her pale form splayed out beneath him, those legs wrapped around his waist, meeting his strokes as he fucked her into the thin mattress. I want that. Want her. Want to be the one that turns all that ivory skin pink, scores marks into her back even as she tears at mine with her nails.

She turns her head and gives me a slow grin. It rolls across her lips in an almost teasing manner as she spots me rubbing the unusual bags beneath my eyes.

"Couldn't sleep, huh? Too excited?"

I incline my head to her, allowing her the easy answer. Telling her I'm incapable of the sort of anticipatory glee she's expecting won't endear me to her. It won't get me any closer to the sort of intimacy that Nash has achieved — the intimacy that Leith so dearly wishes from her, as well. Happiness, in any of its forms, is a summery emotion that can't exist in the boreal reaches of my half-heart.

She does evoke a new emotion. Not happiness, exactly. Something more tepid, but still incredible. It's hope. Or, no... perhaps just the *desire* to hope. I've desired little but pain and vengeance for years. Until she came into my life, I'd written my heart off as a necessary loss, committing the time I had left to building tools my cousins could use to avenge me.

But now? Perhaps there's a chance I can do it myself. If my heart can be thrust back into my chest and forced to beat, I'll be myself once more. A man worthy to stand by her. A man capable of doing good again. I don't care if my cousins commit themselves to the war or not, I can't turn my back on it any longer. Wherever Kassidy goes, I will follow, and damn the consequences. I'll have my heart ripped out a thousand times if only I can make some sort of difference.

Kassidy accepts this with easy acquiescence, but Leith and Nash don't. They both eye me suspiciously as they pass me on the trail, as if I'm somehow going to leap off my horse and abscond with the little dove at any second. She's tucked securely in front of Leith on his horse, and she seems quite happy there. I've no desire to unseat her. If Leith wants to contend with the aching balls he'll have later because of it, then he can. I'm saving my energies for the time they can truly be put to use.

We're approaching the end of the tunnel of Grimm, and the fortress just beyond it where Discordia is rumored to have built her defenses into the side of the rocky wall. The darkness presses in on all sides, threatening to consume the winding path we tread. I imagine the encroaching rock walls would make a human claustrophobic. I'm more attuned to the small eccentricities indulged by humans, since being rendered one by a technicality. Shifting will destroy this false heart in my chest, and so my bear is dormant. I'll be just as hobbled by a trip through this dour place as our dear little dove. It's an offensive indignity to twist an ankle on a jutting rim of stone or the like. There are times I hate being trapped like this.

The cave of Grimm is old and deeply magical. Even in my human form, I can sense it. Magic raises goosebumps along my arms, the dark, swirling eddies of power causing dread to pool in my stomach. I don't like the energy here.

A glance to either side of me reveals that Nash and Leith feel the ominous pall of magic, too. It's worse for them. Their beasts are awake and in tune with the world around them. Nash hunches his shoulders slightly forward, as if an unseen force leans heavily against his spine. This place will be the hardest on

Nash, who has thin control in the best of circumstances.

"It feels worse than normal," Kassidy's voice breaks the silence, saying out loud what the rest of us have been thinking but unwilling to admit. Maybe, like me, the rest were hoping it's just our imaginations running wild.

"There's extra magic in the air," she continues, seemingly talking to herself. "Dark stuff. I mean, coming through Grimm is never sunshine and fucking marigolds but this is... different."

"An early warning system, maybe?" Leith murmurs. "Stay away, or else?"

"Maybe," Kassidy says with a nod. "But I guess we'll have to ignore it. I wish I had another siphoning stone. It could take some of the psychic pressure off."

"I should take point," I say after a moment. "Without my bear and much magic to speak of, I'm ideal to fend off any attacks."

Leith and Nash exchange another glance, clearly reluctant. I'm practically a mundane human in this state, and though I'm the family shame, we are still cousins. It might have been touching, if I possessed the capacity to feel something so trite. But I don't, so I continue, ruthlessly pragmatic.

"We need Kassidy," I continue. By now, we are all using her true name. That, in and of itself, is a subject which amuses me to no end. Such a little recalcitrant she is to give us a false name. The little thief is full of surprises. "I'll go first, Leith will keep Kassidy in the middle, and Nash can bring up the rear."

I can tell they want to argue with me, but in the end, no one speaks out against the plan. Both of them care too much for our little dove to risk her, and they know I'm right. She's our best hope of getting my heart back. I need that heart if I'm to understand that level of care. And I want it, I want it more than I can remember wanting anything for a very long time.

I move my mount to the front of the line, with Leith and Kassidy trailing close behind while Nash's resentment fairly boils in the air around him. I can't force myself to care about their insipid emotions at present. Maybe I'll feel differently soon. The faint flickering desire to hope stirs in my chest again.

Something crashes around a bend in the cave from yards away, and from the sound of the approach, I judge it to be only a pair of individuals. Perhaps three, though it's difficult to tell when the sound splinters and refracts in the hollowed cave. They're making no effort to disguise themselves, creating enough noise that even the hard of hearing would sit up and pay attention.

By the time the figures stagger onto our path, all of us have drawn weapons. Leith has his short sword; Nash, his throwing knives; and Kassidy wields the short bow she favors. The strangers are surprised for perhaps a few seconds before they begin to charge us. But we're ready. I swing my leg over the side of my mount and impact the earth, pulling the stiletto knife from its sheath at my belt before I sprint to meet them.

I'm right, there were three—all of them male, as burly and covered in hair as dwarves. I might have believed that's what they were, if they weren't so tall.

161

Six feet, at least. But they're still a head shorter than I am, and I use that height to my advantage. My superior reach gives me a few extra seconds, and I use them.

The sharp, tapered knife enters the first man's neck, sinking in deep. I smile, cold satisfaction spreading through my body as I carve a bloody crescent through the meaty column like it's a ripe melon. The slash begins to spurt scarlet onto my front. The man's eyes fly open, but his expression doesn't otherwise change. He lets out a gurgling exhale and drops like a stone, head impacting the dirt with a dull thunk.

The next man lurches toward me, undeterred by the death of his fellow. He meets a similar fate, though his ungainly lunge puts his face closest to me. I drive the knife through his orbital socket, squelching the eyeball on the way through. With a smirk, I swirl my blade and reduce the slimy gray matter beyond into slurry. His body bucks weakly, and when I release him, he goes down as well.

I expect the third to run. I *want* him to run. It's not half as satisfying to chase down prey in human form, but there's still a certain thrill to it. It even feels earned when I can take the prey to the ground in this form. But the imbecile doesn't learn. He lumbers toward me, arms outstretched and groping the empty air like some flesh-eating revenant.

Leith shouts something at me, but too late for it to be heard. My blade slides through the third man's enormous belly and his insides slither out, pooling on the ground like a mass of gray snakes. A putrid odor fills the air as his waste spills from one of his severed intestines.

I sense the presence at my back and recognize the bristling energy as Leith's. The fury of his beast is an acrid bite that saturates his scent. When I turn to him, he's a mere foot away, his face a rictus of rage and disgust.

His fist comes out of nowhere, impacting the side of my face with enough force to send me sprawling sideways. It's an effort to stay on my feet, but I manage, catching myself on the trunk of a tree. I whirl to face him, human throat protesting as a growl rips from me. Humans aren't meant to make such sounds, and it burns weakly every time I try.

Tightening my grip on my blade, I size him up. His bear is stronger than mine, even if I could shift. There is something to the idea that blood is important. My diluted blood means that I'm weaker than Leith or Nash. But, unencumbered by emotion, I am more dangerous. I could go for his throat, sink the dagger in and end him. His love for me will impede him long enough to allow for that.

The thought makes my grip slacken on the hilt, and a new emotion washes over me. It's hard to put a name to. Not fear, precisely. Nor disgust. I'm... disturbed. Deep disquiet steals through me as I consider exactly what I wished to do. He's my blood. I've never looked at him as an enemy before.

I force myself to relax and reassess the situation. Leith doesn't afford me the courtesy; he's stalking toward me again.

"What part of 'stop' did you not understand, Sorren?" he snarls.

"I didn't hear you."

"Yes, because you were too busy carving them like a roast! They were bespelled, you bloodthirsty madman! You could have just incapacitated them without fucking butchering them!"

Bespelled? The thought brings me up short, forces me to let go of the last threads of indignation I cling to.

Yes. That makes sense. For men of their size, they were too uncoordinated. Muscle of that caliber suggested professions of some skill. Blacksmiths, stone masons, or other craftsmen. There was no strategy, no communication. Fuck, none of them had even seemed to react as they were killed. Perhaps the first two were incapable when I was through with them, but the last ought to have been screaming. But there was nothing.

I cast my gaze to where the bodies lay. Nash and Kassidy have dismounted and Kassidy kneels by the bodies, examining them with a look of mild disgust on her face. Nash stands as a still and silent sentry, scanning the surroundings for further threat. I should assist. I've come to learn as much as I can about magic in the last decade, first in an effort to understand what had been done to me and then to perfect my traps when I realized the curse upon me could not be reversed.

When I try to push past Leith, he lays a restraining hand on my bicep.

"Let me past," I growl.

He glowers at me. "Not until I have your word you won't try to harm her. I saw that look in your eyes just now. You wanted to kill me."

I'm blessedly free of chagrin, so I shrug one shoulder. "Tell me it shocks you, cousin."

There's a flinching around his eyes, but he doesn't release me. "Your bloody word."

"I won't harm her. I don't want to harm her. I want her too badly to cut her up, Leith. I won't risk it. So let me past."

Leith examines my face for a few long seconds before seeming to decide I'm telling the truth. His grip slackens and I jerk my arm out of his hold, crossing the distance so I can kneel beside the bodies, as well.

Kassidy runs her fingers along the skin of the dead and they come away trailing a shimmering, translucent ooze. I'd almost say it was pus, but the stench isn't foul enough for that. Besides the smell of the leaking excrement, there's almost no odor to these bodies. It's too late to warn her not to touch the stuff. I watch her for ill effects, but the only change I can spy is her expression. The mild disgust deepens.

"It's like a snail's trail," she mutters. "Like mucous." She brings the stuff to her nose and sniffs delicately. "And it smells... sweet."

Gingerly, I take her wrist. She stiffens, eyes flicking up to meet mine. Her body is coiled tight like a spring, and I know the slightest movement toward her will have her backpedaling in an effort to get as far away from me as possible. She still doesn't trust me, even after what passed between us in the aviary. I relax my grip still further, until the pads of my fingers barely touch her.

"I just want to scent it," I assure her, my tone so low that even Nash can't hear, keeping the intimate whisper between us. "I won't hurt you, little dove."

She doesn't believe me, I can see that plainly on her face. But she does let me pull the wrist closer, so her palm hovers a half inch from my face. I draw in a deep breath.

She's right. It's sweet. A crisp, tart aroma that brings to mind the orchards in fall, when the green skins of the apples turns a dusky red. I've smelled this once before, when we faced Discordia ten years ago.

"It's Discordia's apples."

"Apples?" she echoes. "Why would the bodies smell like apples?"

I straighten from my crouch and offer her a hand up. She takes it. Both my cousins stand by, trying not to appear interested. They're as bemused as Kassidy, neither having seen what I have. They sheltered in our compound during the war, and they didn't bother to ask for accounts of the war when I returned altered. I have a feeling they don't want to know.

"Discordia can taint food. Crops are the most efficient, but she has a fondness for the theatrical. She likes to poison fruits, the way it used to be done in those children's tales. Her fruits will allow her to control any who ingests them."

"So, this was an early warning system," Leith mutters. "And now she knows someone has breached her defenses."

The three exchange poignant glances. I feel like an uninitiated observer, watching longtime friends communicate so I am left out of the conversation. It rankles. I can't even catch the tenor of their thoughts.

Thankfully, Nash speaks aloud what they're thinking.

"Do we proceed? If she knows..."

"Then we're in deep shit," Leith concludes.

Kassidy wipes the ooze from her hand onto the ruined skirts of her frock with a shake of her head. Her jaw is set, determination glinting in her emerald eyes like light off a blade.

"We have no choice. We have the power, and we're getting Sorren's heart back. I don't care what it takes."

I act on impulse, stepping closer to her. I wind my arms around her waist, draw her tight against me, and then bring my lips down onto hers. She's shocked, hands fluttering like two frightened birds before they settle on my shoulders. They're amazingly small and dainty in a feminine way that belies her strength. I like it. It's maybe a second or so but then she returns the kiss, allowing my tongue to mate with hers.

When I pull away, she blinks at me in shock, but she doesn't try to extricate herself. "What's that for?"

"For trying to help me, damn the consequences. For thinking I'm worth helping."

Her eyes soften, the emerald becoming almost molten. "You're a hero, Sorren, a soldier who doesn't deserve to be left behind. I want to meet *that* Sorren. And his heart is in Discordia's fortress. So, I'm going to steal it back."

I want to kiss her again, but I can feel both Nash and Leith glowering at me for touching her. I can, occasionally, learn to pick my battles.

She shakes herself visibly, like a dog shedding water.

"Let's go."

And so we follow her into the ever-darkening cave, toward almost certain doom. We are all likely to die tonight, but I can't force myself to care. I'm too busy staring at the retreating back of the golden-haired thief.

She doesn't have to steal my heart. When I return to my body, it's hers for the taking.

FIFTEEN
Kassidy

The small city of Morsoe, where Discordia's palace is located, lies at the furthest reaches of Grimm, in the bottom of a curious bowl-shaped depression in the ground, settled deep within the cavernous mountain. It's almost as if a giant's hand scooped away massive chunks of earth long ago and left a scabbed-over rocky crust in its wake.

It looks eerie.

We observed if from a rock outcropping, overlooking the city for a time, trying to ascertain the number of foes we'll face when we enter. It proved impossible. Too much mist hanging over the town. I didn't need Sorren's confirmation to know the stuff's not natural. There's no reason for fog at this time of year, and in a cave, no less. There exists no body of water for the mist to lift from. It's Discordia's doing. If we had any doubt about her presence here, that doubt has been erased.

There are no lights in the city. No fires burning, no lanterns hung to guide the way. Not that lights would do us much good through the mist, but damn it, it would be something. We're creeping into the town blind. I think I'd rather cut off one of my less-treasured body parts than attempt this without the element of surprise and almost no visibility. What I wouldn't give to have my brothers or Neva at my back. At this point, I'd even take Tenebris, and I don't like her much. Tenebris, or Belle (her first name), is something of an arrogant bitch, though the arrogance is well deserved. She's possibly the most powerful sorceress Fantasia has ever seen.

But, Gods, she's a cock.

The road into town has thankfully hardened due to the cold, so we're not squelching through mud. We've opted to leave our horses behind, sure the things will spook if they end up being surrounded. If one of them gets overturned and lands on us... well, that'll be the end. At least for me. I'm not built as strong as the rest of my traveling companions.

I twitch every time shapes loom out of the darkness. Even the innocuous form of a wishing well within the square makes me jerk in surprise. The longer we go without seeing a humanoid shape, the more paranoid I become.

This village is completely barren, devoid of everything—people, animals, sound even.

"Where are all the damn people?" I whisper.

"They're coming," Sorren says suddenly, his voice eerily flat. Flatter than I've ever heard it. The words raise the hairs on the back of my neck.

"The people?" I ask.

"No."

I strain my ears, cursing my mere mortal status. My life would be so much easier if I'd just been born a huntsman, instead of being adopted by them. Sure enough, after a few more seconds, I can hear *them* as well—the thudding of many feet on the packed earth,

coming toward us fast. I bring my bow, which I've
held pointed toward the ground, up to its ready
position. It's hard to know where to aim because it's
dark as hellhound balls and I can't see a fucking thing.

My heart pounds painfully against my ribs, doing
its level best to try to escape the cage. It's hard to
swallow and I nearly jump out of my skin when
shapes in the darkness begin to emerge, simply more
dark than the darkness around them. They speak in
unison. Hundreds of voices layer over each other,
issuing a single hissed command.

"Get out."

My mind is screaming panicked obscenities.

I'm a fucking idiot. And soon I'll be a dead
fucking idiot.

We *knew* walking in here was a bad idea. Sorren
told us what awaited us. And I came anyway, too
impatient, too arrogant, too headstrong to do anything
else. But faced with these overwhelming odds, I'm
suddenly forced to reconsider. Sorren has five years
before his heart ticks down to the end of his life. Five
years is a long time to plan. It's definitely long enough
for me to come up with something less monumentally
foolish than charging headlong into this fucking mess.

The voices speak again, rising in pitch with every
command. I still can't see them — they simply appear as
pitch black blobs that shift in the darkness.

*"Get out. Get out! Get **out**! GET OUT!"*"

*You heard the fuckers, Kassidy! They want us to get
out so why the hell aren't we doing exactly that?*

Then, their line breaks and they're emerging into
the square, a hundred dark shapes so crowded
together, it's impossible to make out one from the

other. I shoot blindly, just hoping for a hit. Shame burns through me. My brothers would slap me for being so reactionary in the middle of a crisis.

Damn it, damn it, damn it!

I can't see a thing in the mist and they've stopped their weird chanting. I don't hear a sound of impact or a cry of pain. Nothing. And that's beyond weird because I know my arrows have to hit somewhere.

Sorren and the others bolt into action, but soon they too are lost in the mist. Fuck. I can't take a shot in the dark now—I could hit an ally as easily as an enemy.

A hand jerks my bow free of my grip and snaps it in two. I whirl, just in time to see a grizzled stranger lunge in my direction. He appears human but his eyes are blank and glowing white. Where his eyeball should be, there's nothing but white. His mouth is wide open to take a chunk out of me. He goes for my neck, aiming to tear my throat open.

I act on pure reflex, hand flying out to get him in a chokehold, and as I do, I draw on his life force. But the instant I touch the power that buzzes beneath his skin, I know I've made a mistake.

He feels wrong, I think.

Let him go, Kassidy! Let him go!

I try to pry my fingers away from him but their stuck fast. No matter how hard I try to pull my hand away, it won't budge. A dark miasma fills my lungs, and I choke on it, coughing against the putrescence that fills me. My brain is fuzzy, possessed by an eerily calm sort of madness. Nothing around me matters any

longer and as I watch the darkness, I feel as if I'm
suddenly miles away from it.

Is this what it feels like to be Sorren? Floating in a
haze of detachment? It's strangely nice.

With the detachment comes a revelation: *I'm more
powerful than I realize.*

But what does that mean?

*It means you've never needed to touch your victims to
pull their life force, Kassidy. That's always been a crutch
you've leaned on to keep yourself from rising to your true
potential.*

What is my true potential then? Am I a witch?

But I know I'm not a witch. Because I don't want
to be one. Don't want to be like arrogant Belle
Tenebris, or Mad Hattie. I don't want to be taken away
from what I love like they were, to be separated from
the only family I've ever known, for being too *special.*

But now? When I'm so vastly outnumbered, I can't
afford to be lost in the wonder of what I am and what I
could be.

I don't have to touch anyone. It's a realization that
suddenly penetrates every inch of my being and I
understand the truth in the words deeply.

I reach out with my mind and take, pulling the
cloud of seething madness I can sense in each and
every human in the area — Ye *Gods,* there are *three*
hundred in total!

*The only way to stop them is to drain them, Kassidy.
Do it with your mind!*

But can I take all that darkness into myself?

If you don't, there's no way we'll survive.

I realize what I have to do. So, I draw that vitality
into myself, breathing in the stuff until my lungs seem

to burst. The darkness fills me entirely, like a vase, and each and everyone one of the zombies collapses where they stand, their eyelids closing over those glowing white eyes. Men, women, and children simply fall to their knees, like puppets with their strings cut.

But there's too much of the darkness. It pours from my mouth, my eyes, my ears, my fingers, billowing into the air like smoke and catching the wind before drifting away. Even as I try to expel it from my lungs, I'm choking on it. The madness circles through my mind and it's all I can do to hold onto some sense of myself, to not allow myself to fall into the trap the madness wants me to.

I want to bite, to claw, to rip and tear and spend this madness on the earth until I collapse dead on the ground. Gods, is this what it's like for Nash, with so little control of his beast?

Arms come around me like steel bands, smacking me into a chest that's broad, hard, and unfamiliar. I loose a primal scream that shakes the ground all around us as I try to throw an elbow back, to pulverize the man's ribcage so the mindless husk of a villager will drop to the ground like it should. The shape twists, avoiding the pointed edge of my attack by mere centimeters.

"Kassidy!" Sorren's voice roars into my ears, struggling to be heard over the wail of sound that is my own scream. "Kassidy, you must release the energy within you! Otherwise it will tear you apart!"

Tears stream from the corners of my eyes. He's right. The power is too much, threatening to flay my mind with every passing second. Three hundred people. I've taken in the madness of three hundred, and I might burst at any second from the strain.

"I can't," I grit out from between my teeth. It hurts to even talk. "Too much..."

Sorren pauses, considering my words, and then releases me, spinning me so we're facing one another. It's hard to see him clearly through the haze of tears, but I think he's staring at me earnestly, with an expression that tries to imitate concern, but can't quite form the true thing. For Sorren, though, it's incredible. It's the closest thing to panic he can experience.

"Let me help you bear the weight of it, Kassidy," he breathes. "Give me some of it!"

I startle. I think it may be the way he's said my name—it feels like true emotion lurked behind the word. Still, I reject his suggestion almost at once. Give the brimming madness to a man literally incapable of restraint or remorse? It's a recipe for disaster…

His next words bring me up short.

"Leith has been injured, Kassidy. Badly."

No! The word pounds through me and I realize what Sorren's asking. I need to help Leith but I can't do that if I'm overcome by this darkness that continues to feed on me, trying to pollute me.

Sorren continues. "None of the rest of us possess magic, Kassidy, and we don't have any Ambrosia with which to heal him." He pauses and I swear his eyes are searching, pleading with mine. "Leith needs your help."

Immediately, that screaming panic rushes to the fore.

Gods, what have those… things done to Leith? Are Leith's insides lying on the ground? Have they hacked his throat open? Cut him up? I almost don't want to know.

"If you… shoulder this… burden with me," I start, winded and fading fast. "What will that… do to you?" I manage to gasp through the pain.

"It doesn't matter," Sorren says, grasping my chin. His eyes are raw, determined. Fierce. "Do it now, Kassidy. You must save Leith."

Before I can even think, Sorren brings his mouth down on mine, latching on with a savagery that both frightens and thrills me. He tears at my lip with his teeth until I gasp, the tang of blood and dark power spilling up from the core of my body and up my throat, seeking a way out. The darkness blisters out of me and into Sorren. It pours eagerly into this new vessel, a sickness that's quick to spread from host to host.

As I watch, Sorren's eyes constrict and he scrunches up his face in an obvious expression of pain. He drops down to his knees, taking me with him, but his hands are still tight on my arms. He won't let me go. But he's also taking so much of it — more than his share, I'm sure. As the darkness drains from me, I feel my strength returning.

Finally, he pulls away and the madness abates, like the tide sweeping away from the shore. There's still an ocean of it inside me, but for now, I can actually see past it. Sorren staggers away from me, dropping on all fours as he breathes deeply, eyes still slammed shut.

He clutches at his ruined chest, but when I try to approach him, he waves me away impatiently.

He sits up on his knees and inhales a deep breath and I can see he's fighting the darkness within him, the same way I was fighting it moments earlier.

"Leith," he pants. "See to Leith. I'll manage."

I don't argue with him. Sorren's done me a great service by taking the madness into himself, and I won't squander his sacrifice by wasting time. There's no telling when my own tide will sweep back in and render me helpless once again.

It's not difficult to locate Leith, even through the mist and the darkness. I just have to follow the string of vicious curse words Nash is spewing. My heart races in my chest and I feel nauseous. I'm scared to death of what I'm going to find when I do reach Leith. What if he's so close to death there's nothing I can do?

I force the thoughts from my mind. And before I know what's happening, I can see them through the opaque mist. My heart pounding, I drop my gaze from Nash's pale and frantic eyes down to the ground beneath him where Leith lies, mostly lifeless.

It's almost a relief to see him — to see that none of my nightmarish scenarios have come to pass. Leith's guts are still firmly intact. And from the gentle rise and fall of his chest, he's breathing and that means he's still alive. For now.

But then I see it. Really, really see it, and my stomach lurches violently as I realize Sorren was right.

This is bad. Very, very bad.

Teeth are lodged into Leith's neck, teeth that belong to a skeletal head that's been severed from the rest of the body, leaving only a trailing a length of startlingly white spine, flesh and blood. It looks as if someone shredded the hair and skin off the head, probably in an attempt to free it from Leith's neck. But the jaw is clamped tight on his pulse point, threatening to tear his throat open if it's removed.

Oh, fuck.

SIXTEEN
Leith

For several heart-stopping moments, I'm sure the shape that approaches is a Shepherd, one of those grim-faced reapers of souls. Or perhaps it's a God of Death, come to personally escort me to the land beyond the clouds, to Valhalla. A land where all the chieftains before me have gone. The land where my own father now reigns.

Enormous plumes of dark energy spread out from the woman on either side of her, like the wings of some giant carrion crow. A midnight corona of the same energy hovers around her face and head. The shadows surround her, flitting back and forth across her face until it's difficult to make out her features.

But as I stare at her and she lowers herself over me, I see her eyes. They glow like emerald jewels in her beautiful face and I wonder how I'm able to see them in this darkness that's so thick, I could cut it with my blade.

Yet, I can see those jeweled eyes and I latch onto them.

My swimming vision snaps into focus, and I realize this woman is no Shepherd or God. She's *Kassidy*. Kassidy, trailing power behind her like an enormous cloak. Though she hasn't gained an inch in height, something in her bearing makes her seem to

179

stand as tall as a giant. There's so much power radiating off her, it makes my skin erupt in gooseflesh, every hair standing on end, and causes my bear to retreat further inside me as though it's ready to bed down to ride out a storm. It's so fucking astonishing all I can do is stare at her, agape.

It's her.
She's one of them.
She has to be.

My convulsive swallow sends pain tearing through my neck and I groan. The man's teeth are too fucking sharp to be purely human. He must have been a scion of some kind. Of a night hag, maybe, or a shifter. Whatever the fucking creature is, it threatens to tear my throat out, even missing its body. There's still so much power and magic in its head, the body matters little. Already, small movements are tearing furrows open in my throat.

Kassidy kneels down by my side and takes a deep breath as she examines the wound closely. She utters a soft curse and reaches out to touch the side of my neck, below the man's trailing spine.

"Shit," she repeats, more to herself. But then those marvelous eyes meet mine and I can instantly see the sadness in their depths.

"Tell me," I grunt.

She nods and swallows audibly. "It's bad, Leith. Very bad."

I give her a look. It's not like her to state the blatantly obvious.

She runs her fingers through her hair, seemingly oblivious to the smoke that follows her like a second skin.

180

"What do I do?" she asks, first spearing me with her demanding eyes before she turns to Nash and asks him the same question.

But Nash can't offer her the solution because he doesn't know. And I don't know the answer either. The beauty before me runs her hands through her thick, bushy curls three times more before she seems to arrive at a solution.

"Nash?"

My cousin leans away from me. He's been hovering like a sentinel, just as unsure of what he can do for me as was Sorren. Nash seems almost grateful to be receiving instruction. Ever the soldier, Nash is — most comfortable when taking or giving orders.

"What do you need?"

She faces him and the shadows continue to spin around her head and body. "I need to take energy from you."

"Okay," he answers with a quick nod but she reaches out and touches his shoulder. He drops his gaze to her fingers and remains quiet.

"It's not going to be that simple," she says.

"Explain."

Kassidy nods. "I may infect you with this… madness. And with the amount of power and life force I need from you, I could take weeks or maybe even months off your life."

"I understand," Nash replies with a curt nod, his jaw tight.

"I think it's the only way to help Leith survive," she continues, most likely speaking to herself at this point, because her tone is so low and quiet.

"What will you do?" Nash asks, not even flinching at the news he'll have a reduced life span.

She faces him as if just remembering he's still present. "I have to rip this thing's head off," she answers with a shrug.

"What do I do?"

"Kneel here," she instructs firmly, pointing to a location opposite the head. "And take your armor and your shirt off. I need to have skin-to-skin contact for this to be instantaneous. And it's going to need to be instantaneous... when I pull that head off."

Nash sinks to his knees without question and begins to strip off his armor, fumbling with the straps to remove it as quickly as possible. Meanwhile, Kassidy tears open my shirt, giving her access to my flesh as well.

She looks up at me then and gives me a weak smile. She's nervous and she's scared—I can see the truth in her eyes. But she's also strong and she believes in her plan. And that's enough for me.

"I trust you," I manage to whisper, trying not to move my lips as much as I'm able. I don't want to give the thing attached to me reason to bite all the way down. I don't understand why it hasn't already. And then I remember that Kassidy has already absorbed its life force, as well as that of all its compatriots, so it's no longer able to do anything—more than it already has, that is.

She nods down at me and then takes a bracing breath as she reaches out and places each of her hands on either side of the thing's head without touching it. She glances over at Nash.

"Are you ready?" she asks.

"Yes," he answers and holds his lips in a tight, white line.

She nods and then says on an exhale. "On the count of three then."

Nash just nods.

"One."

I close my eyes. If this doesn't go as she plans, I don't want the last visual I have of her to be panic. I want to remember Kassidy smiling. I want to remember those glorious eyes.

"Two."

I breathe in deeply and then hold my breath until the sounds of voices and the wind in the distance seem to fade into oblivion.

"Three!"

I feel the jolt as Kassidy seizes the severed head attached to my throat, ripping it away in one motion.

And then there's intense pain as my eyes pop open and I see the thing's jaw full of a gobbet of flesh and sinew. Kassidy drops the hideous thing to the side and it rolls into the darkness. A gout of scarlet blood spurts from the wound and onto Kassidy's face. She lets out a half-cry of her own before slamming one hand down onto Nash's chest and the other onto mine. Her fingers curl, nails biting into my skin as she drops her head back and screams with pain or from the intensity of pulling power from Nash and thrusting it into me.

My vision pulses in and out, and I only catch snippets of what she does next.

Nash bows forward, a groan escaping him as Kassidy begins to siphon off the energy she needs. At the same time, warmth seeps into my chest where our skin meets, like she's pressed a brand into my skin, though my flesh doesn't burn. And the stinging ache that echoed out from my neck begins to abate until I'm no longer able to feel it. As I inhale, I feel my energy building, my heartbeat regulating and the warmth returning to me. My vision begins to clear and I can see Kassidy where she continues to kneel beside me, her eyes screwed tight in concentration as she channels Nash's scalding life force into me.

She's breathing hard when she draws her fingers back, as though she's just run miles as quickly as she can. Sweat beads on her brow and the corona of dark magic has ebbed somewhat. I raise a hand to touch the side of my neck, expecting to find blood slick and wet beneath my fingers. Instead, I find a knot of scar tissue where a gaping wound should be. I trace the contours of it, finding a crescent missing. It's a scar not unlike Sorren's—deep and irreversible, making me a little less pretty. But I couldn't care less about such trivial matters as vanity. I'm alive. And it's a fucking miracle.

"Kassidy," I breathe her name as the realization I experienced earlier revisits me full-force. I start to push up to my elbows but Nash reaches over to push me back down again.

"Take your time, cousin," he says.

I immediately look up at him. "Nash."

"Yes."

I nod. "It's her, Nash."

"What, Leith?"

184

"It's her!" I repeat.

"Who is her?" he asks, shaking his head as he looks at Kassidy, worry on his face. He thinks my mind is scrambled, that the overflow of energy has addled me. He couldn't be further from the truth.

I look at Kassidy again. "You're a Chosen one."

That draws her head up but then she immediately shakes it. "That's impossible."

"It's possible because it's true."

"My brothers, Tenebris, Peter or *someone* would have noticed it, if such were the case."

"No," I start as I shake my head but she won't let me speak.

"Leith, we've been on the lookout for the ten champions for most of my life. Don't you think they would have spotted it in me if I actually were one of the ten?"

I look back at Nash and find his gaze settled on the distance. He breathes hard and moments later, his eyelids droop as he collapses beside me. Kassidy yelps slightly and then immediately reaches over to him, checking his pulse as well as his breathing.

"Is he...?" I ask.

"He's alive," she interrupts with a nod. "He's going to need rest and lots of food before we continue." She takes a breath and there's sudden concern on her face. "I need to find Sorren."

I don't understand why the sudden concern until I remember what Sorren did—how he took the darkness from Kassidy into himself. And then I realize the potential disaster of a nightmare we could face. Sorren

185

is now darker than he ever was before, but he still doesn't possess a heart...

I sit up as I watch Kassidy disappear in the thickening mist that surrounds this place. I roll over onto my hands and knees and take a deep breath. I'm definitely feeling better than I was, but I'm still not myself. Regardless, I need to follow her—to make sure she isn't in the process of endangering herself.

Sorren is a wild card. More wild than he's ever been before.

I turn to look at Nash and though I don't want to leave him in his unconscious state, I have little choice. Kassidy could need me.

But before I can push myself to my feet, she returns and Sorren is behind her. I don't like the strange look on his face. The last time I saw such an expression, he murdered three people.

He doesn't make any violent moves toward any of us, but just stands there for a few seconds, looking first at me and then at Nash.

"Is he dead?" he asks in a monotone voice, devoid of emotion.

"No," I answer as I push to my feet and stay myself against an outcropping of rock that dips low from the ceiling of the cave. I take a deep breath and then stand on my own, waving slightly but I'm able to remain erect.

"We need to move him," Kassidy says as she motions to Nash, who is still out cold. Sorren nods and moves toward his cousin and I do the same. I don't know how much help I'll be, given my condition, but I'll do my best. It's the least I can do.

Sorren shoulders most of Nash's weight as the two of us pull him to his feet. Kassidy comes to stand on my other side, to help hold me up as I act as one half of a crutch for Nash. Between the three of us, we manage to carry his bulk into the nearest hovel that's perhaps twenty feet away.

The place is deserted and owing to the dust that coats everything within, it's been deserted for a long time. I can only guess it once belonged to one of Discordia's zombies before she turned them into zombies. It's small, one story and built with the proportions of one of the prison cells back home. It's hard to believe people live in such cramped quarters. It would drive my beast utterly mad.

"Leith is right, you know," Sorren says as soon as we enter the hovel and he closes the door behind us, securing it with the stray furniture around the room, leaving a table and a couple of chairs.

"Leith is right about what?" she asks.

Sorren looks directly at her. "You are one of them. There's no doubt about it."

Kassidy shakes her head stubbornly, leaning against the wall for balance. "It's not right, as much as I wish it were. This power is something I was born with."

"Perhaps, but what you just demonstrated went beyond the abilities of any defalcator I've ever seen," Sorren argues.

"What do you mean?" she demands as the two of us hoist Nash into the back area of the room and lay him down on one of the two mattresses within the house. As we place him on the bed, a puff of dust burps out from the straw.

"There's a limit to the power reservoir," Sorren continues as he approaches us, his eyes narrowly set on Kassidy. "You took so much of that dark madness inside of you, Kassidy. You never should have been able to absorb so much, and furthermore, it should have killed you once you did!"

Kassidy's eyes flicker with something that looks like hope. "... Do you really think so?" But then she shakes her head, and dashes the hope in her eyes. "No, it can't be true. It's just too... impossible."

"I believe it," I say fervently, and I trace the divot in my flesh. "Gods, Kassidy, if you weren't so powerful, I'd be dead. As it is, I barely feel the pain of what just happened to me."

"And if you want proof, we'll have it in a day or so," Sorren continues.

She looks up at him. "What do you mean?"

He shrugs. "Once you open the gates." Then he pauses. "I should hope we're still storming the fortress?"

"Yes," she says with a quick nod. "But, we can't do anything until Nash regains his strength."

"Well, he hasn't much time," Sorren continues as we all turn to face him.

"What are you going on about?" I ask.

Sorren takes a deep breath. "Taking that darkness within me, sapped me of much of the time I had remaining, cousin," he says.

"What does that mean?" Kassidy demands.

Sorren faces her and his expression is unreadable, as usual. "I currently have a week left on my internal clock."

Breath explodes from me, like he's struck me with a war hammer. I stagger back a step. A week?! He only has only one fucking week left to live? That's not enough!

This is impossible! Unfair!

"We won't let you die, Sorren," Kassidy says, echoing my thoughts completely.

"I need to excise this energy before it drains me to nothing," Sorren states simply. "I have to expend it somewhere—I can feel it eating me from the inside out."

"How do you expend it?" she asks, facing him with concern.

"Violence or..." Sorren's voice trails off, as he gives her a significant look. His meaning is clear.

Kassidy spares one glance out the window before she turns back to face him and nods. "I'll do it," she says.

Then she approaches him, but I stop her. "Wait," I begin, the word coming out as a growl. I face Sorren. "This is difficult for me to say, given the circumstances..."

Sorren smiles but there's no joy behind the expression. "You don't trust me with her," he says.

I nod. "Without your heart, you're still a wild card, Sorren."

"She's a Champion," he argues, saying without words that she's strong enough to take him.

"I won't risk it or her," I say with a quick shake of my head.

"I won't let Sorren die, Leith," Kassidy says as she turns to face me.

"I won't let him die either," I announce, almost crossly. "There is another way."

"What other way?" she asks.

I face Sorren. "I'm willing to let you be with her if I'm there too," I say. "If I'm able to ensure you don't get carried away, that you won't hurt her."

Sorren nods. "I accept, cousin."

I face Kassidy. "Will you have us both?"

She looks at me and there's slight anxiety in her eyes. Then she nods.

"Go to him," I say as I motion to Sorren. Kassidy doesn't argue but crosses the room and approaches Sorren, throwing her arms around his neck, and kissing him fiercely.

A growl rumbles in my throat as I watch them. I have energy to spend as well, the terror of my almost-death still holding my muscles rigid.

I follow her, sweeping all that golden hair off her neck so I can adorn her skin with sharp kisses. Her back arches, pushing her breasts firmly against Sorren's chest.

"Kassidy..." I breathe against her. "Tell us this is what you want." I have to be sure. I have to know she's not just doing this for Sorren, but that she wants it—that she wants us both.

"Yes," she says on a breathy exhale. "I want to feel you both... inside me."

And that is enough for me.

SEVENTEEN
Kassidy

I could swear they've done this before, because the pair act in tandem.

Leith peels the dress off me with reverence, kneeling to draw the bunched fabric down to my waist and then finally to my feet. I step easily from the pile of cloth and kick it out of the way. His broad, calloused hands slide up my calves, ghosting over the hollows behind my knees, and his nose skims across my thighs, scenting me. My legs threaten to give out from under me when he licks a warm trail along my hip.

My sex clenches tight in anticipation as he presses a searing kiss just above my mound, then slides his fingers through my slick folds. When his thumb finds my sensitive bud, I keen and my legs do finally buckle. If Sorren weren't clutching me, I'd make an acquaintance with the floor.

"Careful," Sorren says with a dark chuckle as I sway. His breath is warm against my throat as he moves his head to kiss and nip at the skin there. "You might want to get her on the bed. Injuries will ruin the mood," he ends with another chuckle.

I can't see Leith's face, but I can tell he's smirking—the same self-satisfied expression Nash had after realizing he'd pleased me.

Leith's hand doesn't stray, still rubbing small circles into my heated flesh. A whimper escapes me, and my knees once again attempt total surrender. Sorren clutches me tighter.

Leith doesn't make any move for the bed. Instead, he lifts me off the ground entirely and wraps my legs around his neck, bringing his face level with my sex. I get an idea of what he's about to do seconds before he does it.

His tongue delves between my folds, zeroing in on my throbbing flesh, and my hips arch. I'm afraid I'm going to break his nose with the violent motion, but he just laughs at me. Sorren echoes the sound, face still pressed against my neck, supporting most of my weight so Leith can work. The vibrations do incredible things to my body, and my thighs tremble with the ecstasy of it. I wind my hands still more tightly around Sorren, sinking my fingers into his hair just to anchor myself.

Sorren licks a trail along the shell of my ear, making my breath catch. When he rolls the lobe between his sharp teeth, gooseflesh riots across my skin. My nipples harden to fine, almost painful peaks. I fist his hair desperately, trying to keep myself from going completely mad from the pleasure of it. It's so much. *Too* much. I'm going to explode if I can't have one of them inside me soon.

Sorren trails bites down my throat to my shoulder, and I'm sure to have lurid purple bruises in a few days' time. A fresh groan leaves my mouth as Leith squeezes my ass, drawing me impossibly closer to him, the new angle allowing him to lave his tongue across my clit with such precision, it's almost painful. He sinks two fingers into me and pumps them in and out of my core, sending ecstasy spiking through my body. Tension curls like a spring in my stomach.

I can feel the pressure cresting in me, like a wave. I'm dizzy, delirious, the madness and pleasure swirling in my head. The muscles in my legs are jumping like mad, promising me the most potent orgasm I've had to date. With a little mewling sound, I yank at Sorren's hair. I'm going to tear it out, at this rate. He doesn't seem to care.

Leith braces his hands on my thighs as I draw nearer to release. Sorren's hand drops to pinch one of my nipples, twisting it, and that spike of pain mixed with the pleasure makes my stomach drop and I'm in freefall, flailing wildly as my climax hits me.

I've not even come down from my climax before they're in motion. Sorren sweeps me into his arms, bridal-style, to carry me toward the far end of the room, away from Nash. I'm not sure if Sorren doesn't want to disturb Nash or just doesn't want him to wake up. He gingerly lays me down on the mattress. For a second, both Leith and Sorren just hover above me, staring down hungrily. I'm not sure who will descend on me first.

"You need her, Sorren," Leith says with a quick nod.

Sorren nods and clambers onto me, stretching the long, muscled line of his body over mine. The mattress sinks beneath our combined weight. My heart pounds like a blacksmith's hammer and it's hard to swallow.

As they're stripping out of their clothes, it finally hits me. I'm going to do this. My second time having sex will be with both of them—two men at once. The thought excites me, of course, but I'm also nervous.

Leith stares down at me, like a collector admiring a particularly beautiful work of art.

"So goddamn beautiful," he breathes.

Sorren braces his hands around me, and I expect him to thrust hard into me, to wrap my legs around his waist and fuck me into the straw bale the way Nash did. But instead, he flips our positions, rolling beneath me and stopping when I come out on top—his very large, very evident arousal poking me in the stomach.

I reach between us to grasp his cock firmly. His lips part in sudden ecstasy as I idly trace the underside with my thumb, gliding it through the drops of precum when I reach the tip. He groans, eyes fluttering shut.

I ease myself down onto him, my back arching and my eyes shutting of their own accord. He's so improbably huge. He fills me so completely, I can barely separate where he ends and I begin. He's mostly made of tight, corded muscle; it's just the ruin of his left side that ruins the image of a perfectly sculpted demigod. But I can't care about it. Scars are part of him, part of Leith, part of me. To throw stones just makes me a hypocrite. Beneath me, he groans, hands coming to rest on my hips. Then he thrusts his hips upward, forcing his cock deeper, brushing across something inside me that sets my toes curling.

"Fuck."

The hoarse exclamation draws my eyes back to
Leith. He looks almost... self-conscious as he watches
us. He's got a hand on his shaft, stroking himself
practically absently. I'm suddenly curious. I want to
know what he feels like, as well.

"Leith," I murmur to him. "Come here."

Sorren guides my hips in a sinuous rolling motion,
taking me most of the way off his cock before
slamming me down onto it again. Prickles of pleasure
dance up my spine, and the sensation continues as I
begin to ride him. It tingles up into my neck and into
the roots of my hair, along every part of me in a
blissful caress.

Leith joins us on the bed, and the frame creaks in
protest. This little mattress isn't built to withstand the
weight of two werebears and a moderately well-
muscled thief. I wonder if we'll continue if it buckles
beneath our combined weight? Probably.

Leith's hand slides along the column of my throat,
his lips ghosting across the nape of my neck. The touch
is so sensitive, so intimate, I buck once, with another
moan. It drives Sorren into me at a fascinating angle,
dragging across something inside me that I can't even
name. Leith's arousal grinds against my back.

"Inside me," I pant. "Please. I need..."

Leith hesitates for a second, and then his hands
fall away from me. I almost mewl in protest when he
climbs off the bed and walks away from us, but Sorren
draws my attention back to him with a few particularly
hard thrusts. Every part of me feels achy with need.
The madness is slowly clearing, spent by passion. But
what about Sorren? He took a good portion of it.

195

"The madness," I start.

"You're fucking it out of me," Sorren responds with a deep laugh.

Leith returns a minute later, clutching something in his hand. I can't tell what, but I'm grateful to have him at my back again. That is, until he presses something slick against my ass. He grips my hips, sliding me slightly off Sorren.

"Don't tense," Leith warns, his soft murmur tracing the shell of my ear.

And then the tips of his fingers, slick with what I assume must be some kind of lubricant, press against my ass.

I make it a point to question him about why he would have brought a lubricant with him on this trip unless he planned for this to happen. But that's unimportant now.

I let out a startled sound when I feel the tip of his finger enter my asshole, not sure if I should tell him to stop. It makes a certain amount of sense, of course. I only have so many orifices he could fit in. Trying to give him pleasure in any other way would be impossible, with the way we've positioned ourselves.

The finger presses into me slowly, eased by whatever he'd slicked his hand with. I'm just getting used to the extra fullness when he pushes another finger in, thrusting both in deep. A fizzle of pleasure shoots straight to my sex, spilling me over the edge. My back bows with a shuddering climax. The sensation is so intense, I can't even draw breath.

Then, Leith pushes into me, inch by inch, moving slowly.

"Breathe," he whispers into my ear. I inhale deeply and he pushes into me fully, until he's seated all the way inside me. I buck in surprise, and gasp in air. I'm stretched so tight, so full, and all I can do is ride out the sensation as both men thrust hard into my body. I can only wonder if they can feel each other.

And at that thought, I climax hard again, and then once more before we're entirely spent. I collapse onto Sorren's chest, skin dewed with sweat. He gives a husky chuckle and pulls me up to claim my mouth in a fierce kiss. Leith slides out of me, and the aftershock is enough to send more pleasure shooting through my body.

"You're fucking incredible," Leith rumbles.

"And you two are incredible at fucking," I tease. "I don't think I'm going to be able to stand up for a while."

"We'll stay here," Sorren declares with a nod, "until you can eat and get some rest. We'll need our strength to breach the castle's defenses."

That little reminder is enough to steal the golden afterglow and bring back the sense of clawing unease I've been fighting since we arrived. This isn't over. It's not a victory lap. This is a brief intermission, a small respite.

The battle is still to come.

EIGHTEEN
Nash

It's hard to tell day from night in this damn mist.

After I wake and the others have sponged off the scent of their union in the washbasin, we raid the tiny pantry. Uncharacteristic guilt washes through me as we settle down to a meal of canned vegetables, stale crackers and dried beef—the only thing in the house that Kassidy and Sorren can confirm is untainted by Discordia's magic. The owner of this home is clearly destitute, and I'm not sure the pile of gold coins we've left in the pantry will make up for what we're taking.

That is, if whoever this house belongs to ever returns. But, after spying all those zombies who attacked us, I have a feeling the answer to that question is a resounding "no."

We all need a night's rest, but we can't afford the time it will waste. Kassidy's magic will keep the villagers down for a time, and it's the only opening we'll get. If we lay down now, we're likely to find ourselves surrounded again—and this time, none of us will be in any shape to stop them.

But I'm lethargic, and all I want is to crawl into bed and sleep for the rest of the winter. The lifeforce Kassidy sapped from me to heal Leith is sorely missed. It's lucky I'm sitting, because I'm as unsure on my feet as a newborn foal.

198

Strength does come back to me in increments as I wolf down what little I've been given. I prefer fresh meat when I can get it, but there's no time to hunt. And no time for the rest I desperately need.

Leith voices my thoughts aloud. "We need to regroup and come up with an alternate plan. Storming the gates isn't going to work; Discordia will have troops in reserve."

"Agreed," Kassidy says, kneading her temples with two fingers. Her face is pinched, as if she's warding off a headache with willpower alone. "Any suggestions?"

"If Discordia is half as clever as she's rumored to be, the walls around her fortress will be enchanted," Sorren chimes in. "We can't scale them. We can't fight her armies or lay siege to the fortress. That really only leaves us one option."

Kassidy nods. "We have to go through the gates."

"Are you insane?" I ask, examining their faces, trying to see if they're serious. "Leith almost died. His throat was torn open by a fucking head! With no fucking body! And you want to waltz through the front gates? She'll slaughter us!"

"We'll plan a surgical strike. Ambush some guards and go in wearing their armor," she answers.

"Doesn't that seem a tad obvious?" I drawl. "Discordia will be expecting a ploy like that."

"Which is why we sell the ruse. Leith and Sorren are mostly healed, and they'll pose as guards. You and I need time to recuperate, so we'll pretend to be prisoners."

I shake my head before she's even finished her sentence. "It's entirely too risky. What if Discordia demands you be brought before her? If she has any inkling you're a Chosen one, she's going to rip your throat out and feed what's left of you to the buzzards." I shake my head. Staunchly. "I won't allow it. We need to find people to back us and, once we do, we return better prepared."

Kassidy's eyes flash and her spine straightens as she pulls herself up to full height. Defiance shines in those beautiful emerald eyes as she stares me down.

"You don't get to dictate to me, Nash. Don't you think I know what could happen? That I haven't lived with that possibility for years now? I wouldn't risk this whole mission, and all of our lives, if there were any other way."

"I still say it's suicide," I argue.

She shakes her head. "You weren't awake for the conversation the three of us had, Nash. When Sorren siphoned Discordia's magic from me, it damaged his clock. He's got a week left to live, and that's a generous estimate."

"What?" I say as I feel my stomach drop down to my toes. I look up at Sorren and he just nods. There's no emotion on his face, as per usual, but somehow it bothers me even more now.

"We don't have time to regroup or think up clever battle strategies," Kassidy continues. "The people in the surrounding villages will be scared shitless of Discordia, if she hasn't already turned most of them into those zombies or whatever the fuck they were. By the time we round up enough willing souls to fight her, Sorren… will be gone. *That* is something we can't allow."

My stomach bottoms out, nausea lurching into my throat before I can stop it. My beast rustles, a snarl of denial rising inside me. This can't be fucking happening. Things weren't supposed to play out like this! Time is supposed to be on our fucking side! How could it just evaporate like that?

I can't stop my gaze from flicking back to Sorren. He's reclining indolently in his chair, boots propped up on the table, looking supremely unconcerned. His focus is on Kassidy as he speculatively eyes her rumpled dress. No mystery where his mind is at the moment. I can't say I blame him. It feels a damn sight better to be between Kassidy's thighs than facing down the knowledge of one's own mortality. If I could fuck away this problem, I would. Cowardly? Perhaps. But I hate the thought of losing her and I hate the thought of losing him.

I feel a headache of my own building, drumming a ball-peen hammer against the front of my skull. I cradle my temples in my hands.

"Please tell me we have other ideas," I say, meeting Leith's eyes with an imploring look. His face is remote, desolate. It's like a death knell for the last hope I've clung to.

There is no other way. None of us is in any shape to breach the magical forces that surround the fortress. None of us possesses a form that can fly in. There's no back entrance, so we can't go around. Over, around, and through aren't really options at all.

A small smile creeps onto my face. "Under."

"What?"

"Under," I repeat. "There are four ways you can generally tackle an obstacle. Over, under, around, and through. Over and around are out. Through is suicide, in my opinion. So, we should try to go under."

"And how do you propose we do that?" Leith asks, frowning. "I don't know about you, but I left my shovels and pickaxes at home."

I frown at him. "Tunnels. There has to be at least one tunnel into the fortress—they have to get the sewage out somehow. I'd wager the tunnel is around the back way, protected by the dense forest on the west side, beyond the back entrance to Grimm mountain. Too many physical obstacles to make it worth a human's while, and there are probably additional defenses set up within the tunnels. But they'll be minimal. There's only so many men you can pack into an opening that wide. Between the four of us, we'll have the advantage."

Sorren barks a laugh. "So, you want us to go wading through a river of shit? I think I prefer storming the gates. There's at least a little dignity in that death."

"You may be willing to die for your pride, but I'm not," I shoot back. "We won't come out smelling like roses, but we'll be alive, and we'll likely maintain the element of surprise."

"Not to mention that would mean we'd have to backtrack," Sorren continues. "If you want us to enter through the backside of Grimm mountain, we'll have to travel back the way we came into Grimm and circle around to enter through the rear forest."

"Right," I say.

"And that would also mean we'll have to go even further into the depths of Grimm mountain," Sorren adds.

"What do you mean?" Leith asks.

Sorren shrugs. "Discordia's fortress is already underground," he says. "And if the sewage system is further underground, we'll be so far beneath the surface, who knows what that will mean."

"It will mean we're further underground," I say.

Sorren looks at me and shakes his head. "There have been stories about creatures unknown to man — those who lurk in the deepest recesses of the mountains, creatures that have never seen the light of day."

"I'm more scared of Discordia," Kassidy responds.

"It's not a bad plan necessarily," Leith mutters, mostly to himself.

He casts a sideways glance at Kassidy. Two for, and one against — she's our deciding vote. Though she looks almost as disgusted as Sorren by the prospect, Kassidy nods absently.

"They're right, Sorren. It is our best bet at getting out alive. I think we have to try."

Sorren blows out a breath, shaking his head. "Fine. But when I assumed I'd die up to my ears in shit, I didn't think it was going to be literal."

Kassidy actually lets out a wispy chuckle, and something around Sorren's eyes softens. I can't fucking believe what I'm seeing. He actually *cares* for her — in so much as he can, without a heart. It's not the sex or the favor she's doing for us, either. It's her. It's Kassidy.

Is it possible he loves her? I don't know.

Is it possible I love her? I swallow hard.

I don't know.

She turns her face away to confer with Leith, and she misses the sudden worry I can feel in my own face.

What if I do? What if I've fucking fallen in love with the little reprobate?

She's quite a woman, our little thief.

Chosen or not, she's a fucking hero.

Now I can only hope she doesn't die like one.

NINETEEN
Sorren

My stomach contents make repeated attempts to escape my mouth as we approach the fortress on the back side of Grimm mountain. We're still a ways off from the tunnel system Nash is sure is there, but the stench of the sewage is already permeating the air.

I'm not usually prone to nausea and can't recall the last time I threw up. And it's not as though I haven't smelled shit before. I fought many battles with the Guild, spilled my share of blood on the battlefield. When they tell the stories of war, they never mention that people shit themselves at the end.

It's not a pretty thing to consider, but it happens. From kings to churls, no one can escape the indignity of death. Men, women, and children—everyone does it. Everyone.

So the fetid smell shouldn't make me react this way. But it does. I gag every few seconds, swallowing bile with every exhale. The malodorous tunnel is exactly where Nash thought it would be, hidden from the purely human eye by a thick copse of honey locusts at its entry point. The thorns are a nice touch, I have to admit, something I should consider adding to my traps. The branches score us as we shoulder our way through and emerge at the mouth of the tunnel. It won't trouble Nash and Leith unduly, protected as they are by their thick fur.

Kassidy rides astride Nash's back, holding onto a thick hank of fur to keep herself from being unseated as we move into the tunnel, leading into the bowels of Grimm, and Discordia's fortress. She looks a little faint, as though the stink hits her like a physical blow. It doesn't bode well for the success of this venture. Kassidy is scent blind, compared to the rest of us. Even in this limited human form, my sense of smell is keener. The stench must be torturous for Leith and Nash.

She retches once and then reaches into her bag, groping for something in the interior. The bag never leaves her side, day or night. It can hold an improbable number of objects. Someday, I want to get my hands on it and find out what extending charm has been added to it. The mage who created it must have been powerful.

After producing a small tin of something, she swabs her fingers through the gel inside and then slathers her nose in the sticky stuff. She tosses it to me when she's through.

"It's extract of pine wood. It's strong; it should help."

I raise the tin to my nose and sniff it experimentally. Immediately, the desire to vomit recedes. I let out the breath I'm holding, dipping a finger into the viscous interior, coming away with enough to coat my entire face. I do just that, spreading it across as much skin as I can, coating the inside of my nose, as well, until it feels like I've developed a head cold. Uncomfortable, but still better than disgorging the contents of my stomach again.

I nod once in thanks and pocket the stuff, in case I have need of it again. The pine scent is almost comforting, in a way. It reminds me of home, and the hunts my cousins and I used to take part in. Those easy times are a distant memory, but pleasant, all the same. If we succeed, perhaps we can revisit them.

We've continuously searched our surroundings and we can't see any defenses. It's not saying much, given the low visibility, but Kassidy assures us she can't sense magic, either. With her newly unlocked powers, she'd be able to feel at least that much. But she can sense there's something lurking nearby, and that we should keep moving.

The damned mist actually works to our advantage, covering our advance from purely human eyes. Kassidy has one hand resting lightly on her dagger, and I have a blade naked in my hand, ready to be plunged between ribs or shoved into the nearest eye socket.

The tunnel looms out of the dark, a gaping maw with nothing but fecund smells and a faint, ominous sound. I can't put my finger on why the noise is familiar. My fingers clench around the handle of the dagger. This is a bad idea; I can feel that truth down to my marrow. We should have gone with the original plan. In the pitch dark, with unstable footing, we're not going to be performing at our peak.

We pause just before the entrance and I suck in a deep breath. This is a *very* bad idea. Just because the smell is muted doesn't mean I can't *taste* the foul miasma. I retch once again.

Kassidy casts me a concerned look over her shoulder. "Are you all right, Sorren?"

"Fine," I grumble. "Let's get this damn mission over with."

I step into the tunnel first, unwilling to be wedged behind my brothers if it comes to a fight. There's barely enough room for their bear forms to stand shoulder to shoulder. Kassidy's arm grazes the stone on one side. It's dark in the tunnel, but I can see that it descends straight down, into further darkness. I can barely see. I'll be useless in a fight.

I sink into the sludgy river up to the knee, grimacing as the stuff slides over the tops of my boots and soaks into my socks. The next step squelches and I curse this idea all over again. Stealth is impossible.

The sound continues, eerily familiar and yet, I can't seem to place it. It's a faint... crackle. Like someone stepping on underbrush. Or perhaps... the sound of wood shifting in a campfire. Yes. It's definitely more akin to a fire.

I realize where I've heard it a second before the light begins to flicker ahead—the red-orange glow of flame. A shadowy mass of black fur looms before us. Flame crackles off its back and tail, and it begins to lope toward us with a feral snarl.

"Hellhound!" I bellow.

We attempt to backpedal, retreating the way we came as yet more hellhounds spill into the cavern, lighting the cramped space like sprinting, huffing torches. We can't back up quickly enough. The bulk of my cousins' bear forms clog the tunnel, forming a sort of furry stopper to the pungent bottleneck we find ourselves in.

Shit, shit, shit.

I fucking knew this was a bad idea! Nothing is ever as simple as it seems.

I flip the knife to my off hand and draw the shortsword strapped to my waist. It's not ideal. In order to strike at the hellhounds, I'll have to be close — close enough to blister or burn should I make direct contact with their fur. But the shortsword is my best option after I lose my knives. A dagger might sink a hound into the muck but it won't kill it, even if I hit it in the throat. Hellhounds are almost indestructible, if you're not prepared. The only thing I relish fighting less is a dragon.

Behind me, Kassidy slides off Nash's back and drops into the river of excrement with a soft splash and a disgusted groan. The stuff hits a high-water mark, sloshing around her knees. Poor, petite human. But she doesn't pay attention to it for long. She palms her dagger and moves forward.

There's a cacophony of pops as Nash and Leith resume human form. Wise choice. In this stooped tunnel, they can't rear and bat the hellhounds back, the way they can in any other landscape. They take their weapons from Kassidy, who's stowed them in her bag for safekeeping. As I watch, she returns her dagger to the leather thong wrapped around her thigh and reaches into the satchel, producing another crossbow.

"Guess you're in unlimited supply?" I ask as I face her, remembering her last bow was snapped in two.

She shakes her head. "It's the same one," she answers, never taking her eyes off the hellhound in front of us. "The satchel also repairs things."

I shake my head with a smile. Meanwhile, there's no time for Leith and Nash to don the clothes from the satchel — they'll be in the raw until the battle's over, and I pity them for it. If one of them loses their cocks like this, I think Kassidy will probably kill every hellhound herself.

With that grim thought, the infernal hounds are on us, leaping the remaining distance to go for Kassidy's throat. She's the smallest of us, presumably the weakest.

The poor fucker doesn't stand a chance.

Kassidy raises her bow in an instant, sights her target, and spears the smoldering canine right through one ember eye.

The hellhound goes down thrashing, falling short of our line, and the impact sends a wave of filth toward us. It splashes our fronts in a wet, smelly slap, and I groan. Life quite literally keeps throwing shit at me. I probably ought to expect as much by now.

The rest of the hounds jump back in surprise as their comrade disappears beneath the sludgy brown muck, his flames snuffed like a candle, guttering as his pelt is slicked with waste.

Nash hauls an arm back and looses a six-inch throwing dagger. It hits the nearest hellhound in the haunches, and the beast lets out a yowl of pain. It doesn't crumple. If anything, the wound just further pisses it off.

The hellhound staggers upright and launches itself at Kassidy. She doesn't have another arrow ready. I step in front of her, putting myself between her throat and the creature's scything jaws.

Sharp, dagger-like teeth sink into my shoulder, ripping into muscle and sinew. It's my left arm, thankfully. It's not as though the left side can get much worse than it already is.

The hellhound's jaw tightens like a vice, threatening to shatter my humerus in two and then grind the pieces like a mortar and pestle. With a furious cry, I seize the thing by the scruff, holding it in place so it can't release the arm. The thick fur bristles and threatens to broil my hand clean off. I grit out another cry through my teeth as I drive my arm and the attached hellhound into the stone wall of the tunnel.

There's a sickening sound of impact, like an egg on the side of a pan, and then the hellhound falls limp in my grip. I bash its head against the stone one more time, to be sure. This time, gray matter slurps out of the crack. The thing is dead, no doubt about it. I let it drop from my grasp to join one of its writhing fellows in the shit stream.

Blood chugs sluggishly from my bicep to pool in the crook of my elbow, and a quick examination shows there's not much damage. It didn't have a chance to savage the flesh or crush bone. The punctures are deep, but mendable. If we make it out alive, it'll heal in a week or so.

I turn in time to shove my blade into the gut of another dog as it tries to arc over me toward Kassidy. I kill it as I breathe out a sigh of what I assume to be relief. Had the fucking thing succeeded, it would have bowled my little dove over and knocked her on her ass, giving the remaining hellhound a prime shot at Kassidy's throat.

"Thanks," she pants, then rounds on the last beast.

The thing hesitates for a fraction of a second too long, seemingly distressed by the death of its fellows. That hesitation gives Kassidy all the opportunity she needs. Lunging forward, she extends those dainty hands toward the creature. She seizes it by the throat with both hands, holding the thing in a chokehold. For anyone else, it would be a monumentally stupid and quite fatal move.

But Kassidy is hardly anyone else.

Her magic saps the hound's energy at once. The flames crackling off its fur dim to sparks almost instantly, and the light continues to fade until she's left holding a medium-sized dog in her lap. Without its aureole of light, the thing looks much smaller, like a stray mutt rather than a creature feared by all of Fantasia.

She pushes the thing's head gingerly from her lap and it disappears beneath the sludge. A stream of lethargic bubbles pop on the surface and then... nothing.

We stand in a semi-circle of dead or dying hellhounds. Kassidy pushes to her feet, wiping the slime from herself as much as she can. I suspect she's thinking what I am: *If we get out of this alive, I'm staying in the bath for a fucking year.*

"This won't go unnoticed," she says with a sigh as she glances around herself at all the carnage. "Come on. Let's get out of the tunnel before more arrive."

With no other choices, we trudge behind her, wading through shit as we follow our smelly savior toward the promise of cleaner destinations.

TWENTY
Kassidy

The first order of business is to find a water spigot.

I've never been so filthy in my life, and I've been tossed into a sty with an ogre's pet pigs. Enormous, feral pigs that had done their level best to gut me. I'd been caked with mud by the time I escaped, a level of soiled I didn't think I could top.

Fate has a funny way of challenging your assumptions.

I grimace at the trail of footprints and droplets we're leaving in our wake. Yet another reason we need to find someplace to clean up. We're going to end up stalking around Discordia's castle completely naked, at this rate.

Well, at least we'll match, I think wryly. The sight of Leith and Nash without their clothes would normally make my stomach flutter with nervous desire. But now? None of us looks or smells even remotely appealing.

Thankfully, there's no one and nothing waiting at the exit of the tunnel, nor at the mouth of the stairs we sprint up. The halls of the fortress are eerily quiet and cloaked in shadow. I don't see any torches in the brackets on the walls. There is, however, more mist.

An almost inaudible sigh escapes me, pluming in the air before my face. Things can never be easy, can they?

The air in the fortress is colder even than it was outside. Covered in semi-liquid and scantily clad, it isn't long before my teeth begin to chatter. Sorren wisely claps a hand over my face to stop my wayward mouth from betraying our location to any guards. He hauls my soiled self to his filthy front, sharing what little heat he has with me. I'm grateful.

Together, we inch our way toward where I assume we should find a kitchen. I've been in a few castles over the course of my years, and think I know where I'm going. Original, stone masons are not. There's a fairly predictable pattern to their craft, and that's what I refer to now.

We emerge into a spacious room about ten minutes later. I do find myself having to eat a little crow, because the room we duck into isn't a kitchen — it seems to be some sort of washroom. Enormous basins filled with sudsy water stand in the middle of the room. Thin cords crisscross the room, trailing drying clothing beneath them like white flags of surrender.

Oh, happy day!

Things are looking up, Kassidy. This must be a sign! Or it's simply a laundry room.

*Don't look a gift horse in the mouth! You needed to
clean up and look at the first place you arrived!*

I guess that's true.

I'll feel sorry for the poor cleaning woman whose
work I'm ruining later. Before any of the others can
react, I strip off my sticky dress and leave it crumpled
stiffly on the floor. Then I sling a leg over the side of
the basin, sinking waist-deep into the lukewarm water.
Sodden sheets swirl around my calves, as if
scandalized to find themselves trampled beneath my
squalid and shit-covered feet.

It's no hot spring, but at this second, I can't think
of anything better than the tepid washing water. The
lye in the tub feels like it's scalding the boils that riot
across my palms and stick like bulbous little tubers
between my fingers. I don't care. I'll take it. I'll take it a
thousand times to escape the stink that clings to my
skin.

The men follow suit, cleaning themselves in the
various basins around the room, and I'm momentarily
distracted by their nudity in a way I wasn't before. In
the heat of battle, it's suicidal to focus on anything but
your own survival. But now?

Now it's cock appreciation time!

On that, we're agreed.

It's hard not to appreciate the way the water clings
to their muscles, the way they dunk their heads and
pull up out of the water, their hair slicked back and
soaking. I haven't seen any of them completely
drenched before. It darkens the slate gray of Leith's
hair to a shade that's almost black, and I can see the
resemblance between Leith and Nash suddenly.
Sorren's brown hair darkens to an almost chocolate.

215

I don't think I've ever seen three more beautiful men before. The dragon shifters come close, certainly, but even they aren't my bears.

We climb out after a few minutes of thorough scrubbing and steal the first things we find that fit. It's an easy task for me. I'm about the size of a young page boy, and with the half-cloak I steal and my hair pulled up and into a leather thong, I look as ubiquitous as I can get.

My men have a harder time of it. Purely human men don't have the width of shoulders they boast, nor do they bulk so impressively without intense effort. The best they can do is don surcoats and ill-fitting trousers that are either too tight around the waist or end at their calves.

"What the fuck?" Nash says as he glances down at himself, the pants too tight and too short. I can't help my light giggle and he looks over at me with a glare.

"Stop being so vain, Nash," Leith says.

Nash turns the glare on his cousin. "Easy for you to say when you can button your breeches."

We shred a bed sheet to make makeshift belts for our weapons as well as a belt for Nash's pants, to ensure they stay up around his waist. Then, clean, armed, and still undetected, we creep through the corridors, hugging the walls. We're forced to go slow, hobbled as we are by the mist. Every time we turn corners, I expect to find more hellhounds, or at the very least a contingent of guards.

Nothing but eerie silence meets us. The fortress doesn't feel like a bustling hive of activity, with

216

mindless drones swarming the place, as I'd half-expected.

Instead, it feels like a tomb. Empty and forgotten. Filled with nothing but decay and the promise of a reaper's touch. Cold tickles up my spine, settling like a glacial premonition at the base of my skull. A cold, mocking voice whispers to me.

This is where you die, thief.

Oh, shut the fuck up, I respond.

The first few doors we try are unlocked and appear to be servants' quarters. There's little in the way of personal belongings; they're mostly just filled with pallets with straw mattresses and blankets. Occasionally, one will have a pillow as well. In very rare cases, there are toys or books tucked into corners. But they all have one thing in common: They're all glaringly void of life.

This fortress is enormous, probably double the size of the one in the werebear compound. It must take a hundred servants to man it, if not more. And yet there appears to be no one here. Has Discordia put all of her staff out into the town to guard against intruders? It seems like a foolish move. It's arrogant in the extreme to believe that no one could breach her defenses.

Clearly such isn't the case.

Had the villagers been a sacrifice to the hellhounds? Some of those nasty hounds are bloodthirsty and deranged, preferring to hunt men for the sport of it. But, no. I'd expect a little more blood, if such were the case.

The void of sound is beginning to unnerve me. You don't really notice the ambient noise of a place until there's a lack of it. I'm expecting a monster or perhaps a Gryphus huntsman to come up behind me and slit my throat any second. The ever-present mist isn't helping—anything might be looming just beyond my line of sight.

"This place is just fucking creepy," Nash mutters from behind me, voicing my thoughts almost verbatim.

"How are your trousers holding up?" I ask, just to lighten the mood.

Leith snickers.

"Keep commenting, Aurelian," Nash responds. "I'm just going to take it out on you later."

I swallow hard as memories of Nash thrusting inside of me revisit me with a thrill. "I'll hold you to it," I respond.

Nash chuckles as Leith elbows him in the ribs and shushes him lightly. Nash falls silent once more. Leith is right. We do need to remain silent. But a silly part of me wants Nash to keep talking, just so I can assure myself I'm not alone. I keep expecting to turn and find them swallowed up by the mist, like they never existed in the first place.

There's a surreal quality to this place, one that makes me wonder if anything here is even real. If maybe *I'm* not real anymore. Just a shade, walking lonely corridors.

We ascend another flight of stairs and tiptoe down more hallways until we reach an armory. Nash seems particularly pleased by this and insists on a brief stop.

Leith doesn't want to risk the delay, but I agree with Nash. One can never be too prepared. The place is full to bursting with weapons of every sort: swords, halberds, spears, enormous battle axes that look fit to be wielded by a giant, and more. I restock my quiver of arrows and cinch a belt around my waist that can hold up to seven knives. I stuff each sheath with daggers and hide them beneath my cloak.

I smile when I think how much Sabre or Titus would approve. I'm more heavily armed than I've ever been outside of a Huntsman enclave. I almost feel like one of them.

Nash chooses a spear, brandishing it like it's a natural extension of his arm. Sorren grins as he swings an ax, and I shudder a little at the sight. Even though I've definitely warmed to him, I can't help but still be afraid of him, just a little. Heartless, he's capable of very little mercy. And he's still completely unpredictable.

We check every room in the corridor, finding a few more stuffed with furniture, but we strike gold in the last room. Literal gold. Dazzling, clinquant gold. Tapestries hung on every wall shimmer with the stuff. I blink in awe, because I know where these works of art have been stolen from. I'm just not sure how in the name of Avernus Discordia has managed to get her hands on them.

There used to be a kingdom on the edge of the Enchanted Forest, small but very wealthy, as this kingdom was the breadbasket of the seven principalities, producing most of the grain and herbal remedies the rest of us relied on. The queen, Leita

Rose, had been arguably the fairest in the land, endowed with many gifts. She was a master weaver, creating tapestries of pure gold or silver, becoming the most sought-after artisan in Fantasia.

She'd surprised everyone by marrying a lowly farmer's boy, Henry, instead of the prince she'd been promised to.

A year later, after she'd given birth to her daughter, Briar, a calamity struck her castle while everyone was celebrating the birth of her daughter. Every person at the feast was poisoned by the spurned Prince Payne, excluding his own retinue, of course. The heartless bastard had even conspired to murder the baby. If it weren't for the intervention of Maura Lechance, the babe would have died, foaming at the mouth like the rest of her people. But saving the baby's life still came at a price.

Briar never stirred again—she was stuck in an everlasting sleep, aging with each year that passed, though she never woke. The tales say she still lies in eternal sleep, even now, awaiting true love's kiss to wake her.

What a load of troll toss!

Well, that's according to the stories, anyway...

How is a spell supposed to recognize true love? True love is earned — it doesn't just appear because one wills it to!

Regardless, the entire kingdom is encircled by thorny briars, stretching miles high and at least twelve feet thick. Even the most determined adventurer has been unable to get more than a few feet in. According to lore, all that remains inside are the decaying corpses of the people and the cursed Prince Payne and his fellows. They're abominations now, fatally allergic to sunlight and any holy objects, condemned to drink blood for the rest of their days. They're starving to death, I imagine.

Good riddance.

The tapestries aren't the only things in the room that grab my attention, however. The place looks like a small horde a dragon might sit on. Treasures of every type imaginable are scattered throughout the room, leaving only narrow pathways with which to navigate the place. None of the others are able to follow me, their bulk making the tight corridors between treasures impassable.

A selection of wands is held in a bracket on one wall. On another, there are wooden puppets, of the sort carved by the master craftsman Carlo Gepetto. The tiny wooden golems are highly sought after, as they make valuable spies and soldiers. I skirt around them nervously.

There are vases full of gems, pottery, a tea set that appears to be snoring in one corner. A pristine, red rose that's trapped beneath glass, a spinning wheel, the preserved corpse of a dewdrop fae.

If this place is where the valuables are kept, I have to imagine Sorren's heart must be here somewhere. I strain my ears, trying to hear a distinct beat. Is Sorren's heart still beating? Or did Discordia stop it long ago? Has this trip been a waste? Has it cost Sorren what little time he has left?

I don't want to consider any of it, don't want to imagine I'm going to be the death of him, so I push the thoughts to the darkest recesses of my mind. I do a tight handspring, launching myself onto the surface of an intricately carved ebony table, and assess the rest of the room.

The mist is a little bit thinner here, with the door blocking most of it from leaking in. Through the wispy stuff, I spy the shape of a gilt mirror, propped against the far wall. I creep toward it after a second of thought. Sometimes, mirrors are enchanted to show your heart's desire. There's nothing I want more than to find Sorren's heart. Maybe the mirror can point me in the right direction?

I grab a fistful of the gauzy fabric that covers the mirror and yank it free, letting it fall to the floor with a flourish. The surface of the mirror is a lovely blue-green and reveals my reflection as soon as I look into it. I react in surprise as soon as I see myself—the pageboy getup steals what little curves my body offers, and with my hair slicked to my head by the recent bath, I look even more boyish. I grimace at myself.

And then, suddenly, a face grimaces right back at me. Not my face. It appears to be a crimson Punchinello mask covering most of a milky pale visage. Silver eyes without pupils blink open and fix on me. I'm frozen, staring at the unexpected stranger in the mirror, heart beating so hard, the others must hear it from across the room.

The mouth just beneath the mask is thin, almost lipless, and just as pale as the rest of the face. The thing opens that pale mouth, sucks in a breath, and then screams.

"Intruders! Intruders, mistress! Thieves come to steal your treasures, to rend you asunder! Intruders!"

"Fuck!" I hiss as I turn to face the others. "Run!"

TWENTY-ONE
Nash

The mirror continues to wail even as we beat a hasty retreat back to the door.

I'm not sure how many guards Discordia has on standby, or why she's waited so long to deploy them. I expected more backlash before now and never believed we would make it this far without issue. It appears our luck has finally worn off. Someone will be coming. In all likelihood, we're about to become food for ravenous hell beasts.

We pelt down another corridor, searching for another staircase or a way out. We're too far up to jump from a window, even if we pass one. It's mostly arrow loops here, and they're far, far too small to offer any sort of escape. They are large enough to let a thousand swarming insects through though.

The fuckers pour in from the outside, pulsing with light like fireflies, and a screaming sound like cicadas. They hurtle toward us at unbelievable speeds.

"Shit!" Kassidy hisses. "Shit, shit, shit! How the fuck does Discordia have those?"

"What are they?" I shout over the growing buzz of the insects.

"Cerise Wasps! That face in the mirror must have been Bacchus or one of his followers. He breeds them himself. They feed on blood wine. Or just blood in a pinch."

I raise my hands to shield my face, but it's no use. The wasps streak by, taking button-sized chunks out of any bare flesh they find. As soon as the scent of blood hits the air, they begin to swarm, the buzzing reaching a new fever pitch. They all began to converge on me and even my flailing isn't enough to keep them off.

Kassidy hits me broadside and, unprepared, it's enough to send me sprawling to the ground with her on top of me. Her legs lock around my waist and I buck up on instinct. It's not really the time, but my body can't help but respond to hers. She arches her back and then shocks the shit out of all of us by belching fire and black smoke into the air.

It doesn't remove all the wasps, but it's enough to sedate or kill most of them. The remaining buggers that stick to my skin meet a swift end beneath the heel of my palm.

Kassidy's welcome weight lifts from my waist, though she still hovers close. She's bleeding too, though only from a few spots on her neck and cheeks. I took the worst of the attack, standing at the front of our little procession.

Concern wells in her eyes as she runs her fingers over the ruin of my arms. A quick glance shows they're littered with small but numerous bleeding gashes. And the wounds are quickly filling with pus. They emit a strong odor of putrefaction.

"Oh, Gods," she pants. "Gods, Nash. You need a healer."

"Don't suppose you sucked one dry?" I ask, taking a weak stab at humor. Kassidy's expression doesn't flicker. She just looks at me with worry in those gorgeous eyes.

"Can we please move?" I ask.

She tears off the cloak of her pageboy getup and rips one corner into strips as quickly as she can, dressing the wounds with businesslike efficiency. She looks so delicate, it's easy to forget she's a trained killer. But she's so much more than that. Kassidy is a thief, and a warrior and quite possibly one of the champions that will save us from the threat that looms on the horizon.

"Let's go," she mutters, as she places the ripped jacket back on and secures it in place with her belt. Then she takes off down the hallway. We follow behind her like three dark shadows.

Just in time, too. There are voices behind us and the thud of many heavy boots as Discordia's men tromp up the stairs and spill into the corridors behind us.

"That was an interesting trick you pulled with the fire," Sorren says, and even he sounds a little winded. "How'd you do it?"

"Hellhound," she pants. "Drained one before it drowned. I can't hold onto the energy for long, though. It's too fucking hot. I feel like I'm baking in a desert right now. My insides feel hot and gritty."

"It might be a good idea to release more smoke if you can," Leith suggests, tossing a glance over his shoulder. The dark plumes of smoke she summoned before still hang in the hall, slowly eaten up by the mist. The mist has hungry fingers, and tears her magic apart piece by piece, like a child crumbling a cookie.

Kassidy nods and turns so she's running backward for a stretch, taking a deep breath, she opens her mouth and forces more of the smoke out, leaving a trail behind her. The trail of smoke cuts a dark line through the mist. Shapes move around inside the haze of mist and smoke. I reach out an arm to snag Kassidy when she stumbles. She gives me a grateful nod. I return it with the barest hint of a smile.

Then we're rounding a corner. One that should take us toward the portcullis, if this fortress is modeled anything like others of its kind. We come to a staggering halt when we're faced with a wall of spears. Sorren almost takes one to the gut before he can stop his forward motion. Of the three of us, he's arguably the fastest in human form.

Kassidy lets out a breathless shriek of fear and then cries to the soldiers; "Don't hurt him!"

I don't think the lead guard can even hear her. He has the same dull-eyed gaze as the other zombies in Discordia's employ, the same glowing, white eyes. I'm willing to bet that were this soldier's armor removed, he'd be sweating the sweet poison of Discordia's making.

They inch closer, surrounding us on all sides. The tips of dozens of different spears jab into us. We can't go for our weapons, not without exposing ourselves or our comrades to harm. The fog is still here, still cloyingly sweet and cold. My vision swims alarmingly, like I've just come up from water. My lungs burn, my head pounds, my mouth feels as gritty as sand.

The reason for the fortress' echoing emptiness suddenly becomes very clear. Discordia needs her servants alive and unharmed. Only those fit to die have been sent in to chase us through the fog.

Through the poisonous, somnolent fog.

Sorren falls to his side first, more affected by it than the rest of us, due to the poor condition of his heart. I'm struggling to stay on my feet and Leith fights a losing battle with gravity as well. One knee buckles, so he's kneeling at the booted foot of a soldier. The second knee bends as well, and then he's barely able to keep his head up.

I'm engaged in a vicious wrestling match with my eyes as I struggle to keep from letting the lethargy take me. This must be *Long Winter's Nap,* a poison developed in Sweetland to be sold for painless death. A favorite of Shepherds if they have to force the issue. There's probably not enough of it in the water vapor to cause instantaneous death. But death is coming, whether I like it or not.

A shape, tall and wraith-like, pushes through the crowd, which parts obediently to let the shape through. The shadow flips back the hood of its gown to reveal the face of a very beautiful woman. Pale, but with startlingly crimson lips that quirk in an enticing manner as she stares down at us. Cruel amusement plays out over that face, though the amusement never truly reaches her dark eyes. They're like a pair of drowning pools in that pale face, intriguing and terrifying all at once.

Kassidy is the only one left standing, because I sink to my knees at last, trying, in vain, to cough the

228

poison from me. I pitch forward, noting dully that the fog did nothing at all to fade my pain. On the contrary, it seems to sink into every divot of my tortured skin and start the stinging anew.

The last thing I spy before my eyes shutter closed, is Kassidy loosing one of her throwing daggers, aiming for those terrifying, unfathomable eyes.

TWENTY-TWO
Sorren

I know the hand fisted in my hair, long, witchy nails digging soft furrows into my scalp as she strokes me like a beloved house cat. I grew very used to her touch years ago.

When I dare to crack my eyes open, I find my surroundings changed from when I was last conscious. Again, this place is somewhat familiar. I spent at least one of my many weeks of captivity here, while the generals carved out their amusement on my body.

The great hall might have been distinguished at one point. I'm too biased to give it a fair assessment. The red granite stone floor and whitewashed walls may be attractive, but I can only see the stain of blood that lines them still. I can only remember what it felt like to be strapped with a dozen other screaming souls to the table as horrors were done to our bodies. I can only remember the bare rafters as the anchor point I clung to when the worst came. The windows are too high up to allow escape for anyone but the most determined bird shifters.

Sigils are hung on the walls here, standing in silent ceremony behind the throne. A full sun, beaming out light and heat, for Sol, the God of light. A pair of intertwined dancers spinning with glasses in their free hands for Bacchus. A sword wrapped by vines for

Vita. A flaming wolf's head for Lycaon. A sparking wand and golden crown for Septimus. An oil lamp for Hassan and a timepiece for Kronos. And then of course, there's the commander in chief…

A single dazzling star in the middle. Morningstar's sigil is the brightest and most offensive of them all.

Pain zings across my right cheek as the person holding me grows weary of waiting. I buck on instinct, shying away from the touch. I know to whom it belongs. And even with my heart gone, I remember the horror of everything as if it were only yesterday.

My captor chuckles.

"Ah, so you do remember me," she purrs.

I'm no coward. Never was, even before the incident. The change in my biology prevents me from feeling true terror. But it takes some effort to drag my gaze up to meet hers.

She's as beautiful as I remember. Shining dark hair piled high on her head, exposing a long neck. Thin-faced and gaunt kept only from looking haggard by her immortality and liberal application of face paint. Sharp cheekbones carve out a profile that's attractive but haughty. Her eyes are dark and fathomless, like the bottom of a well. White teeth show behind cerise lips. I know what those teeth feel like. She bites when she gets in a certain mood.

She's undeniably stunning and I know what it's like to be inside her. I hate her for that knowledge.

Her nails scrape along my scalp, a painful caress that raises every hair on my body. I squirm and find myself trussed tight like a waterfowl. I try to snap the binds, but the agent used to put us to sleep still lingers. Discordia laughs at my flailing attempt to free myself.

"Struggle all you like, dear Sorren, you know better than anyone it's no use."

I don't dignify her with a response. She can throw my rape in my face if she likes, detail it in full to my family. Tell them that both female goddesses had their fun with me, along with some of their retinue, only after giving me Bacchus' wine to make me fight less. All of that is secondary at this point.

Where is Kassidy? What has this bitch done with my little dove? If she's so much as laid one finger on her, I will find a way to carve out her heart before I die. I've got little time left, and I'm going to take this bitch with me. I cast my eyes around the room but can't see anyone within my sightline. Where are Nash and Leith? Held in the dungeon? Murdered?

Discordia tuts. "Oh, my little pet, why won't you play with me? We used to have such fun together."

"Fucking is only fun when both people are willing participants, you bitch," I snarl. "Where are they?"

Discordia draws a hand back and slaps me hard across the face. The slap catches me just beneath the eye and it begins to stream blood at once. I'm sure three bloody track marks run across my cheek now, echoing the shape of Discordia's talons. I can feel the blood sluicing down my face. She didn't mean for that part to happen, I'm sure. Discordia likes my face pretty.

She sinks onto her haunches in front of me, a sickly-sweet smile on her face. I recoil when she draws closer, shudder when she cups her hands around my jaw like a parody of a lover's touch.

She tsks at me. "Now look what you made me do, lover," she purrs reproachfully.

A pale pink tongue darts from her mouth and she licks the blood from my cheek as I withdraw… inwardly. Outwardly, I try to keep very, very still. One might think a decade or more would be enough to cool her ardor. Apparently not. I have a sinking feeling I've just offered myself up as a party favor to the bitch who helped make my life a living torment.

"Just get on with it," I hiss. "I know why you brought me here."

She gives me a serpentine smile and a light laugh that rolls like silk over my skin. "So eager."

She leans in close, and I take in the last breath I'll breathe for a while. Her skin smells like soured apples, stinking of sweet rot.

"I can't wait to feel your cock again, Sorren," she whispers in a hiss. "I've missed it so."

But before her lips can press into mine, something small comes flying at her head and impacts dully. For an instant, I'm hopeful someone's speared her in the skull with a throwing knife or a chakkar. But no.

Discordia retrieves the shape from the floor with an indignant huff and holds it up to the light to be examined. It's a cloth slipper, not unlike those used by palace members to keep the cold off during winter. She turns it over in her hand and then scowls at a spot directly behind me. She gets a grip on my hair again and drags me with her so we both can get a look at the attacker.

Leith, Nash, and Kassidy are chained to the far wall, their arms extended over their heads. Nash and Leith are still unconscious, owing to the poison they've inhaled. And Kassidy's shoulders look like they've been wrenched out of their sockets. The chains were meant for a taller creature than she, and her slippered feet don't touch the ground. Or I suppose, one slippered foot. Discordia holds the other in her hand.

"Pay attention, bitch," Kassidy huffs. I can tell she's hurting by the strain in her voice. She's doing her best not to let it show in her demeanor.

I'm too frightened for her to feel any gratitude for what she's trying to do. Fucking Discordia—or rather being fucked by her—will put a stain on my non-existent heart. But watching Kassidy die? That will mangle it beyond repair. I want to shout at the golden-haired beauty to stay silent. But I can't. It's not in Kassidy's nature to stand by while atrocities happen. And if Discordia learns that Kassidy matters to me, Discordia will ensure that Kassidy's torment will be unending.

Discordia looks at Kassidy for a long while, tapping the slipper against the palm of her hand like she used to wield a riding crop. She releases my hair and sidles away from me. I try to shuffle after her on my knees, which just makes her laugh. I look like a dog desperately snuffling in her wake. I make if a few steps before I overbalance and hit the stone floor with another muted blow.

Discordia saunters right up to Kassidy, plucking one thick golden strand of her hair. She examines it critically, the shining gold texture of it threaded through with lighter accents where the light hits it. It looks mostly like burnished gold and stands out like a beacon, with Discordia's own glossy hair a literal shadow to the color.

"You shouldn't be the one to wake first," she muses as she drops the lock of hair and Kassidy pulls her head back. "You're...what? The size of a small farm girl? *Long Winter's Nap* should keep you out for a day or so at least. Yet, here you are."

"Yet, here I am," Kassidy spits back at her.

Discordia nods and continues to study her with interested detachment. "A bear's metabolism could burn the poison off so quickly, but you..."

She trails off, running a finger down Kassidy's chest, down between the small valleys of her breasts and comes to rest over her heart. Discordia closes her eyes and screws up her face, concentrating.

"Ah, magic," Discordia says as she opens her eyes and pulls her hand away. "You're a witch. Powerful. An acolyte of the thrice-damned Tenebris, I presume?"

Kassidy huffs with effort and actually manages to bring her knee up and lodge it into Discordia's stomach. The blow drives the air from Discordia in a surprised huff and she staggers back a step, seemingly more shocked than pained. Then all her gentle playfulness and idle curiosity drops away and I see the true face of the monster I despise.

Without charm to disguise it, she's like a grinning skull. Lifeless and eerie. Anger transforms her from minx to murderess in an instant. I heard tell she was once a goddess of peace and mercy before Morningstar corrupted her and made her into her current incarnation of pure, unadulterated evil. But I can't see it. Can't imagine a world in which Discordia isn't a heartless bitch.

Discordia's hand shoots out and she catches Kassidy's foot. She squeezes hard, like she's trying to squeeze juice from a fruit. At once, at least three of the bones in Kassidy's foot break and Kassidy whimpers, then catches herself and bites down on her lip. Meaty popping sounds mean Discordia probably also snapped the tendons. Kassidy's back bows off the wall and her head clacks against the stones as her body shies away from the agony of what's been done to it.

She doesn't scream, which I laud her for. In her position, I've been much noisier.

"Insolent little welp," Discordia hisses. "I will snap you like a pile of matchsticks!" She takes a step nearer Kassidy and goes for her throat. I can't handle it any longer.

"Stop." The word escapes me without conscious permission. My heart must be very near, because with just its proximity, feeling is beginning to creep back to me. Inconvenient feelings that cloud my reason. Feelings of guilt. Fear. Protectiveness.

Reason declares that I should use the time Kassidy commands Discordia's attention to escape my bonds and attack. But my distant yet still beating heart can't allow the woman I care for to be brutally tortured while I wait for an opening to kill Discordia.

Discordia half turns to me, eyebrows raised. "Dear Sorren, I do believe your clockwork heart is beating faster. Is it that close to the end then?"

"Five days," I pant. "Five days left, Discordia. So if you want to have your fun with me, you should do it now."

Discordia's lips twist in a playful smile and she's all sex again. She slinks toward me in a motion that's meant to titillate but mostly makes me ill. At least I'm grateful for the break now allotted to Kassidy. Not that it will last long. As soon as Discordia's done with me, she'll return her hatred to Kassidy.

"Admit you still love me, Sorren, and I'll have the little doe healed."

"Leave him alone!" Kassidy yells.

Discordia ignores her and continues to stare down at me, a strange smile on her face. "Fuck me here and now and bring me to orgasm, in front of her, and I'll have her thrown into the dungeon rather than left outside the gates for the crows."

"My cousins too. They receive the same bargain."

"Of course," she croons.

I take a deep, shuddering breath, then pause when I spy something over Discordia's shoulder. She's too preoccupied with our little melodrama to notice Kassidy behind her. I almost grin.

That clever little thief.

She's clutching a small key ring between the toes of her good foot. With one kick she'd managed to steal the keys to her manacles. Now she twists like an acrobat, wiggling to get the key into the lock. She needs time. I need to distract Discordia.

"Take off your dress," I coax, forcing my eyes from her face to her cleavage that sits prominently above the plunging line of her dress.

237

"Tell me you still love me first," Discordia insists.

I stare at her and narrow my eyes, giving her the disobedience for which she yearns. "Sit on my cock and I'll tell you what I think of you when I'm buried inside you."

Discordia smiles a frigid little smile. It barely moves her face. I try not to let my revulsion show. I know she has supplicants, men who worship her like a goddess. There are men, sick men, who would kill to be in my place—to be able to fuck Discordia.

I can't imagine who would be able to pine after something so obviously false, so obviously a sham. She's an image trapped in marble, cold and unfeeling. I'd happily fuck a dunghill if I could escape this.

She hikes the slick black material of her dress up around her slim legs. Her ankles are as dainty as a girl's, her bare feet soft and shapely. She drops down on top of me, straddling me so I can feel the heat of her loins directly above my cock. And my cock doesn't stir, doesn't grow harder. It's as put off by her as the rest of me.

She leans closer, forcing her cleavage into my line of sigh, and something that has been tucked beneath her breasts falls into the light. I stare at it, transfixed.

It's a glass pendant about six inches in length, shaped like a heart. Magic hums from it. And in the center of the heart shape is a real heart. It's miniaturized, bespelled to remain smaller than it truly is, trapped in the enchanted glass like an insect caught in amber.

It's my heart.

The heart Discordia and Vita carved out of my chest so many years ago. My hand half-lifts from the floor, curiosity overwhelming my reason. Will the glass feel warm if I touch it?

Discordia grins at me. "Dearest Sorren," she croons, big inky eyes roving over my face in a look of mocking pity. "Just how stupid do you think I am?"

I have just a half-second for those words to sink in. A half-second when I realize how badly I've misjudged the situation. I've been counting on her desire, fickle and shallow as it is, to give me an edge. And she let me. Let me think I had that edge so she could torment me still further.

She strokes along the swells of the miniaturized glass heart.

"I wanted you to see it," she whispers conspiratorially. "I wanted you to see your heart before you die."

And then she drives her hand down, nails transforming to a vulture's talons, tearing into the already ruined left side of my chest. Those talons drive in hot and deep, like a poker through butter, sizzling the flesh in their path before rending through my ribs like they're nothing but stubborn saplings. Her fingers close around the fragile clockwork piece in my chest before she yanks it out and squeezes.

My heart flies to pieces in an explosion of gears and pendulums.

My time is up.

TWENTY-THREE
Kassidy

"No!"

The shriek claws itself from my throat. I twist the key in the lock without much thought, without caring for silence or stealth. It's not necessary anyway. Any sound I make, including the cry of horror that twisted itself loose from my mouth, is drowned in the two simultaneous roars that Leith and Nash bellow into the silence of the hall.

They'd been keeping quiet, feigning sleep so I could work the locks and free them as well.

Sorren bucks weakly, his face showing only soft, childlike confusion. He doesn't even seem to react to the pain, aside from the sharp inhale he took as Discordia reached into his chest and pulled out his clockwork heart.

His jaw works for a few seconds as though he might say something. Then his body unfurls, sinking into the stone floor with languid stillness. His face goes slack, the light in the depths of his eyes dimming. He's still breathing, but for how long? It seems like a futile gesture. The body's useless denial that it is, in fact, dying.

Discordia straightens and allows a dozen golden, bloodstained screws, bolts, and cogs to spill out of her palm and onto the stone. They tinkle on contact. It sounds like something one would hear at a May Day fair, not the background to an accursed nightmare like this. She slides her palms down the sleek black dress she wears, as though the streaks of scarlet are something vile. The blood doesn't show against the midnight material. I wonder how much blood she's wearing at the moment.

The lock clicks at last and I drop several feet and impact the ground. It's agonizing to land directly on my broken foot, but I school myself. I won't scream. And my arms are aching as they were very nearly pulled from their sockets. Regardless, I won't give this evil bitch the satisfaction of knowing how badly she's hurt me. I stalk forward with a lopsided step, drag, thump cadence. She deigns to fix me with a supercilious smile and watches my approach with chilly amusement.

"Poor little dear. Did you love my dear Sorren as well?"

"He was not *your* Sorren, you vile bitch!"

Everything within me quivers, the power I still have in reserve threatening to explode outward in a cataclysmic explosion that will bring the fortress down around our ears. I know I can do it. I can drag this building apart stone by stone and bury us all in a granite grave. If Nash and Leith weren't chained behind me, I might consider it.

Discordia barks a laugh and begins to circle me like a dark exotic cat, assessing my weakness and searching for a time to strike. She's gathering power too. Should I drive her mad with her own power? Or burn her to a clinquant pile of char and white bone fragments?

Fire sparks at the fingertips of my right hand while seething darkness collects in the palm of my left. Discordia watches me advance still faster, mild alarm twitching her fixed, superior expression into something new and a little less confident.

"That's impossible. No mage can duel wield elements like that, unless..."

"That's right," I snarl. "Unless they're Chosen."

Discordia shrieks; "Guards!"

But it's already too late. I thrust both hands forward as my mouth opens. "*Regressus*!" I yell! I don't know what the word means, where it came from, or the language it's spoken in, but the effects are instantaneous. The power shoots from my hands and misses Discordia by mere inches. She twists her body in an impossible, almost serpentine manner to avoid the jet of flames. My power hits the far wall instead, leaving a scorched and smoking starburst in its wake.

"That's impossible!" she screams again. "You're just a girl!"

I shriek wordless fury at her and redirect the flames and spinning darkness toward her. She evades again, launching into an impressive back handspring, tearing her silken dress as she goes. She's beyond caring though. At this point, survival is her only goal.

The guards she summoned file into the room, spears and polearms at the ready. My surroundings are a forest of pointed blades jabbing at my elbows, my knees, my back. I'm about to be skewered like a pincushion.

And then my saviors arrive.

Leith and Nash used the distraction afforded them to shift into their bear forms and to yank their chains free from the wall. The manacles are enchanted, built to keep their beasts in check. But they manage to pull stone from mortar from sheer *will*.

Nash rears onto his hind legs and swats the line of guards to my right like they're mere tin soldiers. I summon another barrage of power and loose it at the fleeing Discordia. She's almost at the door to the great hall.

"You're not getting away that easily!" I snarl. Then I turn to face my gray bear. "Leith, with me!"

Leith, who's been thrashing a guard within an inch of his life, swivels his great head toward me. I jab a finger at the door and repeat myself.

"Come with me! Let's end this!"

Leith's head dips in agreement and he drops to all fours, lumbering toward me with surprising speed for an animal so large. It continues to shock me how fast the enormous furry monsters can be. It doesn't seem right that an animal should be gifted such immense physical strength and also be able to barrel forward like a Sweetland freight car as well.

I grab fistfuls of his hair and climb astride, apologizing for hurting him. But the pain will fade and we have no time to be graceful. If Discordia leaves Grimm, the only hope we have to restore Sorren is gone. Truly gone, with no hope of return.

I snatch a polearm from one of the soldiers as we pass. If I see a damn Shepherd coming for Sorren, I'll lop their heads off.

Discordia is halfway down the adjoining corridor when we thunder after her. She checks behind her and then lets out a very pig-like squeal when she spots us. Unless she can sprout wings and fly, she has absolutely no chance of outdistancing us.

She seems to realize that too, because she spins on her heel, the slippery black dress with its wide sleeves flaring out like the membranous wings of a bat. She draws something out of the folds of her skirts. It looks like an apple, twice the size of the largest I've ever seen with golden skin that's kissed with a blush of pink at the very top, near the stem.

She hurls the apple at us and it bounces several times before flying apart into pieces, the pulpy insides splattering the walls in enormous chunks. Chunks which then begin to grow, expanding like a sponge absorbing water.

Morningstar's sweaty rancorous balls!
What the fresh fuck is this?

Leith only dips a foreclaw into it, and then rears back, roaring in pain. The stuff clings to his fur and begins eating away at it like corrosive lye. It's already eating holes in the floor. If we dally, the holes will become cavernous sinkholes that will eat the rest of the corridor. Possibly the whole fortress, if given enough time. No wonder the Guild never found anything at Morningstar's camps when they raided them. By the time his army cleared out, this bitch's magic had eaten everything in sight.

"I'm sorry, Leith, but this is going to hurt. Rear up on my count," I tell him, inching up his neck. "Three... two... one!"

On 'one' I get a grip on his fur and swing myself sideways, gathering as much momentum as I can and launch myself over the valley of bubbling stone. At the same time I bring the polearm down with a vicious battle cry. Discordia is half turned to flee, but doesn't have time to begin running again.

I hit her hard and drive us both to the ground, with me on top of her, knocking her face into the stone. I hear her nose snap sideways with a satisfying crunch, hear her teeth rattle as the impact slams them together. The sharp, tapering point of the polearm drives through her calf and stabs into the stone beneath.

She lets out a breathless shriek of agony, which I ignore. My hand weaves itself into all that thin, fine hair and I drive my stubby nails as deeply into her skin as I can manage before drawing on her power.

There's so much of it. It's like a vast inky lake reflecting a starless sky. I can't see where it begins or ends. It's just darkness, black night without the possibility of daybreak. Though I can't see it, I know corruption swims in those black waters. I don't want to venture in; I don't want to know what lies beneath the murk. But I have to. For Leith, whose body will be consumed if I don't. For Nash, who's fighting to defend me in the throne room. For Sorren, who lies prone but not quite dead on the stone.

I wade chin deep and begin to drink the power down, taking small sips at first. It tastes foul, like every rotting, putrid thing I've ever smelled. The water clears by degrees, melting from midnight to slate, the sky above the color of shale as I ingest the darkness by degrees. I drink until I'm bursting. The sky is still only a bruise-like blue, the water aquamarine. There's a promise of sun, if only I can part the clouds.

I need to shove the corruption elsewhere. But where do I take it? I can't put this into a human. They'll die. Even dividing it among my lovers seems like a bad idea. This corruption is strong. The rumors Sorren told us about Discordia must be true. She's a goddess corrupted by Morningstar. And if he can fell a goddess, what chance do I or any of the men stand?

I break away from her, emerging back into reality with a ragged gasp. The contamination bunches in my veins, curling and uncurling in steady rhythm like a fist opening and closing. I know if the corruption reaches my heart before I replace Sorren's, it will all be over.

Discordia is still face down and gasping like a fish. I note with just a fraction of my conscious mind that her hair has dulled from glossy black to a gray similar to Leith's. There's a little animation in her face, spots of color high in her cheeks. Her lips are pink now, not crimson. I don't have time to stoop and tend to her. I snatch the heart pendant from around her neck, get a running start, and then hurl myself over the ever-widening gorge with all my might.

I barely make it. The edge crumbles beneath my heel and I windmill, almost toppling into the abyss, but Leith's massive bear paw bats me out of the air and I go sprawling onto the stone. I lay gasping and breathless for a few too-long seconds before he noses me back onto my feet. I nod to him, then sprint back the way we came.

Thump-thump.

Pain. Scraping blackness, corruption, pain.
Thump-thump.
Give up, let it take you. Surrender.
Thump-thump.

It feels like a lasso of fire binding my entire right leg from the ankle up. The bones grind against one another as I try to race back to Sorren's side. When I reach the great hall, there are only a few soldiers left standing. Most are bleeding-but-breathing huddles on the ground, staring blankly at the hamburger that Nash has reduced their flesh to. I want to feel bad for them; it's not their fault that Discordia turned them into mindless zombies. And if fighting the corruption is truly as painful as this feels, I can't blame them.

I half-fall onto Sorren's chest with a sob. He's barely breathing. His eyes stare at a fixed point, though he's not dead yet. The pupils expand like an inky pool to cover most of the iris when a man is truly dead. And Sorren is close, but he's still in the land of the living.

I take the glass heart and try cracking it like an egg on the stone. It takes four tries before I can get the damn thing to shatter. But once the glass shatters, Sorren's heart slides into my palm, slick and bloody, and pulsing wildly, even as it grows in size. It takes very little effort to settle the thing back into the gaping cavity in his chest.

With the last spurt of energy I can muster, I reach wordlessly for Nash, who places one massive bear paw in mine without having to be asked. His energy beats back the corruption for a few blessed seconds, and a selfish part of me wants to keep it. I want to safeguard myself from Discordia's darkness and what lurks inside it. But the impulse is fleeting. I channel the energy into Sorren's chest, into that beating heart, sewing the broken pieces back together.

I have just enough power left to knit the layers of Sorren's skin and bone on top of his newly replaced heart, though the resulting wound is perhaps worse to look at than the first.

Well, Sorren will have to forgive me posthumously for sabotaging his chances at winning the "Fantasia Princess Pageant".

The corruption hits my heart and it stutters, slows, and sinks into a tide of forever midnight.

TWENTY-FOUR
Leith

Sorren is screaming, long, drawn out peals of agony that echo through the stone corridors. I lope toward the great hall, heart plummeting down to my misshapen feet as I shift mid-stride. There's only one reason I can think that my cousin would be shrieking like this, and I know I'm of no use to Kassidy in my bear form.

The smear of apple is still eating at my toes, eagerly devouring the flesh. It's probably too much to hope that the stuff would simply sluice off with my change of shape, it hasn't. But it's losing its potency now that Discordia has been felled.

My bare feet slap the floor, the boots I'd donned shredded by the change. I know I'm too late the second I step into the great hall.

There are a dozen soldiers lying in a crescent around Nash and Sorren, in various states of injury. They moan and plead for help as I weave through their ranks. I don't have time to spare them, though I know their actions aren't strictly their fault. I only have eyes for my cousins and Kassidy.

Sorren has pulled Kassidy onto his lap, cradling her small form like a fragile doll. She flops every few seconds, gasping in painful rasps of air like a fish trying vainly to breathe on land. Anywhere bare flesh is exposed, I see the blackness running in lines across her skin. Every vein stands at attention, a raised pattern on her skin. The tendons strain in her neck and a low whine escapes through her teeth.

"No," Sorren hisses, shaking her body, as though the jostling will help anything. "No. This is not the way it ends! She doesn't spare me, only to die!"

There's true animation on his face for the first time in a decade. Anger. Disbelief. Despair — the despair is the frightening bit. His chest is an angry mass of barely healed flesh. There's a mess of blood streaked across the pale skin, running in rivulets down his half-naked body. He pays it no mind, just continues to shout directives at Kassidy, who's far beyond hearing.

Her pupils are huge, almost eclipsing the beautiful green of her eyes. If it weren't for the labored heaving of her chest, I'd think she was already gone.

Nash is on his knees as well, a look of almost childlike confusion on his face, as though he can't quite understand how this has happened. That frightens me, too. Nash isn't the sort who caves during a crisis. He gets angry. His bear takes the lead, and he rips apart whatever is causing him upset.

"What's happened?" I demand as I reach them.

I glance down at Kassidy and my heart drops.

She's dying.

Anger burns inside me. *I won't let her go! I won't fucking let her go! Not when the three of us have just found her!*

"She leached Discordia's life force," Sorren spits. "Took power from her to restore my heart. As if I want it, if this is the result." He looks up at me then, tears streaming down his face. "Carve it the fuck out, Leith. I don't want it! Not at this cost."

I want to argue. Having Sorren back has been a distant, impossible dream for years. The idealistic enthusiasm of the little thief has swept us all away, made us forget that miracles are a thing of fairy tales. Storming castles rarely ends well. Battles are messy. Soldiers fall. Chosen ones die. Were we truly blinded by her?

"It's not over yet," I say shortly. "There's work to be done. We're not giving up on her."

They both stare at me with blank expressions, eyes flat and hopeless.

"Up!" I snap. "Get up and bring her. And fucking hurry."

Both rise to their feet, Sorren cradling Kassidy to his chest like she's the most precious thing in the world. Nash trails in his wake. I stalk down the corridor and take the stairs two at a time, leading us back the way we came. The mist has mostly cleared now, and I can see our path with almost perfect clarity. It's a relief. One less obstacle to contend with in our race against time.

Down two floors and then through several long corridors, we should find the kitchen, which is a stone's throw from the washroom where we'd bathed. The memory of Kassidy so vital, sexy, and strong sends a shudder over my skin. I'm not sure what I'll do if we're too late. If I lose her...

I can't fucking lose her!

If that happens, I'll undo Kassidy's last act of mercy and kill Discordia with my bare hands. Rake

251

vengeance into her back until it's nothing but blood and tatters.

But, my first attention needs to be Kassidy. I can heal her, I know I can.

The kitchen is enormous and smells faintly of meat, scalloped potatoes, and onions. I make for the counter in the center of the room and sweep an array of knives and pans off the wooden countertop. Sorren places Kassidy gingerly on the cleared space without having to be told.

"Sugar, oil, salt, flour, and yeast," I snap at Nash. "Now."

Sorren's head snaps up and he regards me with surprise. "Ambrosia? You think that will work?"

"I'll give the final ingredient," Nash offers over my shoulder.

The coveted secret of our people was the recipe for Ambrosia. In truth, it's little different from regular bread, but for one exception. The ingredient that provides it potency? Life force, drawn from our bodies and stuffed into the very essence of the dough. Healthy bears can live for hundreds of years. Shaving off weeks or months can heal injured or ailing members of the clan. Injuries and ailments that would take weeks or months to heal can be dealt with in mere minutes. To heal Kassidy, though, it will take more than a month or two. She'll need more time.

"I'll be adding the final ingredient," I say sternly. "It's not safe for either of you. Too much from you, Sorren, could stop your heart. It's too fragile at the moment. Too much from Nash could steal the last vestiges of his control. I'm the only logical option."

"But…" Nash starts.

"Are you going to waste time arguing, or will you help me?" I demand. He simply nods as I face Sorren. "I need your spellwork. We don't have an hour to let this bake."

Sorren's jaw works furiously as he tries and fails to find a flaw in my logic.

"It's our only hope," I tell him. "So, help me."

He nods curtly. "If this fails, I'm going to flay that bitch alive."

"You'll have to get in line," Nash growls, echoing my sentiments exactly. It's the first time we've been truly unanimous on any subject.

We all love Kassidy—it's a truth that's just become quite obvious.

If she dies, the bonds that cement us will dissolve like suds in the rain. Nash and Sorren will blame me for being unable to stop her. I'll blame Sorren for precipitating the actions that led to her death, and I'll blame Nash for lying around passive and in shock while she lay dying. None of us will be able to stand each other.

Nash plunks the items requested onto the counter with a mixing bowl and dumps in the appropriate amounts with impressive speed. We all know the recipe by heart. It's pounded into every bear's skull early in our lives.

Meanwhile, I carefully shift only the nail of my left index finger so that a black claw darts out with a snick. I choose the vein that runs the length of the ulna and open my skin. The blood pours out at once and puddles on the counter near one of Kassidy's twitching hands.

It's not the blood, but the life force within, that gives ambrosia its power. It takes magic to separate the two—a simple spell I also know by heart. "Vita est vita, et sanguis sanguinem. Et hoc est donum tibi."

I don't even try to stem the flow of blood. To save Kassidy, I'm going to give as much as I can. As much as will pour out before my bear's healing factor begins to do its work. It gathers around Kassidy's prone form like a scarlet halo, sinking into her skin.

It's Nash who finally wrenches my arm away from the table when the pool has grown wide enough to dribble off the counter and onto the stones beneath.

"That's enough. You can't bleed yourself dry. She'll need all of us if she recovers."

I want to snarl at him. It's not good enough, not nearly enough after what she's done for us. She *has* to live. Not just for us, she's also one of Fantasia's few hopes for a future—a fine-tipped weapon to be used against Morningstar when the time is right.

I glance down at the pool. There's a lot of time trapped in those drops of blood. Years, easily. But will it be enough?

It takes thirty seconds for the precious golden liquid to separate from the blood. What's touching her skin seeps in at once, and what remains, we sweep into a bowl. Sorren's already over it, muttering and chanting. Neither time nor fire magic are taught at length in our compounds. He's one of the few who's traveled outside as often and explored as thoroughly as one must to learn such things.

I crouch like a gargoyle at her head, leaning close to pick up on any minute change in her condition. She's still breathing, though her breathing grows shallower with every breath she takes. Her lovely lips have taken on an alarming plum color and grow darker still as I watch. The shadows that line the undersides of her eyes grow darker, her face sinking. Her pupils have completely eclipsed her irises.

"Hurry," I growl.

"I'm almost through," he snaps back at me.

I see just the hint of dark umber in those glacial eyes. His bear form is close to the surface. Just like mine. Just like Nash's. She's done it. The brilliant, beautiful woman has truly restored Sorren to the man he used to be.

He scoops the stuff from the bowl. It's misshapen, hardly a loaf. Gods, it's barely cooked. The raw ingredients will give her a blinding headache if they're not properly cooked, but if that's the worst she suffers, we'll take it and be grateful.

Sorren pries her jaw open roughly, some of his practiced ruthlessness seeping through despite the restoration of his heart. He smears a globule into her mouth and then presses her lips together again. He waits until he hears a thick, painful swallow before doing it again and again until the bowl has been completely emptied.

"Now what?" Nash demands, stalking around the kitchen like, well... a caged bear.

"Now," I conclude bitterly, "we wait."

TWENTY-FIVE
Kassidy

The void is peaceful.

I am weightless, floating on the surface of a vast, dark sea. It's difficult to tell where water ends and the sky begins. Both are endless black, without the twinkle of stars, suns, or the distant spheres to give light or orientation. Perhaps I'm on my back in the sea. Or perhaps I'm suspended in the sky, staring down at the water.

All I know is it's incredible here. There's a quiet in my soul I've never felt before. The world I've left is a violent place, full of garish colors and turbulent emotions. Not once has it ever cared for me. Not my father, who'd loved his bottles of spirits far more than he'd loved his daughter. None of the people I'd begged for food. No one pays attention until there's coin in their hand or a pussy clenched around their cock. Sex is the only currency the powerful will accept from a woman.

None of the people cared a decade ago, when they'd turned their backs on the Guild and left us to flail helplessly at the coming of Morningstar.

No one cared. The world is a stinking dung heap, and I'm glad to be leaving it.

No... that's not true, Kassidy! I yell at myself.

There were small handfuls of happiness in my life, purloined from the fickle pockets of fate and stashed away for when they'd be most useful. Training with my brothers and the spacious home we shared at the Order of Aves.

256

Afternoons with Peter and the Lost Boys. My brief but memorable time with Neva. And, of course Sorren, Nash, and Leith.

Regret pierces the tranquil haze.

Oh, Gods, Sorren was dying. Have I restored him? Or is he about to paddle past me through the sea or sky on his way to... wherever shifters go when they die?

The spell is broken; my body no longer feels weightless. I sink to the bottom of the murky depths, choking on inky water that tastes like stagnation and death.

And when I wash up on shore an eternity later, there's still no peace. In the dim light of morning, I can see a pall over Delorood. More of the damn mist that plagued Discordia's fortress drapes over the castle like a gauzy shawl. Sunrise threatens to shrug it off, but for the moment it remains trapped in this twilight state.

I crawl on my belly, sand scraping my skin raw as I try not to be pulled once more into the sea. I make it three body lengths before I encounter an obstacle. A pair of dainty slippered feet appear in front of me. It takes more strength than I have left to crane my neck up to look at their owner.

She's a little thing.

Smaller even than me, which I don't think I've encountered before, aside from dwarves. She's tiny, with the proportions of a doll. Startlingly white hair falls around her face in loose curls, looking more like wispy clouds have settled around her head than anything else. Her eyes are the palest blue I've ever seen, the blue-white of a perfect winter's day before the snow falls. Slender arms, slender legs. She looks more fae than human, though she lacks the haunting echo their magic typically sends across my skin.

She looks harmless by anyone's estimation. Or, she would be, if it weren't for the crook and lantern she clutches

*in her right hand. The stone within casts a blue-green light
over me.*

This wisp of a girl is a Shepherdess.

"So, I'm dead?" I croak. "You're here to take me?"

*Funny, I thought the dead are allowed to live in a happy
memory before they fade into their afterlife. If this is my
farewell fantasy, I want a trade.*

*She laughs, and the bell-like sound tinkles over my skin
pleasantly.* "A shepherdess?" *she repeats.* "Goodness, no!"

"Then you aren't here to take me to the afterlife?"

She laughs again. "No, Kassidy Aurelian, of course not.
There's still so much to do, silly."

*I grimace, both at the sugar-sweetness of her voice and
the term of endearment.*

"If I'm not dead, then what's happening? Who are you?
And where am I?"

She tilts her head a fraction. "Which do you want
answered first?"

"The second," *I decide. Introductions are important.*

"I'm Bowie," *she says with a smile, exposing perfect
milk-white teeth.* "Bowie Peep. And, to continue answering
your questions in order, this is a twilight vision, Kassidy."

"A what?" *I demand.*

She smiles. "A maybe. A future you will have, if you
survive."

"What the fuck does that mean?"

She laughs again. "Be flattered. Most souls don't
experience this much without crossing over completely."

"I feel honored," *I reply dryly.* "Truly."

*Bowie ignores my flippant tone and continues on as
though I haven't spoken, which is just as well because I'm
being an asshole.* "And you know where we are, Kassidy.
You just don't know when we are."

"Is that supposed to make any sense to me?"

Another bell-laugh. "No. These episodes so rarely do."

"Can you just tell me where the fuck we are, Bowie?"

She nods. "This is Delorood. It's the setting for a final battle."

"Whose?"

She gestures grandly at the city's silhouette, gray against the color beginning to creep along the sky. It's not pastel, like I expect. It's a red-orange, steaked through with crimson, like a giant has wiped his bloody fingers through the air.

"Yours. Mine. Everyone's."

And that's when I see the hulking shapes moving through the fog, approaching the city from the east. War elephants, giants, hellhounds, and hundreds of other creatures I have no name for.

"Morningstar's army," I say breathlessly. "He escapes his prison then?"

"Has escaped," she corrects. "Or will very soon. Time is tricky in twilight visions."

Has or had, it makes little difference to me. The fact is, Morningstar's going to break free and start wreaking havoc on Fantasia again. And I can't let that happen.

"How do I get out of here?" I demand. "I have to return. They need me."

They. The world. The Guild. My brothers. But especially the three bear royals who risked their lives for me. Three bears who I love with all my heart.

"Simple," Bowie says. "You have to swallow."

"Swallow?" I repeat. That seems... deceptively simple.

"Swallow, Kassidy," she repeats. "Do it now."

I swallow obediently and find... that it hurts. A lot. It feels like my throat has been scalded, stung with smoke, like *it desperately wants to remain closed. Still, I force myself to swallow again. And again.*

And finally, after the third swallow, some of the pain eases. The burn becomes an ache. My throat stops trying to seal together, and I draw in a desperate inhale. It's echoed by three others and then hands are touching me everywhere. Hands cradling my cheeks, hands sliding sweetly around mine, hands seizing my shoulders. The latter are the strongest, and they pull me upright.

When my eyelids flutter open, elation suffuses every cell of my body when I see Sorren's chiseled and beloved face only inches from mine. He's flushed with color and for the first time ever, there's a true smile on his face.

And I've never seen him appear more beautiful.

Sorren's alive! I did it!

He's alive, and he's whole, and he's here and...

He's kissing me. His lips crush mine, though not in the feral, possessive need to have me like the first time. His mouth has a new, staggering tenderness, the kiss so full of longing, want, and *love* that it brings tears to my eyes.

"Tell me you've come back to us, little dove," he murmurs against my mouth when he pulls away.

"I'm here, with you," I mutter dazedly.

"Kassidy," Leith's voice sounds from beside me. I glance up at him and the tears increase.

"What... what happened?" I ask.

"You almost hopped the twig, that's what happened," Nash snaps, as though he's absolutely incensed I had the gall to attempt to die on him.

"I'm... sorry?"

"Ignore him," Leith advises. "He's churlish when he's scared. He's happy to see you, as well."

"Sod off, Leith," Nash snarls.

Despite the pain still weighing on every limb, I sit up, noting as I do that I'm covered with gold and crimson ichor from the waist down. I look like I've gone wading into battle with a herd of small gold prospectors.

"What is this?" I ask.

"Leith's blood," Nash says, once he's heaved in several frustrated breaths. "He made the Ambrosia that healed you, and damn near bled himself to death to do it."

"It was worth it," Leith says.

"Making it took years off his life," Sorren adds with a small smile as he runs his fingers down the side of my face.

"Years?" I repeat as I look at Leith with wide eyes. "Of your life?"

"Fuck, don't your lot have any idea how Abrosia is made?" Nash demands, surprisingly angry considering everyone else is relieved. But, that's Nash. "I thought you'd try to learn at least *that* much before stealing the bloody stuff from us."

My stomach does a tumble. In truth, none of us really cared what it was made of, just that it could help our own kind. We never paid much attention to what position it would thrust the bear shifters into if we took it, nor why they guarded it so fiercely. It just seemed like selfishness from the outside. But with this new, intimate knowledge, it takes on a horrifying sort of clarity. We've been trying to steal their lives! In a literal and metaphorical sense. No wonder they've been so hostile.

"How many years?" I ask Leith.

His gaze shutters and his face goes completely blank. "Not important."

"Morningstar's sweaty balls, it isn't! How many?" I demand.

"Twenty-five," Sorren fills in. "Perhaps thirty."

I'm halfway through sliding off the counter when Sorren answers. My knees wobble and then give out from beneath me. Leith has to scoop me up before I hit the ground.

"Thirty?" I repeat in a choked whisper. Suddenly, it's hard to breathe again. "I stole thirty years from you?"

"You didn't steal anything, it was given freely," Leith argues. "You saved Sorren from certain death. And now you're going to save Fantasia."

"You can't know that," I argue.

His eyes shine with consummate confidence. "I do. Because you aren't going to do it alone."

"What do you mean?" I ask.

It's Nash who answers. "We're with you. Our kingdom is with you."

I turn to face Leith, the tears bursting from my eyes as I wonder how this can be true? "You've really changed your mind?"

He nods. "However much aid the Guild needs, we'll give it."

I choke again. Damn him. The salt in the tears hurts my face. I start to shake my head as I realize what they're offering me. Their lives essentially. "I can't accept... it's too much. You can't do this for me. I can't repay this debt."

"Then how about making it a gift?" Sorren asks, hands going around my waist. Nash's heat presses against my back, nose skimming my throat.

"What... ah... kind of gift?" I ask.

Sorren slides a hand into mine. "Tie this hand to our kingdom."

I look at Leith. "I don't understand."

He smiles down at me as the three of them stand before me, making me feel so small in front of them, but so protected.

"Be our little barbarian queen," Leith says.

"Lead our banners into your army," Nash adds.

"We're yours, if you want us," Sorren finishes.

I'm quiet as I let the words sink in. They want me. Not just now, but forever. That's what they're asking.

What can I say, except, "Yes."

TWENTY-SIX
Kassidy

The men wanted the handfasting to take place in the kingdom, but there simply hadn't been time. After Discordia's defeat, the people of Grimm sent her as far away as they could, to serve a life sentence in Ascor.

The twilight vision had confirmed one thing we already suspected: The seals keeping Morningstar imprisoned were beginning to suffer catastrophic breakdown. It was no longer just spirits and the occasional hellhound escaping anymore. Monstrous things were gushing out, and there was no stopgap we could put in place to delay the inevitable any longer. We had to begin preparing for war.

And to that end, Leith, Nash, and Sorren were accompanying me to Delorood. Prince Andric would be our human general to rally all the other kingdoms together, if we could somehow manage to do so in time. We were hoping the show of trust from the leaders from one of the most secretive kingdoms in all of Fantasia, the werebear kingdom, would do some good.

So, instead of marrying before a crowd of their adoring subjects, we were instead poised at the stern of the ship, huddled before the captain, even as the Jolly Roger tried its damndest to pitch us sideways into the sea.

"Aye, ye make a right beautiful bride, Kassidy," Captain Hook says as he eyes me lecherously.

Hook is a very handsome man. A flirt, too, which is why all three of my men glare murder at our officiant even as he prompts us through our vows and drapes the cords over our hands. I can see why women like him. He's tall, well-muscled from a hard life at sea, and his skin has been tanned almost brown from constant sun exposure. He has a swarthy beard, smoldering dark eyes, and a smile that would charm the undergarments off a wench at ten paces.

That and he's as Scottish as his thick brogue would suggest.

Aside from the times I must look at him to repeat my vows, I barely take note of him. Because there's just too much in front of me to ever consider wanting more. My men stand straight, tall, and proud. Leith holds me in his arms because I'm still a little too weak to stand on my own for long periods of time. Coming back from Discordia's darkness definitely did a number on me, but I'm getting stronger with each passing day. It will probably be another week or so until I'm fully healed and restored to myself.

Each of my bears has a hand on mine. The tips of Leith's fingers brushing my own, Nash's trace burning patterns on the back of my hand, and Sorren's fingers lock around my wrist. He smirks when he feels my heart skip every time I look at their beautiful faces.

"I promise to trust you and be honest with you. I promise to listen to you, to respect you, and to support you," I say between my tears. "I… I…"

"Kass?" Sorren asks as I hold up a finger to let him know I'm trying to get control of myself.

Kassidy Aurelian, what the fuck is wrong with you? You're crying like a girl!

Maybe because I am a girl, you cock!

You can't call me a cock because I'm you, stupid.

Okay, then just shut up and let me try to make my way through these vows, will you?

"I promise to cherish every day we have together. I promise to do all this through whatever life brings us—through good times and bad, until death do we part," I repeat my final vow. Hook finishes the rest.

"As this knot is tied, so are yer lives now bound. Woven into this cord, imbued into it with magic an' blood, are yer hopes for a life an' future together."

In reality, it's bespelled rope from the stock down below, but we can't afford to be choosy. It's about the sentiment. If we want to do this again later, we can—assuming we survive. For now, I want to be tied to these men. I want to be their bride any way possible.

"As ye tie this knot, ye bind yer dreams, love, wishes, an' happiness together, for long as yer love lasts."

Forever.

I know I have less of that stretch of time than they do. I'm human, which means I'm finite. I've had a brush with death already, so I know how fragile life is. But for my portion of forever, I want them by my side.

"By this cord, ye are bound together. You may kiss the..." Hook glances between us and then gives a laugh. "Well, someone kiss her."

And then their hands are on me, moving in concert like they've been planning this all evening.

266

Leith takes my mouth while Nash and Sorren's lips fall to either side of my neck, and I squirm beneath the ticklish onslaught.

I don't even struggle as they pull me below deck and into our quarters. Because, finally, I'm exactly where I long to be — in the arms of the three men I love, the three men I adore with all my heart.

TWENTY-SEVEN
Nash

Kassidy's back lifts off the bed in a perfect arch, her pert tits bouncing with the force of her orgasm. I touch my aching shaft a little desperately. It's fucking torture to watch Leith between her legs, bringing her to completion not once but *three times* before he's satisfied she's ready for more. She's slick everywhere, beyond ready.

Selfish bastards that they are, Leith and Sorren have already claimed their turn with her pussy and ass. I feel like a fucking deviant in the corner, stroking myself as I watch them together.

Then, her eyes crack open and she looks at me. Really looks, and a lazy, fuck-me smile spreads across her face.

"Come here," she croons. It's just as sweet as a fucking siren call, and I go to her without question.

"There's another place for you," she says in a throaty whisper that already has my balls tightening. Fuck. How was she a virgin when we met? She's got more raw sex appeal than a succubus.

She taps her kiss-swollen lips with a wink and I about cum then and there. She reaches out for me, squeezes the base of my cock and then draws me nearer by the root of me, sliding my head inside her mouth. My eyes shut and my head lolls back. Ah, fuck yes.

Her lips wrap around me, tongue swirling around my tip like I'm a succulent bit of candy. I can't help but thrust shallowly into her mouth. I don't want to gag her, but she's making it damn hard to think. She runs her tongue along the underside of my shaft, down to the root and back up again, playing me like I'm a damn flute. My hands fist into her hair, drawing her nearer to me. I thrust hard and deep into her mouth and she lets me, rocking back to escape the gag that's sure to result.

I thrust shallowly again, trying to pace myself. The warmth of her mouth, closed tight around me, has my vision flashing white. I'm still aware enough to notice the others.

Sorren has her bent over the bed, fucking her from behind while Leith thrusts up and into from below. It's strange, exhilarating, and intensely erotic to be together, fucking her like this. This little thief we all love. I clamp down tight, tugging her hair as I thrust into her one more time before release hits me.

My release triggers hers. She's getting sensitive to her powers these days, able to sense and siphon emotion as well as energy now. Her body quivers, her eyes glaze over with pleasure and she spasms once more in ecstasy before she's through. The release spills over to Sorren and Leith as well, who roar with their own climax.

We slump in a boneless pile on the bed. The captain graciously gave us his quarters, as it was the only one with enough room for all four of us. His

269

generosity may also have something to do with the priceless jewel-encrusted sword Kassidy gifted him— one that belonged to a fabled dragon.

We all bask in the moment until I'm the first to speak.

"Next time," I pant. "I'm fucking her properly. Understood everyone?"

Kassidy grins wearily. "Understood."

"Ah shut up, Nash," Leith responds.

Sorren just grunts. He's usually the first asleep.

"Now sleep, you brute," Kassidy whispers. "There's a week left of travel before we reach Delorood."

EPILOGUE
Hook

I smile thinly at the ghostly shape of the moon on the horizon, glimmering white-gold like a galleon flung into the sky. The stars are a thousand crushed diamonds spread across midnight blue velvet. The night is warm, the wind high. We'll make it early to Delorood at this rate.

I spend many a night imagining what it would be like to find that spot where sea meets the sky, to see if I could climb to the stars. It's a fanciful notion, but I think the sky above is much like the sea: dangerous and cold, full of monsters. But a damn fine place to be, when all's said and done.

I'm used to hearing a great many things when I voyage. The incessant, pleading cries of gulls as they scavenge. The lapping waves on the sides of the Jolly Roger. The creak of wood as the old girl settles herself after particularly violent tosses. The flap of a mainsail.

What I'm *not* used to hearing are loud, protracted female moans coming from my cabin. Particularly when I'm not the one drawing them out from some lucky lass. It's been some time since that's happened. Aye—a depressingly long time.

I've been too busy. The Guild has me running all around Fantasia more often than not, though I refuse to set a course for Neverland ever again. There are

271

some things you can never return to, no matter the
price.

My good hand strays down to my trousers and I
discreetly adjust the bulge that's growing there. Can't
help it—the lasses cries of pleasure are impossible to
ignore.

Kassidy's not mine, and I'm not fool enough to
challenge her three werebear husbands for the
privilege of bedding her. As if she'd even let me, if I
somehow managed it.

Kassidy Aurelian is beautiful and a damn fine
bedmate, if the sounds coming from within are any
indication. But she's an ally, not a conquest.

Not far off, my first mate, Sam, is also trying to
block the sounds coming from the deck. I've only got a
few surviving crew members after the Lost Boys got
through with them, the little bastards. Not that the four
I've got are strictly necessary. The Jolly Roger can fly in
a pinch and sails itself well enough, if need be. A gift
from a faerie for whom I did a favor.

"Quite... spirited, isn't she, cap'n?" Sam says
slowly, tiptoeing around the subject as gingerly as he
can. That's my Sam. Always the diplomat. Probably
why he has two hands and I only have the one.

I glance down at the false hand. I've normally got
a blade or a hook installed there, but I thought it
would be more respectful to wear a fake appendage for
Kassidy's wedding.

"Aye, quite a loud fuck, she is, Sam."

Sam colors prettily around the edges of his ears—
it's quite easy to embarrass the lad. It's part of the
reason I try to frazzle him so often. He's only just now

eighteen and has such light blonde hair, it looks almost white. He pulls his red cap down over his eyes and looks everywhere but at me. Sweet lad. If I can't have a lass moaning for me like the one in the cabin, the least I can do is draw a blush or two from Sam.

"I've never..." he says, trails off, and then blushes again.

I grin. "I'll give ye shore leave when we reach Delorood. Find yerself some pretty young thing in a bordello an' show her a proper good time."

Sam is positively ruddy now. This night isn't so miserable after all.

"Think it's true, what they say?" he asks.

"Aboot what?"

"The sirens."

"What aboot the Sirens?"

"That they live around Delorood?"

"Aye, 'tis true. Seen one in me day. Dove beneath the waves seconds after, boot they're real. Dinnae expect to fuck one, though. Triton is a monster, an' his children are monsters. Nary a single one of them sided with humans during the war. Sooner drown ye than look at ye. Stick to human women, Sam. I like ye, lad."

"What about the other rumors?"

I shrug, pretending I don't know what he's going on about. To say the thing out loud makes it more frightening. I'm not a superstitious man. I don't bar women from my ship or throw them overboard if the portents prove dire. What I do believe in, though, is fate, and that tempting it with whispers is a bad idea.

"Dinnae know what you're talkin' aboot, lad."

Sam casts his gaze around, but for nothing but heaving sea. The water is black only feet down where the light doesn't touch. It's probably fanciful to imagine something moving below — my own fevered, sex-starved imagination taking over and playing tricks on me.

"The other rumors," he insists. "The ones about the monsters. That the seas are getting more dangerous because Morningstar is back."

"He's nae back."

Sam's eyes are huge, almost as big as silver coins in his face. I want to pity the poor lad. He's a good first mate, a good person, but he's lousy at keeping a poker face. He's scared and has been for weeks while we docked in the harbor, doing only short-term, local work while we awaited Kassidy's arrival. Being on the open sea again almost has him pissing his pants.

"How do you know? He could be…"

"He's not," I cut him off firmly. "If Morningstar was back, there'd be reports, lad. He's hard to miss — a winged giant, he is. Cannae exactly fold himself down into human shape, now, can he?"

Sam is silent for a few seconds, and I'm confident the matter's settled.

"The water, Cap'n. Look!"

At first, I ignore him. He's more prone to flights of fancy than even I am, which is a feat. Born anywhere but in Neverland, and I'd be a poet or a bard. Perhaps a playwright. But not in Neverland. Nothing so gentle for a boy who grew up in Neverland.

But when I finally *do* look, I see what he means.

White foam begins to churn around a point around fifty miles off to the east of us, the waves tossing even more violently. The wind reaches a shrill pitch, whipping the main sail so hard, it threatens to tear. There is definitely a shape stirring in the inky darkness below, a shape even more solid and midnight-black than the water itself.

Fuck.

I didn't want to believe the rumors were true — that Triton is allowing the monsters free reign to terrorize merchant vessels. He truly does mean to isolate Delorood. Which means the Jolly Roger has gone from safe harbor to a target. I have to get the happy foursome and my men off this ship.

"Below!" I bellow at Sam. "Get Harlen, Vince, an' Sham oot of bed, an' get their cargo sealed in one o' them fancy capsules. I'll get the passengers!"

Sam is frozen in shock, clearly unsure of what to do now that his worst nightmares are coming to fruition. I give him a shove. He staggers and almost falls to his knees, then recovers himself, scrambling down the stairs and calling for his mates.

I stalk over to my cabin and rap on the door only once to give them a chance at privacy before I yank the door open.

They're all huddled in my bed. The room reeks of male musk and the potent scent of female pleasure. If I survive this, I'm going to see to it I make a woman smell like that one more time before I die.

Well, death might be waiting around the corner.

"Up!" I yell. "We're abandonin' ship!"

"W-what?" Kassidy stammers. "Why?"

"Sea monster rising from the depths, lass. Trust me, ye dinnae want to be here when it surfaces."

She goes pale as death but doesn't argue with me further. The bunch are surprisingly speedy in a crisis. It's a trait I value highly, giving them some added credit in my mental ledger.

They're up and ready to board in only half a minute, while Sam and the others have piled into their lifeboat and I lower them down to sea. Four to a boat, is the general rule. None of them have done the math yet. That's all right. I'd rather Sam believe I'm still coming with him, but the truth is a captain never leaves his ship.

Once Kassidy and her men are loaded into the second boat, I lower them down with the pulley system that allows the boat to gently touch the roiling waters below. The one with the darkest hair grips the oar and pushes away from the Jolly Roger.

"Cap'n Hook?" Sam calls out as his boat begins to shift away from the ship. "Are you goin' to jump?"

I see the shock and betrayal play out on his face an instant after I shake my head. "Aim for the shores of Bridgeport, Sam!"

"Hook!" Kassidy yells at the same time as she stands up in the small boat and screams at me. "What the fuck are you doing!"

The small boat jars back and forth with the heaving waves, and Kassidy is forced back down, pulled into one of her bears' laps, I know not which one. I don't have time to watch both boats float away. I need to lead this sea creature away from them.

276

Every rune etched into the wheel flares to brilliant life as I steer the Jolly Roger up and out of the waves. I'll be faster unencumbered by the water. The wind whips my hair into my face as I sing a sea ditty and try to quell the surge of fear plaguing me. The truth is, I live on that fear—it's what drives me, what wakes me each morning. I'm grinning like a lunatic, heart throwing itself at my ribs like a prisoner against the bars of a cage.

The thing finally breaks the surface. A hundred tentacles rise above the waves, a massive oblong squid's head emerging from the deep. It fixes glowing red eyes on my position as I turn the ship to face it. It stays hovering in place even when I release the wheel and stride over to the nearest long nine.

With more calm than I feel, I draw a sleeve of matches from the pocket of my velvet frock coat and strike one. I light the fuse. Take aim.

"I'm Hook," I yell out at the creature as it releases an air-shaking bellow. "An' now I'm gonna call ye one-eye, ugly."

The cannon bucks.

A monster screams.

A tentacle comes hurtling down and bats the Jolly Roger into the sea.

To Be Continued in…
ARIA
NOW AVAILABLE!

Get FREE E-Books!
It's as easy as:

1. Go to my website: www.hpmallory.com
2. Sign up in the pop-up box or on the link at the top of the home page
3. Check your email!

About the Author:

HP Mallory is a New York Times and USA Today Bestselling author who started as a self-published author.

She lives in Southern California with her son and a cranky cat, where she's at work on her next book.

Printed in Great Britain
by Amazon